A WORLD OF HURT

A stream of green tracers cut through the night, and Rosemont twisted around to bring fire on it. Even with all the sensors and Mark One eyeballs in the sand around his small perimeter, the hostiles managed to sneak in fairly close before they had been spotted.

Several figures rose from the sand in his night-vision imager. He triggered off a long burst at them. A grunt to his right sent a 30 mm grenade into their midst, and Rosemont's visor blanked when the enhanced explosive detonated.

When his visor cleared, he saw that the bunch of hostiles were down, but more kept popping up. Over the roar of battle, he heard Top Ward shouting as he dashed from one position to the other, coordinating the defenses of the rapidly shrinking perimeter.

Already two men were dead and at least three wounded. There was no time to pull the wounded out of the line. They would live or die along with the rest.

WAR KEEP 2030

MICHAEL KASNER

WITHDRAWN

A GOLD EAGLE BOOK FROM
WORLDWIDE®

TORONTO • NEW YORK • LONDON
AMSTERDAM • PARIS • SYDNEY • HAMBURG
STOCKHOLM • ATHENS • TOKYO • MILAN
MADRID • WARSAW • BUDAPEST • AUCKLAND

First edition November 1992

ISBN 0-373-62014-4

WARKEEP 2030

Printed in U.S.A.

1

Karbala, Iraq—5 June 2030 A.D.

It was the tenth day of the holy month of Muharram in the Islamic year 1451 A.H.— After the Hijra, the first pilgrimage of the Prophet Muhammad to Mecca. The smell of dust and blood was thick in the air, and the sun baked the crowd of Shiite worshipers packed into the walled square around the golden-domed Karbala mosque.

The tenth day of Muharram was Ashurt, the most sacred day of the Shiite Muslims, the anniversary of the death of Hussein, the grandson of the Prophet who had died fighting the Umayyads for the Caliphate of the Islamic faithful in the year 860 A.D. Hussein had fallen outside Karbala and, on the anniversary of his death, Shiite men mourned his demise by inflicting wounds upon themselves and shedding their blood in remembrance of his. They gathered by the thousands around this most holy place, beating the flats of their swords on their heads and whipping their bare backs with chains, opening cuts to bleed freely as they wailed their grief.

Suddenly the hot air shimmered in front of the entrance to the mosque. Where there had been an empty space before, the figure of a tall, beardless, good-looking young man now stood. He wore a long gold-embroidered white Arabic robe over billowing trousers, and a green turban was wrapped around his head. Slung over his right shoulder was a long Oriental bow, and an ornate curved dagger was sheathed in the brightly colored sash around his waist. He drew a long, straight-bladed sword from the jeweled scabbard slung at his left side and raised it high over his head.

"Allah Akbar!" he shouted. "God is great!" His amplified voice rang out clearly over the drone of the crowd and the chanting of the frenzied Shiite worshipers.

Cries of alarm spread as the people saw him standing there, his sword held high. Then shouts of stunned recognition were heard. "The Hidden Imam! The Mahdi! The Twelfth Imam has returned!"

A hush fell over the enclosure as the Mahdi began to speak. Although only those in the packed throng who were right in front of him could see him, all could hear him clearly. The man's voice held the crowd mesmerized as he told them that the end of the world was near, as had been foretold so many years ago. Allah had ordered him to prepare the faithful for their just rewards in the Muslim paradise. He said that Allah was angered that his people had polluted themselves by taking up the unclean technology of the infidel. He called upon the faithful to cleanse all Western contamination from the lands of Islam so they would all be worthy to gaze upon Allah's face in paradise.

The crowd was listening raptly, their devotion and conviction rising by the minute. Muhammad al-Mahdi, who was to become the Twelfth Imam, the last of the Prophet's descendants, had disappeared in 872 A.D. after his father's death when he was still a young boy. The Shiite faithful had always believed that he had ascended to heaven and became the Hidden Imam.

The Shiites said that he watches over the faithful, waiting until the right time to reappear and usher in a golden age of true and pure Islam by wiping the world clean and starting over. They say he will reappear just before the end of the world to warn the faithful against evil and wrongdoing.

His title *Muhdi* means *the Savior.*

A CNN NEWS TEAM was holoveeing the Shiite ceremony at Karbala as part of their coverage of Muharram for their Muslim viewers around the world when the Twelfth Imam appeared. Buck Williams, CNN news anchor and star reporter, stopped his narration and stared at the figure, not believing his eyes.

He knew the figure had to be a hologram projection, but it was the best full-scale projection he had ever seen. He scanned the walls around the square for the holo projectors necessary for the projection, but he couldn't find them. Microtechnology had reduced holo projectors to the size of a deck of cards. They could have been hidden anywhere in the decorative features of the ornate Arabic architecture.

Williams instantly ordered the holocams trained on the figure of the man. Well read on the history and culture of the Middle East, the reporter knew that the appearance of the Twelfth Imam to the Shiites in Karbala was as important as the Second Coming of Christ would be to Catholics in the Vatican.

The Twelfth Imam was the Mahdi, the right-guided one, the Islamic messiah. It was prophesied that the Mahdi would appear at the beginning of a century and that his coming would bring great violence and the end of the world. Many times in Islamic history, men had stepped forward and claimed in vain to be the Mahdi. The last would-be Mahdi had been the Saudi fanatic who had taken over the Grand Mosque in Mecca in 1979, and his coming had been accompanied by great violence in the most sacred site of Islam.

According to the prophecy, it was the wrong year for a Mahdi to appear, but Williams knew that there was still great potential for violence. Ashurt was an explosive holiday for the volatile Shiites, and the appearance of their long-awaited savior was not going to be a calming event. No one would take the time to count the years since the Prophet's first pilgrimage to Mecca and conclude that the Mahdi was fifty years too early to fulfill the prophecy that he would come at the turn of the Islamic century.

No matter how this turned out today, it would be the biggest event in Islamic history since the attack on the Grand Mosque over fifty years ago.

Glancing down at the monitor, Williams saw that the holocams weren't picking up the image of the Imam. "What's wrong with this fucking equipment?" he snarled, making sure that his mike pickup was turned off before speaking.

The Jordanian-American technician behind the control console shrugged. "Beats the hell outta me, Buck. The camera's working, but I'm just not getting anything."

Williams felt a chill run down his spine. The Imam *had* to be a hologram projection, a damned good one; he couldn't be real. People from the past were dead, pure and simple, and didn't return to the land of the living no matter who they had been. Or what anyone now living said about them.

This religious hologram trick had been done in Mexico City several years earlier. A projection of the Virgin had appeared in front of the Mexican national cathedral, and by the time the authorities had stopped the riots, more than ten thousand people had been killed or injured. But there the CNN holocams had been able to record the image and find the holo projectors that had created it. Here, though, something was preventing him from recording the event.

"Whatever it is, fix it," he hissed. "I've got to get this on tape."

Williams looked at the front of the mosque. From where he stood, it looked as though the Imam had his eyes on him. He shivered when the figure seemed to smile right at him.

The Imam pointed his sword at the CNN news team. "They profane the sacred city," he cried. "Death to the infidels and all their works! *Amr Allah!*" he declared. "God commands it!"

With a cry like that of a beast with ten thousand throats, the crowd turned and surrounded the CNN team. Hemmed in by the walls of the enclosure, they had no place to run. Williams's three Jordanian-American assistants were simply beheaded. Williams himself was skinned alive before he was killed.

One of the CNN remote holovee cameras that had been set on a high tripod to look out over the crowd, had been aimed at Williams when the controls were dropped. It was still running and it captured the executions in full color and three-dimensional images. Before it was ripped down and destroyed, it had transmitted its images to the outside world.

Killing the CNN news team seemed to further ignite the crowd. Screaming "God is great!," they stormed out of the walled square surrounding the mosque and fanned out into the narrow streets of the city. No one noticed as the figure of the Imam faded from sight.

When the mob hit the streets, black-robed men armed with torches and carrying the green banners of jihad—or holy war—suddenly appeared to lead them. Cars and trucks parked along the sides of the streets were quickly overturned and set afire.

Police and troops summoned from the local army garrison tried to stem the orgy of mindless destruction. But firearms were no defense against maddened Shiites armed with swords. They gladly died throwing themselves at the police and soldiers. The Imam had told them that paradise awaited all those who died in this last jihad. Many of the police and troops, Shiites themselves, got caught up in the madness and joined the rioters.

The last place the mob struck was the electrical power plant on the outskirts. By that time they had secured explosives and were able to completely destroy the facility. By sunset that evening, the city of Karbala was in flames from one end to the other.

WHILE THE TWELFTH IMAM was appearing to the throngs of the Shiite faithful in Karbala, fourteen hundred kilometers to the southwest, Prince Khalid ibn Sa'ud, the West-leaning Saudi foreign minister, was meeting a group of Shiite pilgrims at the hill town of Taif overlooking the holy city of Mecca on the plain some five thousand feet below.

The capture of the Grand Mosque in Mecca in 1979 by fundamentalist Shiite dissidents following a self-proclaimed Mahdi had put the house of al-Sa'ud in a bad light throughout the Muslim world. They were entrusted with guarding the sanctity of the holy city and they had publicly failed. The harshest criticism came from the Shiite nations who claimed that the Saudis had become corrupted through their extensive contacts with the West.

In the fifty years since the outrage at the Grand Mosque, the Sunni Muslim ruling house of Saudi Arabia had made every effort to show Shiite pilgrims to Mecca that they were still worthy custodians of the holy city. The appearance of Prince Khalid at this meeting was only one of these gestures.

Though Muharram was not the month of the annual Great Pilgrimage, those who could not come then were allowed to visit at other times. This delegation was in Mecca to meet with the Saudis to discuss the next Pilgrimage. As with the celebration of Ashurt at Karbala, CNN was recording this audience of the prince for transmission to the faithful as part of the Islamic news coverage.

Suddenly a young man, wearing the two "seamless white towels" that were the prescribed robe of a pilgrim, stepped out from the group.

"Ya Khalid," the pilgrim addressed the prince. "Peace be upon you and upon your house." In the informality of the Saudi royal house, it was not customary to use royal titles even when speaking to the king.

The prince smiled. "And upon you be peace," he answered with the traditional reply.

Without another word, the pilgrim flung back the edge of his robe, his hand darted inside and came back out holding a curved length of bright steel. The jambiya, the traditional dagger of the Arab man, flashed through the air.

"*Allah Akbar!* God is Great!" the pilgrim shouted as he thrust the dagger into the heart of the prince.

Giving it a savage twist, he pulled the blade free. A gush of bright blood followed it, staining the prince's white robe. A look of stunned surprise on his face, Prince Khalid collapsed and died.

The beatific smile on the assassin's face shocked all who saw him as he again cried out "*Allah Akbar!*" and plunged the dagger deep into his own throat.

He was dead before he fell to the ground beside the body of the prince.

By nightfall of the tenth day of Muharram, the entire Middle East was in flames. The CNN broadcasts of the appearance of the Mahdi and the assassination of the Saudi prince inflamed the Islamic mobs. Taking up the Imam's cry of jihad against all things Western, they went on a rampage. Religious violence always simmered just beneath the surface of the Middle East and this was all it had taken to make it explode once again.

In other cities, as in Karbala, black-clothed leaders waving the green banners of jihad appeared to direct the rioters to their targets. No one thought to stop and ask who these leaders were, or how it was that they had been prepared and waiting for the riots to start. They just followed them.

2

Cascade Mountains, Oregon—7 June

Staff Sergeant Katrina Wallenska of the recon platoon, Echo Company, United States Expeditionary Force, lay motionless on the hillside overlooking the thickly forested valley below. According to the calendar it was supposed to be summer in the Oregon Cascades, but true to form, it was raining. A fine mist obscured the details of the forest of towering firs around her, but the sensors built into her recon helmet cut through the rain. They also cut through the camouflage, both visual and electronic, that had been erected around the target she was observing, a Thunderbolt antiaircraft missile launcher command center.

The Thunderbolt was manned by a launch crew and security detachment of Regular Army troops from the 314th Air Defense Artillery Battalion that had come down from the Fourth Division at Fort Lewis, Washington, for the training exercise. The purpose of the maneuver was twofold. First was to give the Regular Army experience dealing with this kind of situation, and second, to keep Echo Company's recon teams on their toes.

It had taken Wallenska three rainy days and nights to infiltrate her five-man team to this location and they were the first of three teams taking part in the exercise to reach the objective. One team had been picked off at the drop zone, and the other was still hung up in the mountains. But she had finally located the target, and the fat lady was about to sing.

Wallenska tongued her mike implant and spoke softly. "Ash, this is Kat, I've got 'em. They're right below us in a stand of trees."

Three kilometers away, First Lieutenant Ashley Wells, the platoon leader of Echo Company's recon platoon, called up the display on her helmet visor showing Wallenska's location. This hidden Thunderbolt launcher had already "shot down" two of the Tilt Wings supporting the exercise, and it was time to take it out. "Flash it!" she ordered.

Wallenska quickly pressed a sequence of buttons on her keypad, and the target data from her sensors was instantly transmitted to Lieutenant Wells's helmet visor display. "Got it," she replied.

Quickly scanning the information, the platoon leader saw that the launch center was a good target for the laser-guided bunker buster Wallenska's team had carried for three days. "Can you take 'em out with a pit bull?" Wells asked.

"We have a malf on the pit bull," Wallenska transmitted. "The tracker's not reading. I think the rain got to it."

"Shit!"

Wells went over the target data again. While a recon team's mission was to find the enemy and bring long-range smoke down on them, sometimes they had to go in and do it themselves. This was going to be one of those times. "Take 'em out the hard way."

A big grin spread over Wallenska's face under her helmet visor. The 5 mm caseless ammunition in her M-25 LAR, light assault rifle, was all training loads, since this was a training maneuver. But as far as the sergeant was concerned, war was war. As the sign over the door to the Echo Company armory back at Fort Benning, Georgia, read, "The More Sweat Lost In Training, The Less Blood Lost In Combat."

And she was planning to make those assholes down there sweat. Maybe bleed a little, too. Even training ammunition could mark a man if you know exactly where to put it.

Checking the location beacons of the other four members of her recon team again, Wallenska quickly planned her attack. Her fingers tapped out an attack plan on her keypad, transmitting the planned movements for each team member as soon as she traced it out on her attack display. As soon as the last blue locator pip blinked "message received," she sent the execute signal.

Although the order to move out had been given, an observer watching the hill occupied by Wallenska's team would have seen no movement. The team's recon chameleon camouflage suits were tuned to show the wet greens and browns of the foliage, and they were almost invisible. The team's ECM—Electronic Counter Measures—units in their suits were also keeping them from showing up on the enemy's sensors. The only way they would be seen was if they stumbled into one of the security detachments. But that wasn't too likely in the rain. In Kat's experience, the RA troops she had met didn't like to get wet.

Once down on the flat, Wallenska checked the progress of her team. So far, so good. The locator beacons showed that all of them had reached the valley and were positioned to move in on the command center.

There was a flash of movement in the underbrush in front of her. A man in a camouflage battle dress utility uniform backed into view, dropped his pants and squatted in the wet fir needles. Apparently he was one of the outer ring of security and had chosen this particular moment to answer a call of nature instead of watching his sector.

Slinging her rifle over her shoulder, Wallenska drew the armor piercing, teflon fighting knife from her boot and waited for the soldier to finish his business. She usually didn't take a guy out when he had his pants down. It made the men too insecure and prone to doing something stupid like resisting instead of surrendering. And a guy could get hurt resisting the Kat.

Wallenska activated her helmet air filters and waited until the soldier was finished and had pulled up his pants. As silently as a cougar, she stepped behind him, grabbed him around the neck and threw him to the ground. His yelp of surprise was cut off when he felt the point of the blade slip under the edge of his helmet and prick his skin right over the jugular vein.

"You move and you're dead," Wallenska whispered in his ear.

"Jesus, lady!" the soldier exclaimed. "Be careful with that thing! This is supposed to be an exercise!"

"I ain't no lady," Kat growled softly, keeping the point of the combat knife pressed into his neck. "And all an exercise means to me is that I gotta call in a Dustoff after I stick ya."

"Okay, okay." The soldier tried to relax. "Be frosty."

Wallenska smiled; frosty was her middle name. She never did anything in the heat of anger or passion. The daughter of Polish immigrants, she hadn't gotten where she was in the nation's most elite military unit by being quick-tempered. But that didn't mean that she took any shit from anybody either. All it meant was that she picked her own time and

place to kick someone's ass when he, or she, needed
it.

Wallenska pulled the soldier back into the underbrush with her and, reaching down, punched the
POW/casualty code onto his keypad. This disabled
the soldier's commo and turned off his locator beacon as if he had been killed.

"You stay frosty," she cautioned, "and you won't
get hurt. You start yelling or running around, and
I'm going to come back here and zero you for real.
You read?"

The soldier nodded. "Yo, Sergeant."

Wallenska grinned and patted him on the helmet. "Good boy."

Wallenska's helmet display showed that the rest of
her team had gotten into position around the launch
command center. It also showed that Ironstone, her
assistant team leader, had taken out another one of
the security detachments as well. Whoever was in
charge of these RA malfs obviously had his head
inserted all the way up his anal cavity. He should
have noticed by now that his status board was reading that he had two men down.

It was time to hit them before they got their heads
out and saw that they were about to buy the farm.

She flipped the selector switch on her LAR to
burst fire and flashed a silent assault signal with her
keypad. The four blue pips on her display blinked to
acknowledge. As her old drill sergeant used to say,
it was show time.

SECOND LIEUTENANT Harvey Barnes, United States Air Defense Artillery, huddled under his thermal blanket and tried to stay warm as he watched his threat sensor screen. The heater in the launch command center was turned off so as not to leave an IR trace for the aggressor's sensors to home in on. And, speaking of the aggressors on this exercise, where in the hell were those supersoldiers, anyway? If they were so damned good, why hadn't they found him so he and his people could go back to Fort Lewis and get out of this damned rain? Even though Lewis was only a few hundred kilometers to the north, it was a hell of a lot dryer than in these Oregon mountains. And if the Peacekeepers would only show up, he could go home and dry out before he grew webs between his toes.

The holovee always showed the United States Expeditionary Force as dropping into a crisis and sorting the situation out in less than an hour. Maybe that was because the holovee programs lasted only an hour. But as far as he was concerned, the Peacekeeper's military skills were grossly overrated and this week-long exercise had done nothing to change his mind.

The United States Expeditionary Force had been formed after the U.S. and the remnants of the Soviet Union had mutually disarmed in the late nineties. At that time, the threat of nuclear war did not end. In fact, if anything, it grew even worse.

The United Nations had failed to control the spread of nukes because they had relied on the belief that men and governments would do the "right" thing if they were only shown the way. It had called upon nations to disarm themselves in the name of peace, brotherhood and civilization, but not everyone answered the call. The nations of the Euro-Combine had quickly complied—even the proud French gave up their nuke weapons—but most other nations had laughed in the UN's face. Nukes were the best chance for small nations to even up old scores with their enemies, and they would not willingly give them up.

Then came the brief Arab-Israeli nuclear exchange of 2004. The strike against Tel Aviv had been launched by a mentally unbalanced Syrian major with hashish-inspired dreams of jihad. The rest of the one-day nuclear war had been conducted by the Israelis as they extracted biblical vengeance from their Arabic enemies. Their missiles had been aimed at military rather than civilian targets, but the destruction had been devastating nonetheless.

The great powers reacted instantly. Led by the United States and the Russian Commonwealth of Independent States, military strike forces went into the Middle East and forcefully removed all the remaining nuclear weapons from the warring nations. Some combat erupted during the operation, but no more nukes were detonated. When they were done there, they moved to the other nuclear nations and attempted to disarm them, as well.

While this was going on, the last remnants of the old Palestinian Liberation Organization infiltrated and captured several of the world's largest oil fields. In what became known as the "Palestinian Outrage," they detonated specially designed radioactive cobalt bombs deep underground in the oil-bearing strata. The resulting contamination rendered over sixty percent of the world's oil supply unusable for centuries.

To ensure that nothing like that ever happened again, in 2006 the Russian and the American governments announced the formation of a new world police force: the Russian and American Expeditionary Forces, or the Peacekeepers. Equipped with the best fighting men and women, and the best weapons and equipment the twenty-first century could produce, the United States Expeditionary Force was ready to move at a moment's notice to potential trouble spots anywhere in the world. When a crisis situation arose, the USEF was sent in. Once in action, they would not be withdrawn until the crisis was over. The only way it was over for the Peacekeepers was when their enemies were dead at their feet.

The Peacekeepers got all the headlines and holovee news time, but as Barnes had seen in the recent Mexican border wars, the United States Regular Army didn't do too badly on its own. It was a small organization now, but it hadn't needed the USEF to hold its hand while it whipped several Mexican drug lords' armies. His unit had taken part in that operation, knocking out hostile helicopter gunships, and he felt good about its performance. He was confident that it would do as well against the vaunted Peacekeepers.

Suddenly all the monitors in the launch command center went blank. He punched the button to activate the emergency power packs. But, instead of his monitors coming up again, he heard the sounds of small arms fire break out. Shrugging off his thermal blanket, Barnes snatched his weapon from the rifle rack and dashed for the door of the command centers.

Stepping out under the trees, he was hit by a burst of 5 mm fire that deflected off his body armor and sent him sprawling. When he opened his eyes, a figure in a USEF chameleon suit was standing over him.

Wallenska flipped up her helmet visor. "You're dead meat, LT." She grinned. "Get your ass over there with the rest of your malfs and put your hands up."

Harvey Barnes looked acutely miserable as the rain dripped off the end of his nose. Shit! He'd been taken out by a woman! The guys back at the battalion would never let him live this down.

"KAT? THIS IS ASH," came the voice in Wallenska's earphone.

"Kat, go."

"This is Bold Strider," the lieutenant said, giving her official call sign. "Alpha Kilo X-Ray Two One Mike. How read, over?"

Wallenska quickly punched the code sequence into her keypad and read the message on her helmet display, "Deployment Alert Three. Prepare for immediate retrieval."

"This is Strider Alpha," the sergeant answered with her own official call sign. "Acknowledge Alpha Kilo X-Ray Two One Mike. Ready for transport in zero five. What's up, Ash?"

"I don't know," Wells sent back. "But it looks like a big one, Kat—it's a Dep Three alert. We've been recalled to Benning, and I think we're going to war."

Wallenska felt her heart start to pound. Kicking the shit out of the Regular Army on maneuvers was fun, but that wasn't the reason she joined the Peacekeepers. Like other troopers in the USEF, she referred to their unit as the Warkeepers. Peace was something Kat Wallenska knew very little about. The sole mission of her recon team was to make war.

3

Fort Benning, Georgia—8 June

Captain Alexander K. Rosemont, United States
Regular Army, strode up the sidewalk leading to the
low brick building in the part of Fort Benning
known as Harmony Church. In the distance, he
could hear the sounds of weapons training on the
nearby firing ranges.

Rosemont was blond and blue-eyed like his
namesake Alexander the Great, but that was where
the similarity ended. The legendary Macedonian
king had been a small wiry man, and Rosemont was
six feet tall and muscular. In the age of Alexander,
he would have been considered a giant.

The sky blue beret on his head bore the twin silver bars of his rank and the dark-blue-and-white-
and-gold crest of his last Regular Army unit, the
Twenty-second Infantry. Before the morning was
out, he would retire the blue beret and don the green
beret of the United States Expeditionary Force. The
official name of this elite unit was the Peacekeepers, but peace was not its profession. The busi-

ncss of the USEF was war in its most swift and decisive form. It was true that the Peacekeepers imposed peace wherever they went, but not until the last of their enemies were lying dead at their feet.

Rosemont chuckled at the irony of the hardest-hitting military force in world history going by the name of the Peacekeepers. Like any American who watched their exploits on the holovee, he knew that among themselves, they were known as the Warkeepers. The politicians could mince words all day long if they liked, and call a shovel a manually operated excavation tool, but the troopers of the USEF knew what their job was.

Rosemont had wanted to join the Peacekeepers almost from the moment he had been commissioned in the Regular Army infantry, but a slot in the elite unit was hard to get. Of every one hundred men, enlisted or commissioned, who applied to join the elite unit, only three were chosen to don the proud green beret.

A company commander's slot had opened up in the USEF and, as a result of Rosemont's commendations in the recent Mexican border action, he had been selected to fill that slot. Now he, too, would be on the cutting edge of keeping peace in the world.

THE WORLD in the year 2030 was somewhat more peaceful than it had been over the previous forty years, but what peace there was had mostly been imposed by force of arms. While the United States, the EuroCombine and the Union of Soviet Demo-cratic Republics had reduced their military forces to purely defensive levels over the last 50 years, the rest of the world had not followed their example. If anything, more men were under arms than at any time since the end of the Cold War.

Successful at their mission of ridding the world of nuclear weapons, the Peacekeepers had recently been deployed for other missions. In the politics of the twenty-first century, no one denied the right of a nation to slaughter its own people or to make lim-ited war along its borders. Warfare had always been mankind's favorite blood sport and this hadn't changed. Most of these were little wars, however, local affairs more on the order of a soccer match with live ammunition.

Even in this era of military and political realism, wars of conquest were still frowned upon. When armies crossed established national boundaries, they would more often than not find the Peacekeepers standing in their path. Like the legionnaires of Au-gustan Rome who had kept the two-hundred-year Pax Romana, the Peacekeepers drew their swords and marked the line on the sand in front of them. An aggressor crossed that line at his peril.

The wall-size map in the entryway to the USEF headquarters told the story of the Peacekeepers and the United States Army and Marine Corps units it had sprung from. Known as the Hall of Honor, it held the honored memorabilia from over two hundrcd fifty years of a proud American military history.

Midway through the hall was a battered flag that had flown over the Lang Vei Special Forces camp in the Vietnam War of the 1960s and '70s. Rosemont's grandfather had been in a Special Forces A Team in Vietnam, and he remembered the stories the old man had told him. Stories of bravery thrown away in the name of political expediency. That was something that didn't happen in the USEF. When a Peacekeeper was killed in action, his survivors knew that he or she had died for something worth dying for.

The USEF had chosen to wear the green beret of the old Special Forces as a badge of honor. In a short while Rosemont, too, would finally wear it.

AT THE END OF THE HALL, Rosemont handed a hard copy of his ordcrs to the first lieutenant adjutant along with the diskcttc containing his 201 file.

"Have a seat, sir," the adjutant said. "The colonel will see you in just a moment."

"What's going on?" Rosemont asked as he watched men and women hurrying from one room to another.

"We're on a Dep Three alert," the lieutenant replied with a grin. "It looks like we're going to the Middle East again."

Even though he had been isolated at the USEF indoctrination course, Rosemont knew about the current situation in the Middle East. Like most Westerners, he knew that the so-called Twelfth Imam who had suddenly appeared was nothing more than a sophisticated hologram projection. But he also knew that this explanation wasn't being accepted by the Islamic masses, particularly the Shiite Muslims. The worst part was that the national armies in the region were massing and preparing to go to war in an attempt to protect themselves from what they saw as an external threat. And, as always in the Middle East, for oil.

Since the Palestinian Outrage of 2005, the world's remaining uncontaminated oil reserves were more valuable than gold. Nations were all too ready to go to war either to protect what oil they had left, or to take their neighbor's if they thought they could get away with it.

The adjutant answered his buzzer and looked over to Rosemont. "The colonel will see you now," he said. "First door on the right."

Rosemont straightened his uniform blouse and stepped up to the door.

"Enter," a deep voice answered his knock.

He marched into the room and stopped the regulation three paces in front of the colonel's desk. "Captain Alexander Rosemont, reporting for duty, sir."

After returning his salute, the colonel stood and extended his hand. "Bernard Jacobson," he said. "Glad to have you on board, Rosemont."

"I'm glad to be here, sir."

"Have a seat."

"As you know," the colonel said, "I'm sending you down to Echo Company. Echo Company is designated as light infantry. But don't let the title confuse you. One of our light infantry companies can stand up to a standard infantry battalion and beat them into the ground. Our heavy infantry companies can take on a full regiment and wipe them off the face of the earth. We're small but we're powerful. And, man for man, or woman for woman, I think I've got the best troops in the world. Not even the Russian Expeditionary Force can stand up to us."

Rosemont knew the colonel wasn't bragging. It was a cold statement of fact. An exhibit in the Hall of Honor commemorated one of the first USEF actions, the attack on the secret nuclear weapons facility in Pakistan.

The mountain facility had been guarded by two divisions of Pakistan's best troops equipped with the latest Han Empire weapons and armor. But neither the overwhelming numerical superiority nor the Chinese weapons had stopped the Peacekeepers. In one pitched battle, Bravo Company had won battle honors by crushing a Pakistani armored division, men in heavy infantry powered fighting suits against tanks.

"That's the good news, Rosemont," the colonel continued. "The bad news is that Echo Company's in the barrel this time. If we go on this one, your people will be the first in. I hate to do this to you and I'd like to send Charlie Company, but they're tied up in the Amazon and I can't withdraw them in time."

"I think they can handle it, sir," the new company commander replied. "They can keep after me until I get up to speed."

"You've got some good people down there," Jacobson said. "Your XO is on the promotion list to captain, and your recon platoon leader is the best I have.

"And speaking of promotions," the colonel continued, opening his desk drawer, "all my company commanders are majors, so here's your oak leaves. You'll be acting major until the orders come through."

Just then the adjutant walked into the colonel's office with a green beret in his hand. Rosemont's 201 file contained his uniform sizes, and he had sent down to supply for the right-size beret. He helped Rosemont pin on the new badges of his rank and handed him the green beret.

"Congratulations, Major Rosemont." The colonel extended his hand. "You're now a Peacekeeper. Take command of your company and prepare for immediate deployment. I'll see you at the officers' briefing later today."

Rosemont shook his hand, then saluted. "Yes, sir."

"Good luck."

"Yo! MICK!" First Lieutenant Ashley Wells yelled over to her fellow lieutenant and company executive officer First Lieutenant Thomas "Mick" Sullivan.

The sound of Ashley's throaty voice calling his name spun Sullivan around. Even after three weeks in the field, Ashley Wells was her usual beautiful self. Her face and hands were dirty, her close-cropped dark blond hair was matted with dried sweat, but her slate gray eyes sparkled. He could smell her from where he stood. Even over the arms room smells of gun oil, ammunition and explosives, came the strong aroma of unwashed female. He had to admit, however, that on her, it didn't smell all that bad. On a few occasions, Mick had tried to get close to her off duty, but she had brushed him off as she did anyone who tried to date her.

"You guys made good time getting back here," he said. "I didn't expect you until later this evening."

"The throttle jockeys in the blue suits stayed in full afterburner all the way," she replied. "What's the drill this time?"

"We're at Dep Three."

Ashley ran her hand through her short hair trying to fluff it up. "What's the word? Where we going this time?"

"The Middle East. That phoney Imam has them going crazy over there. Their national armies are on the move, and the whole place is about to blow up again.''

''Oh, shit!''

If there was any place on earth that the fair-skinned Ashley Wells hated, it was the desert. And her least favorite people on the planet were the Arabs.

''Oh,'' he said. ''Word is that we got our new CO in this morning.''

''Just fucking outstanding!'' Wells snorted, ''We're on a Dep Three alert and we've got an FNG CO. You met him yet?''

''No, but I've seen him and he looks like he knows his business.''

Ashley's gray eyes looked up at him. ''Did he come in wearing a Superman cape with blue flame shooting out his ass?''

Sullivan hated it when she got sarcastic. ''No,'' he said patiently. ''He came in wearing a blue beret with a Twenty-second Infantry crest, a CIB on his chest and a SoCom combat patch.''

''Woopie fucking doo.'' Ashley twirled her index finger around in the air. ''So he's from SoCom—Southern Command, and a real war hero. Just what we need, RA all the way.''

The recent war—a low-intensity conflict, as Congress called it—with the Mexican drug lords across the nation's southern border had been an all Regular Army affair. Relations with Mexico were touchy enough without sending the Peacekeepers in to lay waste to a large area of the country. Not that the drug armies had been a pushover, however. The drug lords had the money to buy the finest military hardware on the market and hire the best trained mercenaries in the world. It had not been an easy fight, and some RA units had taken heavy casualties.

"Ash," Sullivan said seriously, "we've got to give this guy a chance. He's not Major Nicks but maybe he'll work out. You'd better clean up your act for a couple of weeks. He might not appreciate having one of his LTs mouthing off to him all the time."

Ashley threw her head back and laughed. "Thanks, Mick," she said. "I really needed that. When the day comes that I walk softly around some FNG RA major, they can have my fucking bars. They don't call me Ash and Trash for nothing, you know."

Ashley Wells hadn't joined the army to have a job. She'd had all the civilian jobs she could handle just trying to spend her share of her family's money. She had taken a commission and had joined the Peacekeepers because she wanted to do something with her life that made a difference.

Her nickname came not only for her effective use of the more pithy words of English, but also for what she left behind at the end of an operation. When Ashley Wells's troops were done with an area, all that was left was ash and trash.

"Just trying to be helpful, Ash."

"Thanks, Mick," she replied with a smile. "I appreciate it. But whoever he is, I think I can handle him."

Sullivan had no doubt in his military mind about that.

4

Al Qatif, Saudi Arabia—8 June

Saudi Prince Azis ibn Khalid, the director of
Aramco, the huge Saudi oil conglomerate, watched
helplessly from his skimmer scout car as the fires
raged out of control in the Al Qatif oil-pumping
complex. Untold millions of irreplaceable barrels of
crude oil were going up in flames, and the fire
danced in the tears of rage forming in the corners of
his eyes.

Since the Palestinian Outrage, no one had dared
to damage an uncontaminated oil field, much less
set one afire. Now that over sixty percent of the
world's oil reserves were contaminated with radioactive cobalt, oil was far too precious to merely
burn. Not for the first time, the Prince silently called
upon Allah to punish all the Palestinians still left
alive. Not that there were that many, however. In the
aftermath of the Outrage, Palestinians in the Middle East had been driven out. The remnants of their
population were now all safely overseas living in
Western nations.

Following Iraq's downfall in the 1991 Gulf War, the only people who had been excluded from the various settlements had been the Palestinians. Over the next fifteen years they simmered as they watched the Kurds carve a homeland for themselves out of what had been northern Iraq and the Shiites in the southern part of the country win a republic for themselves, as well.

As always, no one had been concerned about finding a final homeland for the Palestinians, not even their brother Arabs. They had sided with the madman Saddam in his war against Saudi Arabia and Kuwait, and had to be punished for it. In a gesture of peace, the Israelis had finally relinquished control of the Golan Heights back to Syria, but even that had not helped the Palestinians. Like the other neighboring Arabic states, the Syrians had not wanted them, either, and refused to allow them into the country.

Over the next ten years the Palestinians had grown even more violent, attacking Arabic, as well as Western interests from their enclaves in the Middle East and overseas. After the short nuclear war of 2004, the Palestinians finally struck in a final orgy of frustration. In a well-coordinated operation, PLO commandos infiltrated most of the world's oil fields and detonated cobalt bombs deep inside the oil-bearing strata to contaminate it. If they couldn't share in the oil wealth of the Middle East, then no one would.

To the industrial worlds of both the East and West, the loss of oil had been only a short-term problem. Experimental alternative-energy sources had been on hand for many years and were quickly converted to use. Methanol was used to power motor vehicles. Senoil—produced from garbage, biomass waste and the remaining oil-bearing shale reserves—took up much of the slack for lubricants. But natural petroleum oil was still necessary for medical and chemical industries, so the price of the remaining usable crude oil remained outrageously high, and the oil-producing nations were still wealthy. And most of that oil was still in the Middle East, particularly in Saudi Arabia.

With the destruction of the oil reserves, nuclear power development also went into high gear, and power requirements were quickly filled by nuclear-generated electricity. Western antinuke activists had resorted to terrorism to try to stop this. After sabotaging a nuke plant in the United States, they were hunted down and eliminated.

Nuclear-powered desalinization plants along the Persian Gulf had produced massive amounts of freshwater for irrigation and reforestation projects in the region. The greening of the desert had dramatically raised the standard of living for most of the Gulf peoples. But not everyone was happy about the changes.

The ancient tension between the settled city people and the desert dwellers became even more acute as more and more desert was brought under cultivation or was planted with trees. With less arid land available for the nomads and their flocks and camels, the ancient ways were dying, but not without a struggle. The insane ravings of the false Imam were generating violence against anything that was contaminated with Western technology.

Saudi history was full of the desert people rebelling against technological progress, but this time even city dwellers were caught up in this frenzy. Although a Muslim himself, the prince gave no credence to the mystical appearances of the Twelfth Imam. He had a PhD in engineering from Cal Tech and he knew that it was a hoax, even if the superstitious believers did not.

The Saudi government had gone on the holovee to try to explain what was happening, but to no avail. The violence was spreading. This was the fourth such attack on a Saudi industrial target in under a week. Raiders had also hit one of the desalinization plants along the coast and a nuclear power plant. Whoever the raiders had been, in all of the incidents they had gotten past the Saudi defenses, planted their charges and had escaped unseen.

The Saudi military had the finest equipment that oil money could buy, but they were small, maybe too small. The prince would recommend to the king, his uncle, that the Westerners be invited in again to protect the kingdom as they had done back in his father's time when Saddam's armies threatened the oil fields. He would have preferred not to have to call upon the West to protect his nation, but as an engineer, Prince ibn Khalid was also a realist. The future of Saudi Arabia was at stake, and it was vital that something be done to prevent another outrage like this from happening.

At least oil-fire fighting had progressed dramatically over the past fifty years. It had taken the fire crews a year to put out the oil-field fires in Kuwait when the madman Saddam had torched the wells there in '91. It should take no more than a few days to put out these fires here at Al Qatif.

"ATTEN-HUT!" First Sergeant Ward's voice rang out in the Echo Company briefing room. As the officers and senior NCOs got to their feet, Rosemont strode through the door, very aware of the shiny new major's gold oak leaves on his epaulets.

"Take your seats, please," he ordered as he reached the podium at the front of the room. "As all of you know, we are on a Dep Three alert, and I have just received word that all personnel will be confined to the base until further notice."

"Shit, sir!" Ashley Wells's contralto voice rang out in the crowded briefing room.

Rosemont stopped in midsentence with his mouth open. The comment had come from a petite blonde with the silver bars of a first lieutenant on her collar. "Did you say something, Lieutenant?"

Lieutenant Mick Sullivan caught the tone in Rosemont's voice and realized instantly what had happened. Apparently the Regular Army didn't have the tradition of allowing subordinates to question orders, and he had thought that Ashley was being insubordinate. "Sir?" Sullivan said urgently. "May I have a quick word with you? It's rather important."

Not knowing what in the hell was going on, Rosemont turned to his XO.

"What Lieutenant Wells said, sir. It's a tradition in the USEF," Sullivan hastened to explain. "She was not being insubordinate, sir. When a senior orders something that a junior thinks is unreasonable, it is traditional that they are allowed to make the comment 'Shit, sir.'"

"Is there a traditional answer to that?" Rosemont asked.

"Yes, sir. If you don't want to discuss the matter, the answer is 'Shut up and soldier.'"

Rosemont smiled. "Lieutenant Wells?" he called out.

"Yes, sir."

"Shut up and soldier, Wells."

Laughter broke out all over the room.

"Yes, sir," she answered meekly.

"Now," Rosemont said with a grin. "If I may return to the briefing?"

There was another burst of laughter.

"As I am sure all of you know, we are alerted for possible deployment to the Middle East. And, as you also know, this is my first day on the job. The colonel told me that I could depend on you to keep me out of trouble until I can at least figure out where the latrines are."

That got a good laugh.

"Therefore," Rosemont continued, "go on about your business, and if anyone sees that I'm doing something that I shouldn't, or even more important, not doing something that I should be doing, please let me know ASAP."

Flicking on the wall-size holo projection map of the Middle East, he picked up the light pencil and pointed out a location in the middle of the Saudi desert. "If we are deployed, Echo Company will drop into this DZ."

He punched up a magnification and zoomed in on an industrial complex in the sand to the south of their drop zone. "This is the Rafhah oil complex, and our initial mission will be to guard it. Recon platoon will lead the drop, with the line platoons coming in after the DZ has been secured."

For the next half hour, Rosemont went over the initial phase of the mission. It was a standard operation, but it helped him to talk through it. "Are there any questions?" he asked when he was finished.

As he had expected, there were none and he dismissed the group. "Wells?" he called out as the meeting broke up.

"Sir?"

"I'd like you to report to my office at your earliest convenience."

"Yes, sir."

ROSEMONT LOOKED UP from his desk at the knock on the door. "Enter!" he called out.

The blond lieutenant who had mouthed off to him in the briefing marched in. Halting the regulation three paces in front of his desk, she rendered a crisp salute. "First Lieutenant Ashley Wells reporting, sir."

Rosemont returned her salute, then rose from his chair. "I don't believe we've been properly introduced," he said, extending his hand. "I'm Alex Rosemont."

She stepped up and shook his hand firmly. "Ashley Wells, sir."

"Have a seat, Wells," Rosemont said as he took his chair again and punched up her file on his desk monitor. She sat on the chair, her hands crossed in her lap, as he quickly studied her military records. As the colonel had said, her record was impressive. She had earned the Distinguished Service Cross and the UN Legion of Honor. Not bad for a first lieutenant.

"I see that you're from L.A.," he said. "Any relation to the UniCard Wells family?"

Ashley's eyes flashed. "That's not in my file, is it, Major?"

Rosemont was a little taken aback by the tone of her voice. "No, it isn't," he replied. "Your next of kin is listed as an attorney's office, Butler, Butler and Associates."

"Then that's my family."

Rosemont sat back in his chair and studied the woman seated in front of him. Obviously he had struck a raw nerve here. If she was the daughter of Winston W. Wells and one of his many wives—all blond, all beautiful and all much younger than the wealthy financier—it wasn't any of his business. But from the looks of this Lieutenant Ashley Wells, she had to be one of Winston Wells's several daughters. Her kind of fine-featured, aristocratic beauty didn't come from a random matching of genes. It could only be achieved by generations of breeding for aristocratic beauty.

"Look, Wells," he finally said, "I really don't care who your parents are. As far as I am concerned, you were born the day you took your commissioning oath and I really don't give a damn about your civilian background. Just as long, that is, as it doesn't affect your ability to do your duties."

He held up his hand to forestall her reply. "And from your service record, I can see that it obviously hasn't. So as far as I am concerned, the matter is of no interest. Does that take care of it?''

"Yes, sir."

"Now," he continued, "on to the purpose of the meeting. I will be making the initial drop with your platoon."

"Have you ever ridden a recon drop capsule, sir?'' Wells cut in.

He reached up and tapped the silver jump wings on the left top pocket of his uniform blouse. "I'm fully jump qualified."

"But in recon capsules, sir, or in heavies?''

"I've done both, Wells," he answered, trying to regain control of the conversation. The colonel had said that Wells was the best recon platoon leader in the regiment, but he had failed to add that she was mouthy on top of it. "May I continue?''

"Yes, sir."

"As I said, I will drop with your platoon while Lieutenant Sullivan remains with the rest of the company."

"Question, sir."

"Yes?''

"May I ask why the major is dropping with us, sir?'' Wells locked eyes with him. "It is customary for the command group to come down with the line platoons. Sir."

Rosemont leaned forward. "It is also customary for me not to explain my orders, Lieutenant. Since I'm new around here, I'll do it just this once. I don't know anything about your last company commander, but let me explain a few things about the way I operate. First off, as long as you remain in this unit, you can expect me to do things my way without taking an opinion poll.''

Wells stiffened at the implied threat and forced herself to relax again. She wasn't about to let this guy bluff her. She knew her record and knew that he couldn't afford to transfer her out. Not now, at any rate.

"You can also expect me to command my company from the point of contact. As you can plainly see from the badge on my chest, I've been shot at before and expect to be shot at again as long as I wear the green suit."

Wells's eyes automatically flashed up to the sky-blue-and-silver-wreathed musket of the combat infantryman's badge pinned on the left breast of his uniform blouse. Under it were the ribbons for a Silver Star, a Bronze Star and the campaigns in both Mexico and Cuba. There was also the plain purple ribbon of a Purple Heart, denoting that he had been wounded in combat.

"Which is why I'm dropping with your platoon, Wells. Any time Echo Company is deployed, you can expect me to be with the lead element. Any questions?"

"No, sir."

"However," he continued, "I also expect my subordinates to guide me in their areas of expertise.

As my recon platoon leader, I expect you to make sure that I am employing your people to their best advantage. Should you have a tactical suggestion, do not hesitate to make it. At the same time, however, once I have made a command decision, I expect it to be followed without question. Understood?"

"Yes, sir."

"That's all for now."

"Yes, sir." She rose and saluted.

Rosemont returned the salute.

Doing an about-face, Wells headed for the door thinking that she should have listened to Sullivan. Obviously Mick had been right for a change. This guy was a far cry from Major Nicks. At least with Nicks, she hadn't had to watch her mouth all the time.

"Lieutenant," Rosemont called out, and she halted, her hand on the doorknob. "Tell your rigger that I will be by shortly to have my drop capsule fitted."

"Yes, sir."

"That's all."

Rosemont watched Ashley Wells close the door behind her. She was a beautiful woman and obviously a talented professional soldier, but he wasn't too sure how long she was going to last under his command. He knew that there were always a few people who didn't make the transition to a new commander, but he hoped that she would make it. He hated to lose a good recon platoon leader.

He pushed the intercom button on his desk. "Can you send the first sergeant in, please?"

"Yes, sir," his clerk answered.

5

Fort Benning, Georgia—9 June

While the world watched the latest turmoil in the Middle East, the Peacekeepers quickly and quietly prepared to go to war. The longer they stayed at Dep Three, the more Rosemont liked it, however. He needed all the extra time he could get to become more acquainted with his unit and form the bonds with his officers and NCOs that would make for effective combat leadership when the balloon finally did go up. And he had no doubts that it would. The reports from the Middle East were more and more disturbing, and the situation was rapidly disintegrating.

The Twelfth Imam had appeared in several more cities. Each time he raised the cry for jihad against the West, riots and mass destruction followed. Much of the Arabic world was rapidly slipping back into a medieval state. Worse than that, though, was that the armies of most of the Arabic nations were massing against their old enemies, blaming them for their internal disruptions. Tempers were high, and all it would take was one accidental contact for the entire region to explode into open warfare.

He had learned that the Russian Expeditionary Force planned to deploy along its borders with Iran and the Islamic republics in the southwest of what had been the old Soviet Union. If fighting broke out in the Arabic gulf states, it would be up to both the Russian and American Peacekeepers to put an end to it.

Rosemont was going over the endless paperwork associated with the mission preparation when the company First Sergeant, Roger "Big Daddy" Ward, knocked on his open door. "I've got the printouts you wanted, sir."

"Come on in, Top."

First Sergeant Ward had been in the Army for most of his adult life. A big, burly man with a shaved head, Ward's broad face bore the scars and wrinkles of twenty-six years as a combat infantryman. The puckered scar that ran along the right side of his jaw had been given to him by a Pakistani bayonet. The matching scar on the left side of his face was from grenade frag he had picked up in the jungles of Colombia. The deep wrinkles around his eyes were from squinting into the sun of more than a dozen battlefields ranging from Egypt to the Amazonian jungle.

No one would ever mistake Big Daddy Ward for anything other than what he was, a professional soldier.

Rosemont couldn't have asked for a better First Shirt for Echo Company. Since he planned to be with his lead elements in the field, he needed someone like Top Ward to handle the company's rear. The way the USEF was organized, the companies did not have large headquarters staff as the Regular Army did. Lieutenant Sullivan, his XO, commanded First Platoon when the company was in the field. He acted as the executive officer only when they were in garrison. In the field, Top Ward and his small HQ crew took care of all the admin and logistics chores for the unit.

"What's the story on our skimmers?" Rosemont asked, taking the equipment readiness printouts from the first sergeant. "The force maintenance chief tells me that two of them are deadlined and probably won't be repaired in time to make the deployment."

The GEV-6 ground-effects scout vehicles, more popularly known as skimmers, were vital for desert operations and, as far as Rosemont was concerned, he needed every last one he could put his hands on. Having the two of them unavailable would severely cramp his style. In the desert he needed his mobility as much as he needed firepower.

Ward smiled thinly, stretching the scar on his jaw. "They'll be ready for the drop, sir. I have the chief's sacred word on that."

Rosemont didn't bother to ask how Ward had managed to get the vehicles repaired. There were some things that a company commander was better off not knowing. That was why a company had a first sergeant anyway—to handle the dirty work and the under-the-table deals.

"Okay, how are we doing on the rest of the Dep One preloads?"

The first sergeant opened his own set of printouts to the proper page. "We're up on rations and med supplies, sir. Some of the ammunition is still short, but I've got supply working on that right now."

"Good. Keep me informed."

"Yes, sir."

Rosemont flipped back to another page. "Now, what's our personnel status?"

WHILE THE USEF PREPARED their equipment for war, the troops were being prepared, as well. All personnel not actively engaged in essential duties had gathered in the classroom for last-minute training and orientation. The force training officer was tall, balding and wore glasses. To many of the younger troops in the classroom, he was the only man they had ever seen wearing them. Even with modern medical techniques, there were still those few whose vision could not be corrected with laser surgery.

"Okay," he said, keying his briefing notes into the classroom monitors. "Listen up, people. The topic of today's discussion is Saudi culture and desert operations. I know that all of you have had your basic briefing on these subjects, but since we will be staging out of Saudi for this emergency, the colonel wants us to go over it one more time.

"Even though the Saudis are, in most respects, the most modern of the Islamic states, in many ways they are still the most conservative. As you will remember, the Arabic word 'Islam' means 'submission,' and in this case, it means submission to God.

"The result of this submission to God is that Muslims live without the separation of church and state as we know it in this country. Every aspect of Saudi life is guided by Islamic principles as laid down in the Koran, their sacred book, rather than by law as we know it. Everything from the law to banking and what they can eat and wear is determined solely by their religion.

"While we will be operating out of one of the Saudi military enclaves or in the field away from the general population, you must still be aware of Islamic sensibilities at all times. Particularly those sensibilities regarding women. The Saudis have been aware we use female troops since the first Gulf War back in '91. The conflicts since then have helped them get used to seeing Western women in uniform. There are still some Islamic customs that female personnel will observe at all times no matter where they are."

Several of the women troopers groaned.

The training officer peered through his thick lenses. "Is there some problem with this?"

"Sir," a rugged, redheaded woman with E-5 sergeant stripes on her collar spoke up. "Does that mean that we can't take our halter tops and suntan oil?"

"Yes, it does, Sergeant. No halter tops, no shorts and no bikinis. Understood?"

"Shit, sir," the sergeant said.

"Shut up and soldier," he replied.

"Yes, sir."

"Any more questions about this issue?" He peered at his audience. "Good. All female personnel will read over the special briefing instructions on your monitors and will log in that you have read and understood. We can't have any incidents this time."

Every trooper in the classroom, male and female, was well aware of the loss of life that had occurred at Riyadh when a truck full of off-duty American service women from the nearby air base went into town. The women had been dressed in shorts and halter tops, standard wear for Americans at home, but shockingly provocative dress by Arabic standards. When the truck stopped at a traffic light, one of the women playfully flashed her bare breasts at a large group of Arab men who were on the street corner staring at them.

The woman thought that she was being playful, showing off to the men. The Saudi men, however, felt that she was purposely insulting them by showing her nakedness and stormed the truck. The handful of men on the truck vainly tried to protect their fellow female soldiers, but they were quickly beaten senseless. One of them later died of his wounds. The women were beaten senseless and raped, with two of them dying in the ordeal.

The ensuing diplomatic flap over the incident seriously threatened to end the longstanding American-Saudi relationship and almost caused a war. The so-called human rightists in Congress demanded that strong actions be taken against the sexist Saudis, and the Saudi government quickly responded. The rapists were rounded up immediately and executed Saudi fashion, publicly beheaded with a sword. But that had only caused even more cries of outrage from the human rightists. Those men had not been given a long, drawn-out Western-style public trial with defense lawyers and endless appeals, but had been condemned and summarily executed by an Islamic religious tribunal.

The situation was finally smoothed over when the Saudi government paid huge damage settlements to the victims and their families.

Since then American female military personnel serving in the Middle Eastern nations had been under orders to obey certain Arabic customs, like it or not. When those orders came down, the human rightists screamed about sexual discrimination. But they were overridden. The Middle East was still too

important to the Western world to risk further
damaging the all-too-often delicate relationship.

"Next," the training officer continued, "is the
topic of alcohol."

Even more groans greeted this subject.

"As those of you who have operated in the Middle East before are well aware, alcohol is not allowed."

He quickly raised a hand to forestall the comments he knew were coming. "Yes, I know that this
rule is more often broken than not, particularly by
Muslims who had been educated in the West. But as
far as the USEF is concerned, this will be a dry operation. Colonel Jacobson has instructed me to tell
you that there will be no exceptions to this rule. Any
trooper found smuggling booze or setting up a still
will be dealt with accordingly."

He paused. "And as you all know, when 'the
Bull' says no, he means no. Any questions about
this?"

There were none.

"Now, on to our next topic, heat stroke and water discipline."

ROSEMONT WAS GOING OVER the last of the load-out
lists when his intercom buzzed. "Yes?"

"Major," the first sergeant's voice came over the
intercom. "The colonel has ordered an immediate
commander's call in the 'Bull Pit.'"

"'Bull Pit,' Top?"

"Yes, sir," Ward answered. "That's the situation room right next to his office."

"On the way."

Colonel Jacobson was in the Bull Pit studying the holomap on the main screen when Rosemont arrived. As he slid into his seat, the sergeant major announced, "Ladies and gentlemen, the force commander."

Everyone fell silent as the colonel turned around and stepped up to the podium. "Ladies and gentlemen," he intoned. "We are at Dep Two as of 1400 hours Zulu. I expect to receive a Dep One message at any moment."

A murmur ran through the crowded officers' briefing room. Deployment Alert One meant war. And, as they all knew, a real shooting war, not a talking war. They had all been expecting it for the past two days, but it was still a shock now that it was finally happening. Some of them smiled thinly, some faces showed concern, but everyone felt a rush of adrenaline. When this was over, there would be another exhibit in the Hall of Honor and more names chiseled into the black granite of the Memorial Wall—the names of the men and women who had died fighting for peace.

"Our latest Intel shows that the situation in the gulf states of the Middle East has completely fallen apart. Many cities are in the hands of rioters, and effective civilian government is almost nonexistent at this time. Iraq has fallen to the extremists, and the

Saudis are fighting armed raiders along their borders. The Intel birds are also showing Israeli armor moving toward the borders with Jordan and Syria. The war hasn't started yet, and our mission is to get this situation under control as quickly as possible and see that it doesn't turn into a full-blown conflict.

"We will be dropping into Saudi Arabia where we will join up with the Saudi national forces and go into a defensive posture. As soon as we have secured the Saudi borders and expelled the raiders, we will fan out into the other gulf states and put down the insurrection wherever we find it. For the most part, we expect cooperation from the local governments. Except, of course, from the Iranians."

That comment got a tense laugh. Iran was governed by a body of Ulmas, religious leaders, who could seldom agree with each other much less with anyone else. In the past fifty years, Iran had been in almost total isolation and, without the oil production of the gulf states, had slipped into being the poorest of the Arabic states.

"Your mission packs are waiting when you leave the room, and the company drop zones have been entered into the tactical data base."

The colonel paused for a moment. "You will prepare your units for immediate deployment. Your transport is landing at Lawson Airfield right now and as soon as it's all down, preloading will commence. As soon as this has been completed, move your troops to the airfield, as well. We will lift off as soon as I receive the Dep One message."

His eyes swept the room. "Are there any questions?"

There were none. Every man and woman in the United States Expeditionary Force knew their jobs cold. They wouldn't be in the Peacekeepers if they didn't.

The colonel looked at each face in the room one last time. The way this operation was shaping up, this might be the last time he would see some of these men and women alive. "Good luck, ladies and gentlemen."

The departing officers were issuing orders to their subordinates by comlink before they were out of the door. Rosemont flashed the load-out message to Top Ward and grinned when he saw the figures read out for the equipment that was already standing by at the airfield.

It was nice working with a true professional. It made his job so much easier and, right now, he needed all the help he could get.

6

High over the Desert—10 June

Alex Rosemont could smell himself. The acrid reek
of his adrenaline-laden sweat cut through the normal odors of an aircraft packed with troops. The
closer they got to the drop zone, the ranker he
smelled. Looking across to the row of half-opened
recon drop capsules on the opposite side of the
plane, he saw the blond hair of Lieutenant Ashley
Wells. She was sitting with her helmet in her lap and
her head laid back against the webbing, sleeping as
peacefully as if she were in her own bunk back at
Benning.

Seeing Wells so comfortable under these circumstances pissed him off to no end. He had told her
that he was fully jump qualified, and he was. But he
had not told her that he had an almost paralyzing
fear of heights. Nor had he told her that he hated
jumping more than anything else in the world, particularly dropping at night.

Throughout his Army career, he had been able to
hide this particular fear and he was sure as hell not

going to let his control slip now. Not only was he the new CO who had to prove himself to his command, but he was also going to war. Any man was allowed to refuse to make a drop whenever he wanted, but he was not going to miss out on this for anything. He would make the drop if it killed him, which was exactly what he was afraid of.

He heard the electric whine of the plane's wing sweep motors and felt the C-36B Valkyrie airborne assault transport suddenly decelerate and go subsonic. Flicking on his nav display, he saw that they were approaching the drop zone, a patch of the Saudi desert close to the southern Iraqi border guarding the Rafhah oil field. He felt the sweat break out again and would have killed for a shower.

When his earphone bonged with the "suit up" signal, he closed the jump capsule shell around his chest and dogged it down tight. Closing his helmet visor, he checked the helmet seals and turned on the oxygen supply for the ride down. The stale, musty taste of the bottle air made him salivate, and he swallowed to clear his mouth. God, he hated this shit!

After making a quick function check on the drop capsule, he stood up at the end of the jump line and shuffled forward to the capsule launchers on the sides of the aircraft. The display on his visor still read that everything was in the green as he stepped into the launcher. He felt the clamps secure him and the magnoelastic joints of his capsule stiffen to lock his legs together and hold his arms tightly to his sides. He knew some fanatics who still jumped with just a nylon parachute strapped to their backs. The mere thought of stepping out into empty space without a jump capsule around him was enough to make him want to puke.

He was on the end of the stick and had to wait until the rest of the platoon was launched before he felt the slam of the launch against his shoulders. As always, his stomach lurched and he clamped his jaws together, sucking in the stale, dry oxygen as deeply as he could. The capsule bounced in the turbulence as it cleared the launcher before the stabilizers snapped out and caught the air.

Once the ride smoothed out, Rosemont flicked on the drop display on his visor and watched the altimeter reading swiftly decline. His speed was within the limits for a recon capsule, but dangerously on the high side. It must be the low air density that was making him fall so fast. The air was hot over the desert, even this early in the morning.

He rested his right index finger on the trigger for the speed brakes, but didn't pop a retard. Right now the recon drop capsules were as stealthy as technologically possible. Their radar signature was less than that of a sparrow, but the instant that he hit the retard, he would show up as if he were in a hot-air balloon. His screen showed that none of the other capsules had their retards deployed, and if they could do it, he could, too.

As the altimeter numbers ticked off like an over-revved clock, he watched the other capsules on his screen. They were approaching the deploy point at well over three hundred miles per hour, but no one had popped their capsule's canopy yet. They were riding them all the way down as though they were bombing the drop zone.

He felt his testicles suck up into his belly when he thought of hitting the ground at that speed. The capsule had a reserve chute if the main failed, but it was useless below a certain height. Hell, even the mains were useless unless you deployed them in time.

When he saw the first capsule pop its main chute, he instinctively triggered his own. The opening shock slammed him against the capsule shell, but it was over in an instant as the breaking chute fully deployed. He had opened low and, falling as fast as they had been, he was still approaching the ground too damned fast. He reached for the "chicken switch" to the emergency retro rocket, but was too late. He hit the ground hard, knocking the breath out of him.

"ROUGH JUMP, MAJOR?" came Wells's voice in his earphone as he de-magged the capsule joints and struggled to get to his feet.

Rosemont heard the amusement in her voice. Fuck her. "I'm fine," he answered. "Status?"

"All down and deployed," she answered. "No hostiles spotted and no scanning detected."

"Send the all clear," he said as he quickly shed his capsule and released his weapon pack.

"It's been sent."

Lieutenant Wells might have an attitude problem, but Rosemont had to admit that it looked as if she knew her job cold. He'd see just how well she knew it when the rounds started flying, however, and would reserve his final judgment until then.

For the next several minutes, Wells's recon teams set up a defensive perimeter while Rosemont and the comtechs set up the company CP. There was only a little less than an hour till beginning morning nautical twilight, the time they switched over to daylight tactical mode. The rest of the company was scheduled to start their drop then, and he wanted to be ready for them.

"Bold Lancer, this is Bold Strider," Wells sent over the comlink. "Strider Alpha reports multiple bandits approaching the Delta Zulu. Plot three, five, eight-point-nine, seven, two."

Rosemont consulted his tac screen to remind him that Strider Alpha was the recon team under Sergeant Wallenska, which was holding the eastern edge of their perimeter, sector five. "Flash it!"

Rosemont's helmet display lit up with the target data for the approaching bandits. It showed a dozen blips. Whoever they were, they were not riding vehicles, but they were still moving at a pretty good clip. Either they were mounted on stealth vehicles of some kind or they were on horseback. Knowing what he did about the Arabs, he expected the latter.

That could be good or bad. Tonguing his mike implant, he called to Strider Alpha. "This is Bold Lancer, do you have anything on those bandits yet?"

"Negative," Sergeant Wallenska sent back. "They are not squawking Saudi IFF. I'm picking up unshielded hardware blips, lots of them."

If the sensors were picking up weapons, they could be Saudi troops. But according to his briefing, the Saudi National Guard troops working in this area were mounted on either skimmers or wheels and they were all equipped with IFF—Identification Friend or Foe Squakers. Anyone on horseback had to be the bad guys.

"If they come our way, zero 'em."

"Affirm," Wallenska answered calmly.

Whoever this Strider Alpha was, she wasn't afraid to start a war, and Rosemont liked that. This company was looking better and better to him.

Flicking his comlink over to the company secure frequency, he quickly tapped out a scrambled message to the other inbound Valkyries with the rest of Echo Company on board. They were scheduled to drop in less than half an hour, but now they would have to orbit until he could get this bandit situation sorted out. Had it been one of the Hulk companies up there, they could fight their way down in their armored heavy infantry drop capsules. But his Echo Company platoons were all grunts, light infantry, and their lightly armored stealth capsules couldn't take the pounding that the Hulks could.

When the acknowledge flashed, he flicked back to his tac screen. Strider Alpha had her five people spread out in a semicircle with the remote sensors in the gaps between her and the two teams on her flanks. He was about ready to flash an alert to Bravo and Delta on Alpha's flanks when he saw that Wells had already done it. She was right on top of it again.

"Lancer, this is Alpha," Wallenska's voice sounded in his earphone. "The bandits are vectoring into our position. They must have seen us come down."

The recon drop capsules were stealthy, but they were not invisible to a Mark One eyeball close enough to see their mains when they deployed. Particularly when they were outlined against a clear desert night sky. "Take 'em out."

"Incoming!" someone shouted over the comlink.

The rattle of 5 mm LAR fire cut through the stillness, followed closely by an explosion as a ballistic rocket mortar round detonated close to the CP. Rosemont was already on his face in the sand when the frag sang over his head. He heard a grunt of pain over the comlink and quickly scanned his screen to see who had been hit.

One of the CP staff was showing a casualty marker, but the medic was already on him. Another rocket mortar landed before the pit bull launched by Strider Delta detonated over the enemy launch site. The missile had been set for air burst and the glare of the explosion blanked his visor for a split second.

When his vision cleared, he saw that Strider Alpha was assaulting the enemy's main body with Strider Bravo team setting up a base of fire. From what he could see, they were rolling them right up very nicely. He could hear the chatter of the LARs over the small explosions of the frags and some scattered return fire.

Silence again fell over the desert as Wells's voice cut in over the comlink. "Lancer, Strider. Be advised that the bandits have been zeroed and we're policing up the bodies right now. Negative friendly casualties, ninety-five percent basic load remaining. Returning to alert status two."

"Outstanding job, Strider," he replied. "Have Strider Alpha report to me."

"Affirm."

STRIDER ALPHA turned out to be a stocky, dark-haired woman with deep green eyes, high cheekbones and wearing a small silver skull in her right earlobe. In the clear dawn light, splashes of blood showed dark red against the muted tans of her camouflage suit sleeves. The top of the knife sheath on her left boot top also showed streaks of blood.

"We got 'em all, sir," Wallenska reported. "All fourteen of the motherless bastards. We also got their horses, but two of them were still alive and had to be put down."

"Sergeant Wallenska, right?" Rosemont asked, remembering her name from the company roster.

"Yes, sir. Kat Wallenska."

"Good work, Sergeant. Any idea who they were?"

Wallenska shrugged. "They look like locals to me. We're going over the bodies right now, but so far they're clean. Their weapons are all Han stuff that you can get on any street corner."

The Han Empire of China did a landslide business in weapons exports to smaller nations, and it wasn't bad hardware, either, particularly the infantry small arms. He had come up against Han weapons along the Mexican border and could attest to their effectiveness.

"Let me know if you find anything," he said. "Our Saudi liaison officer is due in this morning. Maybe he can tell us something about them that we've missed."

"Yes, sir."

Ashley Wells approached as he was dusting off his cammies. Her helmet visor was slid open, and he saw a look of amusement in her gray eyes. "I think we're ready for the drop now, sir."

It was on the tip of Rosemont's tongue to ask her what in the hell she thought was so funny, but he refrained. "Flash the all clear, DZ secure."

"Affirm." Her fingers tapped out the code. "ETA one four," she reported.

"Prepare to receive the drop."

"Affirm."

A few minutes later Rosemont caught a flash of light high in the sky as one of the Valkyries banked over for her run. Since their remote drop zone had been compromised, the rest of Echo Company came down with a full escort. Two pairs of Navy A/F-38 Puma strike fighters from the carrier *USS Reagan* offshore in the gulf orbited the DZ several klicks out to make sure that no one else tried to disrupt the landing.

The drop capsules were too small to be seen at that altitude, but their beacons showed on his screen as they launched. Soon the screen was full of blips as the Valkyrie's launchers spit them out at the assault rate. As the recon platoon had done, his line platoons were riding their capsules down hot with no retards out. Apparently that tactic was company practice, not some test of his courage that Wells had thought up. At the last possible moment their main chutes popped, and the slowing capsules could be plainly seen. Seconds later they started touching down.

The First Platoon was no sooner on the ground than Second Platoon landed with the weapons platoon and the company headquarters hot on their heels. For the next several minutes, the men and women of Echo Company scrambled all over the drop zone as they secured the empty drop capsules, broke open the heavy-weapons containers and started digging into their positions. Lieutenant Sullivan and the first sergeant were everywhere as the company prepared for combat.

For the most part, Rosemont simply let the troops do what they had to do. This was the first time he'd had a chance to see his new command at work, and he had to admit that everyone seemed to know exactly what was required without having to be told. But then, they were Peacekeepers and he had expected nothing less.

THE DROP ZONE WAS CLEARED and the troops were fully deployed when Rosemont received a satlink message from force headquarters informing him that a company of heavy infantry Hulks, Bravo Company, Bull's Bulls, were on the way to reinforce him, ETA two hours. With them was coming a jump CP and tac staff, to be followed by a lift section from the aviation company. Two more Peacekeepers companies, Alpha and Delta, with a second jump CP and more air assets would follow the next day, dropping into northern Saudi Arabia along the Jordanian border.

The tac Intel update showed why the dramatic buildup of force was taking place. The situation was rapidly deteriorating all over the Middle East. The Twelfth Imam had appeared again, at several places simultaneously, and had raised the cry for jihad against Western technology. By that, the Imam apparently meant anything more technically complicated than a mud hut, a camel or a sword.

Mobs of Shiites, and even Sunnis now, were on the rampage in several countries, destroying everything in sight. Television stations, modern hotels and electrical power plants seemed to be their favorite targets. But any building or shop marked in a non-Arabic language seemed to be fair game for destruction, as well.

The governments in the region were trying to stem the hysteria, but to no avail. Even the Ulmas running the Shiite Republic of Iraq were powerless to control their own population. For all practical purposes, the mysterious Twelfth Imam now ruled the Middle East.

7

Rafhah, Saudi Arabia—10 June

Rosemont was updating his tac screen information when Sullivan approached. "Yo, Major," the XO said. "I've got a hard-copy scramcom for you from force HQ."

Rosemont took the flimsy from him and punched the code sequence on it into his keypad. He frowned as the decoded message read out. "Shit!"

"What is it, sir?"

"We're not getting the Hulks," Rosemont replied. "The Bravo Bulls are being diverted up north."

"That figures, sir," Sullivan snorted. "The Bravo Bullshitters, we call them. How about the air assets they promised? Are they pulling them, too?"

"No," Rosemont replied. "We're still getting two Tilt Wings and a Bubble Top scout section."

"So what are we supposed to do with them?"

Rosemont looked out over the sand. "Take control of the local situation, stay frosty and await further orders."

Sullivan followed his commander's gaze. "That's about right, sir." He sounded disgusted. "We're the first ones on the ground and we're the most mobile of all the companies, so we're the ones who get to sit and wait."

Rosemont laughed. "Welcome to the Army, LT. Hurry up and wait."

"Shit, sir!"

"Shut up and soldier, LT."

"Yes, sir."

THROUGHOUT THE DAY, Rosemont received a string of tactical situation updates. Bravo Company's landing in the north had been opposed, but they had fought it off successfully. Before their position could be consolidated, however, the Hulks had been assaulted by a battalion of hostile armor. The tanks, all Han Empire T-105s, had not worn national insignia, but were painted with Islamic slogans and flew the green flag of jihad, Islamic Holy War, from their antennae.

The Bravo Bulls had had their hands full for a few minutes, but they finally came out on top without taking too much damage. T-105s against heavy infantry powered fighting suits was not really a fair contest. Short of a direct hit from their main guns, the Hulk suits could stand up against almost anything the tanks could put out.

After cleaning up the hostile armor, the Bulls had gone on to secure a large part of the local landscape, including the road junction leading into northern Iraq.

The Delta Company grunts had been diverted to the southern Saudi coast to guard the nuclear power plants and their desalinization units. Alpha, the other heavy infantry company, was being held in reserve for use as a ready reaction force. The situation was still too chaotic for them to be committed as yet.

Rosemont received tac Intel updates from all over the Middle East. While none of it was good news, the worst came from the neighboring country of Kuwait.

A mob had stormed a Kuwaiti nuclear plant and, after skinning one of the reactor techs alive, convinced his co-workers to tell them how to destroy the plant. Bypassing the safety locks, they dumped the reactor coolant and caused a core meltdown. Not many of them had escaped the resulting burst of radioactivity, but they had died smiling.

Another crowd had been repelled from the second Kuwaiti nuke plant, but only after what was left of the Kuwaiti National Army had killed several hundred people and napalmed the rest. At last report, the crowd was forming again for another try.

Across the region, smoke rose over many cities, particularly those in the Shiite nations, as mobs rampaged. Smoke also rose from the newly planted forests that covered large areas of what once had been arid desert wasteland. Nomadic raiders suddenly appeared out of the desert to set the trees alight and destroy the irrigation systems that made possible the forests and bordering fertile farmlands. The farmers fought back, but as in many ancient wars between desert dwellers and farmers, the farmers were the losers.

In the middle of this chaos, every Middle Eastern government blamed its neighbors for the destruction. There was absolutely no proof as to who was behind the Twelfth Imam, but it was too easy to accuse old enemies.

IT WAS AN UNEVENTFUL day for Echo Company, spent improving their defenses in the sand and waiting to be called into action. By early afternoon their Saudi liaison officer finally showed up in a skimmer. Ali al Muhalhal was typical of the old Saudi desert aristocracy, but he had been educated in the United States and his English had a definite American flavor, but not modern American. He spoke like an actor in an old movie.

"Hey, dude!" the Saudi called to Rosemont as he stepped down from the skimmer. "You the main man around here?"

Rosemont stepped up, his hand out. "Major Alex Rosemont, Echo Company, USEF."

"I'm Ali al Muhalhal," the Saudi with the shoulder insignia of a first lieutenant said. "Like, pleased to meet ya, you know." He looked around at the encampment. "This is a totally out-of-sight place you have here."

"You went to school in California, didn't you, Lieutenant?" Rosemont asked.

"Yeah, man. Can you dig it?"

Rosemont tried hard not to smile. Berkeley was his guess. That was the only place on the planet where people still spoke that particular archaic kind of English. Berkeley and a couple of other places in southern California were caught in a time warp, frantically trying to make believe that they were still living back in the last century, a time that they called the golden age. An era when a large number of people in the state calling themselves fruit children, bippies, or something like that, had wasted their lives taking addictive drugs, passing sexual diseases back and forth and living on government welfare. Rosemont didn't see what was so golden about that time in American history, but others did, particularly foreigners.

"And you majored in golden-age studies, right?"

"Yeah, man. Like, you read my mind. What's your sign anyway, dude?"

Rosemont had to bite his lip to keep from laughing. "I think I should introduce you to the rest of my officers."

"Groovy, man."

Rosemont's officers tried to hide their amusement at Muhalhal's antiquated English. When he looked Ashley Wells up and down and whistled loudly, she was annoyed. Rosemont signaled for her to stay frosty, but the rest of the meeting was a little less cordial than it could have been. Arabic sexist attitudes were not popular among the Peacekeepers.

As amusing as the Saudi's English was, for most of the discussion Sullivan had to act as a translator for the others. Muhalhal seemed oblivious to the fact that he was being less than clearly understood. Fifteen minutes later he glanced down at his watch. "Oops, got to boogie, guys and gals."

Rosemont and Sullivan walked the Saudi back to his skimmer. Once mounted, Muhalhal turned around in the command hatch. "Like, catch you later, dude. Have a nice day."

Rosemont watched the vehicle drive off. "I'm not too sure that we should export American popular culture."

"At least not ancient American culture, sir."

"What dialect was he speaking, anyway?"

"Well sir, part of it was val girl, some of it was flower child and . . ."

"I thought that was fruit child?"

"No sir, fruits were homosexuals, gays, and they had their own dialect."

Rosemont shook his head. "For the duration of this mission, LT, you've just been assigned as our official English-language linguist."

"Roger that, sir."

THE SUN WAS SINKING into the desert. Rosemont had just finished inspecting the perimeter when he received a scramcom message from force HQ that decoded into a mission order. He flashed a mission alert to his platoon leaders, and they were at his side almost instantly.

"We've got us a situation here," he said. "The Aramco oil-pumping station a hundred and thirty klicks south of here at a place called Ash Shu 'bah has been taken over by an unknown group of hostiles. Force has ordered us to move in and take it back tonight."

Sullivan grinned. This was more like it. Digging holes in the sand was getting old real fast.

"Wells." Rosemont turned to his recon platoon leader. "I want your people to lead this assault. Two of your teams should be enough, but I want to have the other two teams on standby."

Seeing that his XO was almost dancing from one foot to the other, he added him to the mission. "Sullivan, your First Platoon will make the assault after the recon teams have cleared the way. Our mission is to clear the facility of hostiles, but we've got to do it without tearing the place up. Oil production is down enough as it is without having us doing any more damage to it."

Sullivan grinned broadly. "You mean we can't destroy the village to liberate it, sir?"

Rosemont chuckled. That old line from a flatvee newscast made over sixty years ago during the Vietnam War still haunted the military. "No, this time we've got to zero the hostiles without doing any damage to the facility."

"That's going to put a real strain on us, sir," Sullivan said seriously. "The only way we can do that is if we limit our heavy-fire support, and that's going to cost us."

"I know, but those are our orders," Rosemont explained. "I know you guys like to go in and kick ass and take names. But this time you've got to do it the hard way." He turned to Wells. "Force wants some prisoners to interrogate. As many as possible, they said."

"Shit, sir," Wells spoke up. "That puts my people out on the raggedy end of the stick. If we run into hostiles on the way in, we can't stop and pat 'em on the ass. We've got to zero 'em and drive on or we're going to get zeroed ourselves. Particularly if we don't have heavy fire support."

Rosemont knew that she had a good point. A fast moving recon team couldn't spare the time or manpower to deal with prisoners.

"Okay, Sullivan," he said, amending his orders. "You take the prisoners and that'll free Wells's people from having to screw around with them."

"We can do that, sir."

"Good." Rosemont called up the map of the pumping station on his tac screen and flashed it to his platoon leaders. "Here's how we're going to do it."

THE FULL MOON CAST deep shadows over the Ash Shu 'bah oil-pumping complex. With their chameleon camouflage suits dialed to matt-night-black, Sergeant Kat Wallenska and her recon team were just five shadows among many as they approached the facility from the northeast.

Flying at a ground-hugging altitude, AV-19 Tilt Wing assault transports had flown the two recon teams to their LZ right after dark. Not knowing what kind of radar or detection devices the hostiles had, the teams had been landed several klicks out so as to not be picked up. The long tactical march over the sand had done nothing to improve Wallenska's mood. Now that the moon was up, she was antsy to get this operation on the road. The sooner they closed with the hostile force, the sooner it would be over.

The team was moving in an extended line formation probing to find the outer ring of the hostiles' defenses. Wallenska, in the center, opened her helmet filters to the night air, and the harsh odor of burning hashish suddenly filled her nostrils. The sergeant smiled broadly behind her visor. Someone was blowing a little weed. How convenient. Hadn't they read the surgeon general's report that it could ruin their DNA? What the report had not mentioned, however, was that smoking it on night guard duty might also ruin your whole life for eternity.

Following her nose, Wallenska turned to the right and increased the magnification on her imager.

Flicking the IR sensor up to max, she caught the faint glow of the smoke hanging in the air before it cooled to the ambient air temperature.

She hadn't picked this guy up on her IR before, so he was obviously wearing a stealth suit. He was blowing his weed behind the face mask to try to hide the glow of the cigarette, but had not thought to contain the smoke. It gave off a good heat signature if you knew what to look for.

Wallenska chuckled. You could take a boy out of the sticks and give him high-tech war gear, but that didn't mean you changed the way he thought. A desert nomad with a stealth suit was still a nomad who didn't have the slightest idea how or why it worked. She was going to make damned sure that this was one guy who would never get a chance to learn either.

Reaching down to her left boot, she drew her teflon fighting knife and locked it to her assault harness. Some of the kids in the platoon had bought those new vibroblade knives, but no one would ever catch her with one. When the shit hit the fan, she wanted a solid piece of plastic in her hands, not a gadget that might run out of power while you were trying to kill someone. She had punched her reinforced teflon blade through the side of a skimmer once and it hadn't broken. She'd stick to what she knew worked.

As she crept toward her target, she could smell the stench of sweating, unwashed male over the reek of the hash, the stink of hydrocarbons from spilled petroleum and the flinty odor of the sand next to her face. Even with all the desalination plants that had been built over the last twenty years, bathing still wasn't a high priority in the desert and it lent a definite aroma to the locals. Some of her team members said that she had the nose of her namesake; she always had been able to smell out an enemy.

The guard was standing beside a pile of supply crates that had been fashioned into a makeshift barrier. She liked going up against hostiles who were too lazy to dig holes; it made her life easier. He was leaning against a crate with his back exposed. Dead meat.

The kill went as smoothly as a training exercise back at Benning. Her knee went into his back, throwing him off balance, and her hand clamped over his mouth as she pulled him to her in a deadly embrace. The knife flashed down into the hollow of his neck, and the sharp, metallic smell of blood suddenly filled the cool night air. The guard's feet kicked in the sand, and he was dead in sixty seconds.

Carefully lowering the body to the ground, Wallenska patted him down for commo gear but found nothing. He didn't have night glasses, either. Regardless of the stealth suit, whoever these guys were, they were taking low-tech warfare to new heights. Even his weapon was a 5.56 mm Han Type 98 assault rifle, an old brass cartridge piece from the turn of the century. Even though it was an old weapon, Wallenska didn't discount it. She wore a scar from a Han 5.56 mm that had almost cost her a leg.

She quickly scanned the area to either side and, when she saw that it was clear, she signaled for the rest of her team to join her. They were inside the outer perimeter now, and it was time for them to open a hole for Sullivan's line platoon to drive through.

8

Ash Shu 'bah Pumping Station—11 June

When the slow moving shadows of Wallenska's recon team reached her, she signaled for them to move out to both the right and the left to probe for the next two enemy positions along the perimeter. Then they were to take them out, too, and hold the ground in between them for the infantry to pass through.

Two hundred meters to Kat's right, Ashley Wells and the other recon team had also made contact with a hostile outpost. Another silent kill had allowed them to penetrate the perimeter and open a gap there as well. Now Rosemont had two avenues of advance.

Wallenska quickly tapped out a sitrep to the company commander and waited for the signal that Sullivan's platoon had moved into assault positions. She took the M-19 10 mm pistol from the holster at her waist, fitted the silencer and laser sight to it and clipped it within ready reach on the front of her assault harness.

Since the hostiles were wearing stealth suits, she was going to have to find them one at a time, and that could get a bit tricky. Once the firing started, there should be no problem IDing them, but she wanted to keep things quiet for as long as she could.

Tapping out her intentions to the rest of her team, she started moving forward again. Recon always lead the way, and she had to clear the area for the grunts.

BACK WITH THE LEAD elements of Sullivan's First Platoon, Rosemont acknowledged Wallenska's signal. Once more Strider Alpha was showing that she knew her business. Sullivan gave the word to move out, and the grunts became more dark shadows moving swiftly across the sand toward the pumping station. When the point elements made contact with Wallenska's team, they poured through the perimeter, spreading out as they headed for the heart of the complex.

Rosemont attached himself to one of the assault squads as they entered the compound. The first ten meters were open ground, and they crossed it quickly without being spotted.

CAUTIOUSLY APPROACHING the supply shack in front of her, Wallenska sensed, more than saw, movement behind her. Spinning around, she raised her LAR just in time to deflect a brutal slash from a sword-wielding opponent. The blow knocked the assualt rifle from her hand.

"Allah Akbar!" the Arab yelled as he brought his sword back for another blow. His war cry was answered by dozens more as the entire complex suddenly erupted in blazing gunfire.

Now the excrement was in the ventilation!

Reaching down for the knife from her boot sheath, Wallenska stepped into her opponent, under the arc of his swing. The knife lashed out, slicing through his throat. The Arab's scream became a gurgle as blood poured into his windpipe.

She grabbed him as he fell and eased the body to the ground. Dropping to the sand beside the corpse, she clipped the knife back onto her harness, retrieved her LAR from the sand and paused just long enough to blow the sand out of the action. Sand played hell with the 5 mm caseless ammunition, but she couldn't clean the weapon now. She would have to risk having it jam.

Red and green tracer fire cut over her head as the lead elements of the grunts targeted the hostile positions that had revealed themselves when they opened up. Sullivan would start maneuvering his people through here in a few moments, so it was high time that she moved her ass somewhere else. Even with her location beacon showing on the grunts' tac displays, it was still all too easy to fire on the wrong target at night.

A burst of green Han tracer fire cut through the sand to her left. Spinning around, Wallenska saw the muzzle-flash and answered it with three controlled bursts from her LAR. Another hostile fired at the sound of her bursts, and she rolled over to the side for cover.

This guy wasn't firing tracers, and she snapped her IR imager down to try to spot him. The burst sounded as though it had come from high on her right flank. She studied the raised platform on the right, looking for likely places to hide and the flicker on her IR display that would indicate a heat source. Her IR display was blank, indicating that this guy was wearing a stealth suit.

As she scanned the platform, she unclipped a flash-bang grenade from her ammo pouch with her left hand and thumbed off the safety. Throwing it far to her right front, she counted off three seconds and closed her eyes. Although her visor would go blank to keep the light from blinding her, she wanted to make sure she didn't lose her precious night vision.

The grenade detonated with a bright flash and a loud explosion, startling the hostile. When he shifted to cover that side of the platform, she spotted a patch of darkness moving in the moonlight. Thumbing her LAR down to single shot, she focused on his center mass and squeezed off a round. A high-pitched scream told her that she was on target, and she followed the first shot with two more.

When the black mass stopped moving, she flicked her LAR back to 3-shot burst and moved out again.

WITH THE STRIDER BRAVO element, the second re-con team, Ashley Wells was trying to flank a hostile machine-gun position that had pinned down a squad of Sullivan's grunts. She huddled under an oil pipe while green tracers cut over her head, cursing the orders that had denied them heavy fire support. A single pit bull or a Long Lash antitank missile would take out that gun, but it would also destroy the oil valve it was hiding behind.

Keeping to the shadows as she inched along the pipe toward the gun position, Ash vectored the Bravo team in on it as well. The gun crew suddenly went into action and fired a long burst off to her left.

She heard a choked-off cry over her comlink; someone on the team had been hit. One of the beacons on her visor screen beeped yellow for an instant, then faded completely. Larson, the number three out on the far left flank, was dead. She blinked her eyes hard—Larson had been a good man. He had pulled her out of a hard spot more than once when she had first been with the platoon.

She would miss him but there was no time to grieve. The hostile machine gun stuttered again, and she continued to inch her way toward the sound.

ROSEMONT SUDDENLY FOUND himself alone in the battle when he stopped to change the magazine in his M-25 light assault rifle. Crouching down beside an immense oil pipe valve, he dropped the empty from the back of the weapon's breech, pulled one of the loaded plastic cylinders from his ammo pouch and clipped it in place. Pulling back on the charging handle, he jacked a 5 mm caseless round into the chamber and flicked the selector switch down to three round burst fire mode.

His tac display showed that the friendlies had pushed a wedge into the heart of the pump complex but were under heavy fire. The hostiles were well deployed, and Sullivan's grunts were going to have to dig them out one position at a time. But this was what Infantry combat was all about, close with and destroy the enemy by fire and maneuver.

He spotted a line of green tracer fire to his right and zeroed in on the source. Two quick bursts of 5 mm put an end to it. The hostiles' Han weapons and ammunition made it easy to determine who was shooting at whom. The 5.56 mm Type 98 Han assault rifles had a harsh metallic chatter, where the light assault rifles were quieter and had a higher rate of fire. Also, the Han tracer ammunition burned green, but the 5 mm caseless tracer was red.

Getting to his feet, he moved across the open compound to the next oil valve. The burst of fire that knocked him over came from behind. Sprawling face-first in the sand, he scrambled to find cover behind the valve a few meters in front of him. As he reached cover, another burst kicked sand into his visor, and he felt his body armor soak up another round. He didn't feel the pain of a wound, but that was cutting it a little too close. He'd worry about the little shit later, though. Right now he needed to extricate himself from this situation.

Flicking his IR imager up to max, he searched for the guy who had almost zeroed him. A small flicker showed in the walkway halfway up the pumping station fifty meters in front of him. From the way the heat source moved, he knew he had found the hot muzzle of the hostile's rifle. Sighting in below the faint IR trace, he triggered off a long burst and was rewarded with a choked-off cry and a metallic clank as the man dropped his weapon.

After a careful scan revealed no other hostiles in the vicinity, he got to his feet.

"Major?" came the voice over his comlink. "This is Kat. Move your left hand."

Rosemont froze and did as he had been asked.

"Good," she said. "I thought it was you. Your location beacon is out, sir. You'd better link up with me before you get zeroed by mistake."

Rosemont spotted her on his display and turned toward her. "Yes, I'm over here," she transmitted. "Just hold tight where you're at. I'm coming to join you."

A black shadow detached itself from the night and raced across the open toward him. He covered her with his LAR, but no shots were fired at her.

"Thanks for the warning," he said when she slid in beside him. "I soaked up a couple of rounds in the armor, and they must have hit something."

"Just stick with me and you should be okay."

"Where to next?"

She studied her display. "There's another pump station to the left, and it looks like one of Mick's squads is bumped up against it. You want to go sort it out for them?"

"Lead on, Kat."

"Just follow me, Major."

Even with the moonlight, Kat was difficult to follow. Her chameleon suit shifted from dead black all the way up to grayish tan as she moved through the broken patches of light and shadow. When she stopped suddenly in deep shadow, he ran into her.

"Quiet," she hissed over the comlink. "I think we're on their flank."

Rosemont peered into the shadow and thought he saw a patch of dead black moving where there should have been only dark gray. His visor display didn't show any friendlies in that location, so the movement had to be hostile. "How do you want to do it?" he asked.

Kat grinned in the dark. "How about I toss a flash-bang behind them and when they turn around to see what it is, we zero 'em?"

"Sounds good to me. Do it."

She tossed the grenade as hard as she could. As she had predicted, the hostiles spun around and opened up on the detonation, exposing themselves to Rosemont and Kat's fire. Twin streaks of red 5 mm tracers quickly cut them down.

"Okay," Rosemont said, scanning the dark again. "Who's next?"

"Follow me, sir."

Now that Sullivan's platoon was spread out throughout the complex, the battle settled down to a rat hunt. Man for man, the Peacekeepers had everything their way, but the rules the colonel had laid down were seriously hampering them. The best thing to do was to break the squads down into two-man hunter-killer teams and go after them that way.

Quickly issuing orders, Sullivan teamed up with one of his young privates. Slinging his LAR over his back, he took his pistol from its holster and attached the silencer. For this kind of work, it would help to be able to make silent kills.

With his partner covering him, Sullivan slithered forward on his belly toward a raised platform of tanks and piping. The sound of his partner's LAR firing short bursts drove Sullivan to his feet as he raced for cover behind the nearest pipe. So much for caution.

Peering around the concrete pipe support, he saw a faint IR trace on the platform and sighted his pistol in on it. With the silencer fixed to the muzzle, not only was it quiet, it would show no muzzle flash when he fired. He triggered off two quick shots and was rewarded by a sharp grunt as the IR target fell to the sand.

LIKE SULLIVAN'S GRUNTS, the recon teams had split up into two-man hunter-killer teams as well. Since Kat and Rosemont were already teamed up, they continued their hunt for hostiles, but targets were becoming harder to find. Scattered bursts of fire still broke out, but more and more time was passing between the bursts. Finally everything fell quiet.

Rosemont took a report from Sullivan and Wells before signaling for the medics to come in to clear the casualties from the complex.

9

Ash Shu 'bah Pumping Station—11 June

The first thin light of dawn was tinting the clear sky over the Saudi desert a deep orange when the Ash Shu 'bah oil facility was finally secured. For the first time in hours, all was quiet. The only people moving through the complex were the men and women of Echo Company as they policed up their dead and wounded and collected the enemy's weapons.

Bodies lay crumpled all over the compound. Most of them wore black Arabic robes, but a few chameleon suits were lying on the sand as well. Those with their camouflage circuitry intact had turned a tan, sand color to blend in with the killing field. The spilled blood had seeped into the thirsty sand and had dried to the consistency of thick pudding. Weapons, empty magazines and other debris of battle littered the ground near the bodies.

This was not the first early-morning battlefield that Rosemont had ever seen, nor even his first desert battlefield. Northern Mexico was a desert, too, and the sand there had smelled the same after a battle. The smell of explosives, gunpowder, sweat and blood filled his nose, overpowering the smell of oil from the pumps. He also knew what it would smell like after just a few hours under the sun. If they were still here then, he would have to drop his air filters to block the stench.

The place was a mess, but it had survived undamaged, as per the colonel's orders. Echo Company had paid the price, however, for the facility's survival. Having to be careful not to damage the pumping rigs had given the advantage to the defending enemy force, and they had used their advantage well. Five of Rosemont's people were dead, two from Wells's recon, and three from Sullivan's First Platoon. Another seven were wounded, two of them seriously.

It had been costly, but not a drop of precious Saudi oil had been spilled. Only blood stained the sand and not all of it was Echo Company blood.

Sullivan had counted forty-six hostile dead and three more so seriously wounded that they were not expected to last the hour. No unwounded hostiles had been captured and, from the evidence, some seriously wounded enemy had committed suicide rather than risk being taken captive.

Like any soldier, Rosemont hated to face an enemy who fought with that kind of fanaticism. It made his job that much more difficult. It always cost dearly to go up against fanatics who were not afraid to die and who would not surrender when the battle turned against them. On the other hand, the apparent suicides might have been the act of a highly disciplined enemy, a way of ensuring that no information would be given away through the interrogation of prisoners.

Little more than common military equipment had been found on the hostile dead so far. All he could say with certainty was that they appeared to be Arab locals. But even that wasn't proven yet. For all he knew they could be Turk or Lebanese mercenaries. It would take the med techs back at the force field hospital a few hours to make a positive DNA ID on the bodies.

The company medics were seeing to their own wounded first. Already, several MH-78 Dustoff choppers were inbound to evacuate the casualties. Even with the casualties gone, it would be some time before this place smelled like anything other than a slaughterhouse.

BLOODIED AND WEARY, the men and women of Echo Company slowly took up the defensive positions they would hold until they could be relieved. The first thing they did after digging in was to eat. Combat consumes tremendous energy that has to be replaced. If they were to stay at their peak, ready for a counterattack, they needed nourishment.

Sullivan walked over to Ashley Wells and Kat Wallenska, who were seated in the sand finishing up a breakfast of ham-and-scrambled-egg Readi Heats.

"Yo, ladies!" he said. "Mind if I join you?"

"Pull up a sand dune, Mick," Ashley invited him.

The XO sat down cross-legged on the sand and reached into his pants pocket. "Ah, shit," he muttered as he brought out a battered plastic canister. The Readi Heat coffee canister had been pierced by a bullet, and the contents had leaked out.

"I felt something wet last night." He grinned. "But I just thought I'd pissed myself."

Ashley turned as she dug into her pack and came out with a full canister of coffee. "Here you go, Mick." She tossed it to him. "I know you get cranky in the morning without your coffee."

He pulled the tab to heat the contents. "Thanks."

"So," she asked, "what do you think of our new company commander this morning?"

He took a cautious sip of the hot coffee. "Damn, they should lower the temperature on these things for the desert."

"You're not answering the question, Mick," Ashley prompted him.

"Alexander the Great?" Sullivan grinned. "I think he did okay for an FNG. You've got to admit that it was a good attack plan and it worked real well." He swept his hand out to encompass the undamaged oil facility. "Not a scratch on this place."

"How many people did you lose?"

Sullivan's face hardened. "Three killed and another four down, one of them seriously."

"And you think he did okay?" Ashley frowned. "Is this the same 'Mad Mick' Sullivan who once punched out the fire-support platoon leader for dropping a short round and wounding one of his people? What the fuck's wrong with you, man?"

Sullivan sucked down the last of the coffee and collapsed the canister. "Ash, you're going to have to chill out on the major a little. I know you two got off to a bad start in the briefing room, but you can't keep on thinking about him this way. If he screws up, the Old Man will pull his ass out, you know that. Until then, we've got to learn to live with him and do our job."

"I think he did okay, LT," Kat Wallenska spoke up as she absentmindedly stropped her teflon knife against the top side of her boot.

Ashley turned to her recon team leader. "Say what?"

"You heard me, Ash," she stubbornly replied. "The Old Man gave him this dog shit mission, and Rosemont did the best he could with it. True, Major Nicks might have argued with the colonel about it a little more. But in the end you know that he would have had to do it this way, too."

She grinned. "Plus, I don't see what you have against the man. I think he's kinda cute, myself."

Now Ashley really was completely perplexed. Usually the only thing Kat Wallenska had to say about an officer was that she wanted to have a "shirts off" bout with him on the unarmed-combat training field and kick his ass. She shook her head in disgust as she got to her feet. "I don't believe I heard you say that, Sergeant."

Kat grinned. "There it is, LT. Like our man Mick here says, we've got to learn to live with this guy and it helps if I think that he's cute."

"Jesus!"

Sullivan and Wallenska watched Wells march off to harass one of the other team leaders. "What crawled up her ass?" Sullivan asked.

Kat resumed stropping her blade. "I just think she misses Major Nicks, LT. She could always bat her baby blues at him and get that poor bastard to do anything she wanted. But from what I've seen so far, it seems Alex the Great is immune to her shit."

Sullivan didn't know if that was really true, but it seemed Rosemont hadn't reacted yet to Ashley Wells the way most males did upon meeting her. But then he had only been in the company for less than a week. Wait until he had a chance to see her up close in her dress whites at a regimental dining in, or in a string bikini at an R-and-R center. That's when he'd see what kind of stuff Alex Rosemont was made of.

"Maybe you're right, Kat. Maybe Ash and Trash has finally met her match. A man she can't blow away just by looking at him."

Kat gave the edge of her blade one last swipe and sheathed it back in her boot. "Maybe she has, LT. Maybe she has."

From where he was standing, Sullivan couldn't see the catlike smile on Wallenska's face.

SHORTLY AFTER 0900 hours, Rosemont received a message that Stone Tower, the Force Commander Colonel Jacobson, was coming to inspect the battlefield. After alerting the perimeter not to fire on income aircraft squawking IFF, he brushed off his dusty cammies as best he could and squared the green beret on his head.

An OH-39 Bubble Top recon scout ship flashed overhead, escorted by two AV-19 Tilt Wing gunships. The Bubble Top's rotors blew up a flurry of sand as it touched down in an open area beside the liberated facility. Colonel Jacobson stepped out, his eyes taking in the facility. Unlike Rosemont, he had fought in this part of the world before. Over the past twenty-five years, he had seen plenty of Middle Eastern sand covered with blood. This was simply one more spot of bloodstained sand, but it was never easy to see when the blood had come from your own troops.

Rosemont approached him and rendered a crisp salute. "Good morning, sir."

Jacobson returned the salute. "Your people did a damned fine job here last night, Rosemont."

"Thank you, sir," the company commander answered. "I'll pass that on to them. It was pretty tough going for a while, and we sure as hell could have used some heavy-fire support. Far too many of my people got hurt.''

Colonel Jacobson surveyed the Echo Company aid station, where troops with minor wounds were still being treated. "I know. I really hated to ask you to do it that way, but we had to take this facility intact, and even light-fire support would have damaged it. The way things are shaping up, we have to be careful not to lose the backing of the Saudi royal family, and they insisted that we recapture this place in one piece.''

"I understand, sir.''

"Let me know if anyone distinguished themselves last night, and I'll see that they're properly recognized.''

"I'll put my XO on it, sir.''

"I understand that you went in with the assault elements, Rosemont,'' Jacobson continued. "How are you finding your new command so far?''

Rosemont looked out over the sand where the First Platoon was dug in. "They're damned good troops, Colonel.'' Pride showed in his voice. "Some of the best I've ever served with. So far, I've only had a chance to see Sullivan's First Platoon and Wells's recon at work, but I have no complaints, sir. They're almost as good as my old Bravo Company, second of the twenty-second.''

Jacobson laughed. "The 'Bravo Regulars' are a frosty lot,'' he said. "And that's why you're here. I followed your operation in Mexico when you went up the side of that mountain at night to take out that triple-A site in the caves. That was a first-class piece of light infantry work."

"Thank you, sir."

After a quick walk through the pumping station, the colonel followed Rosemont to his small tac CP that had been set up in the pumping facility's empty office. Offering him the only chair, Rosemont reached into a ration case and produced two canisters. "Coffee, sir?"

"Thank you."

Pulling the heat tab on one, he handed it to the colonel, who took a sip and quickly took the cannister from his mouth. "Damn, this stuff's hot."

"So what do you think of the operation so far?" the Colonel asked.

"There's something screwy going on here, sir."

"How's that?" The colonel cautiously raised the coffee to his lips again.

"Well, sir. Our opponents are supposed to be Muslim fanatics who have answered the Twelfth Imam's call for a jihad against Western technology, right?"

The colonel nodded.

"But as we found out last night, this apparently doesn't mean that they have a prohibition against using Western weapons technology. Some of the stuff we've captured is pretty damned sophisticated and most of it's Western in origin. Most of the hostiles were wearing French-made stealth suits. And the pumping stations were wired with Korean-made sonic sensors set to detonate when they picked up people speaking English. If my people hadn't really been on their toes last night, this whole place would have gone up and taken us with it."

Colonel Jacobson sipped his coffee and thought for a moment. "What do you think it means?"

"Damned if I know, sir. But I think there's a hell of a lot more behind this supposedly Islamic uprising than we know at this time. I'm not a middle eastern expert, but there's too much about this that just doesn't make sense."

"I couldn't agree with you more," the colonel replied. "And I've been here before. I've got everyone working on the battlefield Intel we've picked up so far. As yet, we don't have much to go on beyond the obvious. You didn't take any prisoners last night, did you?"

"No, sir."

"No one else has taken any prisoners, either," the colonel said. "That's part of the problem."

"It tells me that this is a lot more than a spontaneous uprising, sir," Rosemont said. "It takes firm leadership and planning to create that kind of discipline."

The colonel finished the last of his coffee and stood. "The Saudis are coming in to relieve you at 1100 hours," he said. "As soon as they're in place, I want you to move these two platoons and a heavy-weapons section to a place called Al Mish 'ab."

The colonel flashed the data to Rosemont's tac screen. "There's an old fortress there overlooking the coast and a major road leading into Kuwait. You and the rest of your company will go into defensive positions guarding a desalinization plant a little to the southeast."

"Yes, sir."

ROSEMONT WATCHED as the colonel's Bubble Top flew out of sight. For his first mission as a Peacekeeper, he hadn't done that badly.

"What did the Old Man have to say, sir?" Sullivan asked as he walked up. As the company XO, he was the unofficial rumor-control officer and had to stay on top of the latest information.

"He told me to compliment you and Wells for a job very well done last night."

"We did it all right, sir." Sullivan's gaze flicked over toward the aid station. "But I'm not too sure how well we did it."

"He knows it was a bitch, and he apologized for having asked us to do it without fire support. But it had to be done that way."

"I'll pass the word on, sir."

"And pass the word for everyone to stay loose and not to dig in too deep. We're moving out again as soon as the Saudis show up to relieve us."

"Where are we going, sir?"

"You're being moved south to the gulf coast and you're going into a defensive position."

"Another oil facility?"

Rosemont shook his head and grinned. "No, this time you're going to keep an eye on the dolphins."

10

Zagros Mountains, Iran—12 June

In the moonlight, the ruined fortress high on the
crag above the narrow valley almost looked like it
was part of the rugged mountain. It was not remembered who had first noticed that the site was a
good defensive position to guard the pass through
the valley below, but over the centuries, broken Ne-
olithic stone spear points had been found there. The
first worked stones for a small fortress were laid on
the site at the end of the Bronze Age about 1000 B.C.
That first, small fortress fell to the invading Assyr-
ians some two hundred years later.

Over the centuries the small fort was rebuilt, enlarged and occupied several times by various armies
seeking to control traffic through the valley. The last
troops to occupy the fortress had been Turks of the
Ottoman Empire in 1917.

Now the two-meter-thick walls of the fortress were
mostly toppled. In one corner a tower still stood to
a height of a dozen meters, but it, too, was in ruins

and sheltered only falcons who had built their nests among the satellite antennae hidden inside.

When the Persians had occupied the fortress in the third century B.C. to guard against Alexander's Macedonians, they cut a set of steps into the base rock of the mountain leading down into a natural cavern that had been the rain cistern for the earlier garrisons. Over a thousand years later, the Turks enlarged the cistern yet again, creating a huge cavern when they rebuilt the walls and occupied the fortress as part of the defenses against the Islamic armies. When the Turks were conquered by the Saracens a short while later, the collapsing walls blocked off the stairs leading down to the cistern. Subsequent occupiers failed to discover the blocked steps and built over the rubble. Knowledge of the cistern was lost to man.

After the nuclear exchange of 2004, a team surveying the extent of the fallout rediscovered the ruins. Acting on their report, an archaeological survey team from the University of Modena mapped the site and, in the course of taking seismic soundings, discovered the underground cistern. The site was not exciting enough to merit a full-fledged archaeological expedition, however, so their findings were buried in the back of a professional journal and soon forgotten.

In 2030 A.D., the ancient stones still blocked the old Persian cut-stone steps, but seismic sounding would not find the cistern again. It had been lined

with a material that would give off the same readings as the solid rock. To all observation now, both
visual and electronic, the ruined fortress was simply what it appeared to be—ruins.

Inside the newly excavated and equipped cistern,
a small team of European technicians sat in front of
their electronic consoles and monitored the taping
of a hologram program. Across the room, a young
man wearing an embroidered robe of ancient Arabic design stood on a platform in front of the holo
recorders. A long, straight-bladed sword decorated
with gold and pearls hung at his side next to a
golden-handled dagger sheathed in a red leather
belt. A green turban covered his hair, and pointed
slippers protruded from his billowing trousers.

A holovee prompter screen was set in front of him
on a moveable mount. As he faced the screen and
read the text slowly moving across it, the holograph
recorders picked up his image. Once completed, the
holo signal would be tightbeamed from the antennae hidden in the ruined tower to a communications satellite passing overhead. The scrambled burst
transmission would take mere seconds.

Although officially listed as an agricultural
weather satellite launched by the EuroAgCombine,
this satellite was equipped with military-type laser
hologram transmission gear. On command from the
control room in the fortress, the satellite would
tightbeam the holosignal down to projectors
mounted near selected sites in the Middle East, and

the Twelfth Imam would speak to his adoring masses.

"Amr Allah!" the young man in the Arabic robes shouted in archaic Arabic, striking a pose with his right hand raised. "Allah commands it!"

"Fini!" an older European man dressed in a white lab smock said, drawing his finger across his throat in the universal gesture.

"How did I do?" the young Arab asked in French as he stepped down from the platform.

The older European, once a professor of Middle Eastern languages at the Sorbonne University in Paris, looked up from his copy of the script. "Not bad, Hassain," he said. "But try to look a little more heroic next time and speak with a deeper voice. After all, you're supposed to be the Shiite messiah, not some damned graduate student. Remember, you are the Mahdi."

The young man, a French citizen of Arabic Lebanese descent, nodded. It hadn't been all that long ago that he had in fact been a graduate student at the Sorbonne University in Paris when he had been approached about an acting job.

"But I'm not an actor," he had told the man, an Arab wearing an expensive European-cut suit.

"You are a student of medieval Arabic language," the man had replied in medieval Arabic. "And you also are, as Allah has willed it, heavily in debt to certain interests who are demanding that they be paid."

Hassain Fadal could only nod agreement. Even though he no longer followed the Muslim religion of his forefathers, he was a student of the Arabic language, particularly the poetry of the seventh and eighth centuries. And it was true that he was heavily in debt to certain gambling interests. Unfortunately his disapproving father had cut off his funds, and he was facing personal disaster, maybe even death, if his debtors were not paid off immediately.

"But rejoice," the Arab had continued. "Allah has smiled upon you and has sent you a way to regain your honor. In his mercy, he has also willed it that you will become a wealthy man at the same time."

"And what must I do to receive this blessing?" Hassain had asked in French.

"You must become Imam Muhammad al-Mahdi for the Shiite faithful," the man had replied in Arabic.

"The Twelfth Imam, the Hidden One?"

"The same."

Hassain had paused. Even though he was not Shiite, everyone of Muslim descent knew of the Twelfth Imam, the Shiite Mahdi, the savior who would return to the Islamic faithful to announce the coming of the end of the world. Having been educated in Europe, Hassain considered the possibility about as unlikely as the mythical Second Coming of Christ that faithful Christians still patiently awaited. To him, the Mahdi was only a fable, but as he knew from history, it was a powerful fable to the Arab masses. Several times over the past thousand years, a false Mahdi had risen to lead the Arabs into futile bloody conflicts against both the West and their own peoples. And it looked as though it was about to happen again.

"Tell me of the wealth that will come to me if I do this thing."

The man had smiled thinly. "It will be wealth enough for even one such as yourself who is addicted to childish games of chance."

Hassain had smiled back. "I am interested in learning more about this God-sent proposal."

"Come with me."

It had been several months since Hassain had first been contacted. Since then, his gambling debts had all been paid off, but he had not yet seen the wealth he had been promised. That would have to wait, he had been told, until the end of the project. In the meantime, he would be paid only a monthly living wage. It was a decent wage, he had to admit, but he was anxious to collect the promised reward. Maybe this time, for a change, the gambling tables would be good to him.

Actually the work hadn't been difficult, just very unusual. His employers and most of the technicians on the project were European, mostly Italian and French. The few other Arabs he had met were either Lebanese like himself, or Algerians. Like himself, none of them was religious. Some of the

Arabs, however, who had visited the remote Italian villa where he had stayed for over a month studying his role, had been religious. Shiite commando leaders from half a dozen nations had visited the villa, usually in the dead of night, stayed briefly and left, again in the night.

Two weeks ago he had been brought to this isolated, ruined fortress somewhere in the mountains and had started playing his role as the Mahdi for the holovee cameras. Hassain wasn't at all curious about why his employers wanted him to pretend to be the Mahdi. All he was concerned about was the money they had promised to pay when his performance was over.

Cut off from the outside world, he had no idea how his hologram appearances were affecting the Middle East. Had he known, he may not have particularly cared. His family hadn't practiced their ancestral faith since they had been driven out of Beirut almost fifty years earlier. When his grandfather had immigrated to France, he had left behind the Islamic faith that, in his mind, had been responsible for the systematic destruction of his country. In France the Fadal family had been raised to be middle-class Europeans, not superstitious Moslems.

The Mahdi meant no more to Hassain than the Christians' Jesus would have. It was all silly religious mythology to him. An educated man like himself did not waste time on ancient myths.

IN AN ADJOINING ROOM in the underground ho-lovee facility, three men watched a recon satellite monitor screen. Two of them wore the white lab-coats that were the uniform of scientists and tech-nicians the world over.

The third man was dressed in desert camouflage fatigues and had a scar running from his hairline to his jaw on the right side of his face. On his shaved head he wore a faded maroon beret bearing the sil-ver, winged dagger insignia of the French Foreign Legion paras, an organization he'd had the honor to serve in for many years. The scar was courtesy of a machete wielded by a drug-crazed Senegalese he had encountered while in that service.

The destruction he had visited upon the people responsible for the insurrection that had sent the Senegalese after him with the machete had caused quite an international incident. Enough of an inci-dent that he had been forced to leave his beloved le-gion in disgrace.

Upon leaving the legion, his only skills were those of a soldier and a leader of soldiers. As always, that translated into his becoming a mercenary com-mander, a man for hire who would solve any prob-lem that lent itself to a military solution. In the twenty-first century, small wars were as common as soccer matches, and far more popular, so Colonel Jean-Claude Francillion was never out of work for long, even at the price he commanded for his serv-ices.

This job was the easiest money he had earned in years. In fact, were it not for his long-standing rule against working for free, he would probably have taken the job on as a favor to himself. The vines surrounding his small estate in the south of France had withered beyond recovery in the fifth year of the drought that was killing the once-rich agricultural heartland of southern Europe. Once his estate had produced a small but well-sought-after vintage. Now his fields were dust-dry and cracked, as was much of the prime agriculture acreage in a large swath cutting across Spain, Italy and southern France.

When his current employers had told him of their plan, he had thought them insane. How could trees growing in the Middle East cause a drought in southern Europe? After their scientists explained the dynamics of European weather to him, he had seen how the reforested areas acted as moisture traps preventing clouds from forming over the Mediterranean and sending rain to southern Europe. Were his vineyards ever to grow again, the Middle Eastern desert had to become desert again, so Francillion had signed on to see that was exactly what happened.

In the smoke of the fires raging through the forests of the Middle East, the mercenary saw not destruction, but fresh green vines growing on the hillsides around his home. Who said that war wasn't good for living things?

One of the men with the colonel was Alfredo Caproni, the Italian project director for the EuroAgCombine. Caproni looked up from the satellite monitor screen and said, "We are more or less on schedule except for the desalinization plants in Saudi Arabia and Kuwait. The American Peacekeepers have proven very effective at keeping our forces away from them."

Francillion didn't have to be told that. In his career as a mercenary, he had encountered the USEF and their Russian counterparts more than once. Sometimes he had been on the same side, but at other times he had been looking over the sights of a rifle at them. He had the respect for the Peacekeepers that only one professional soldier could have for another and they were the only part of this operation that he'd had doubts about from the beginning.

His doubts, however, had been discounted when his employers had pointed out that the appearance of the Mahdi would rouse the entire population in the target zone. Not even the Peacekeepers could kill the entire population. And so far his employers had been both right and wrong.

It was true that he was commanding a vast army this time, even though most of the army did not know of his existence or that he was commanding their actions. But, as it had turned out, the Peacekeepers were able to counter the overwhelming numbers by managing to be at the right place at the right time. That was the purest essence of any successful military operation. Nothing counted as much as being in the right place at the right time.

He glanced over at the screen showing the latest update on the USEF and multinational unit deployments. So far, the Peacekeepers were in static defensive positions mostly around oil facilities, and the multinationals were facing off against one another along the national borders. The multis he could ignore. They would only become a factor when they started shooting at each other. His problem was the Untied States Expeditionary Force.

"I want to mount an operation against the Peacekeepers in Saudi Arabia tomorrow," Colonel Francillion said. Even though he had not been back to Canada for years, his French still bore the accent of his native Montreal. "I will send the Islamic Brotherhood in Kuwait against them."

Along with the Arabic masses running amok and destroying everything in sight, the mercenary had several large, well-trained Shiite commando units more or less under his control, and they were his real military strength. These were various dissident groups who had joined the operation in hopes of being able to carve their own little kingdoms out of the wreckage the Twelfth Imam was making of the modern Middle East.

Thanks to the finances of the EuroAgCombine that was backing the operation, they were now equipped with the best weapons money could buy and they were more than willing to die for their cause. And die they would. Francillion had no illusions about the realities of fighting the Peacekeepers. It was a losing proposition, but he was counting on the numbers of men he commanded to offset what they lacked in military expertise.

The French Canadian mercenary's finger stabbed down on the screen. "Here, where this Peacekeeper unit is guarding this desalinization plant. Echo Company."

11

Al Mish 'ab, Saudi Arabia—13 June

"This is just like something out of *Beau Geste*," Sullivan said as he looked over the battlements of the small sandstone fortress on the southern Saudi coast. The gently breaking waves of the Persian Gulf were a hundred meters to his right, and the desert sand stretched out in front of him toward Kuwait.

"What in the hell is a *'Beau Geste'*?" Ashley Wells snapped. "Another one of your boring old movies?" The recon platoon leader was not at all happy about being stuck way the hell out in the middle of nowhere and ordered to hold down this crumbling pile of old stone. Shit like this was okay for Sullivan's line platoon and the people from Hank Rivera's weapons platoon, but recon troops were supposed to be out in the brush, sneaking and peeking, not sitting on their asses like line infantry.

Sullivan grinned. "As a matter of fact, *Beau Geste* is considered to be the classic movie about the old French Foreign Legion and their battles against the Arab and Berber tribesmen in North Africa.

Adapted from a book written in 1924 by Percival Christopher Wren, the first Beau Geste movie, starring Ron Coleman, was made in 1926. Four remakes were made over the next fifty years, including one entitled *The Last Remake of Beau Geste,* featuring..."

As Ashley closed her ears to Mick's cinematic history monologue, the thought occurred to her that one of the many reasons she had never taken him seriously was his obsession with old movies. His specialty was old war movies and, at the drop of a hat, he could deliver an hour-long lecture on any topic from the John Wayne Indian war-cavalry movies to Rambo as a symbol of urbane social unrest in late-twentieth-century American society. Usually she could listen, more or less politely, when he started in on his favorite topic, but not today.

"...*The Last Remake,* however, was a parody of the Beau Geste genre, as it were, rather than being a serious reinterpretation of the..."

"For God's sake, Mick," she burst out. "Will you please shut the fuck up? We're stuck out here in this leftover from the Dark Ages and all you can do is go on about some stupid fucking ancient movie. Don't you ever watch anything filmed in this century?"

Sullivan was used to Ashley's outbursts. He thought she was either in the wrong phase of her lunar calendar or worried about her people. Consid-

ering how many days it had been since she last bit his
head off, he thought it was probably the latter.

"Actually," he said, "I saw a great holoflick just
the other day about Humphrey Bogart. You know,
the guy who did *Casablanca?*" He assumed a Bogart pose. " 'Here's looking at you, kid.' "

"You're going to be looking at the inside of a
body bag if you don't shut up."

Sullivan stopped in midsentence. Ash was a little
more testy than usual today, and as long as he was
sharing a fort with her, he knew he had better back
off. The last time she had gotten this pissed at him,
she had caught up with him on the unarmed-combat
training ground and the bruises hadn't faded for
weeks.

"When did you say Alexander the Great was going to show up here?" she asked, her mouth drawn
up in a sneer.

Sullivan's new nickname for Major Rosemont was
catching on quickly throughout the company, but
Ashley had not meant it as a compliment. She had
to admit that Rosemont had carried more than his
own load in the battle at the pumping station at Ash
Shu 'bah, but she had expected no less of an infantry officer. Other than that, though, he hadn't
shown her much yet.

"The last flash I got was that he'd be here before
dark with a mission order."

"Why the hell didn't he flash the mission to us instead of bringing it in person? This is the twenty-first century. We have a comlink, you know."

The XO shrugged. "Ours not to reason why, ours but to do and . . ."

Ashley slammed her elbow into the pit of his stomach.

"Jesus, Ash!" he gasped for breath. "What the fuck's wrong with you?"

"I told you to knock that shit off, Sullivan. I'm in no mood for it today."

"Okay, okay. Stay frosty."

Just then, Ashley's comlink beeped. "Send it," she snapped.

"This is Bravo, I've got three bandit skimmers approaching from the west at high speed." The Bravo team leader paused. "Wait one, they're squawking IFF. It's the major."

"Strider, affirm."

Spinning around, Ashley headed for the steps. Sullivan hurried after her. Beau Geste or not, after two days of inactivity, he too was anxious to hear what the CO had to say.

"This looks like something out of one of those old Beau Geste movies," Rosemont said as he surveyed the old fort. "The heroic French Foreign Legion fighting in the sand and all that."

"Yes, sir," Sullivan chimed in, glad to hear that his boss was an educated man. "As a matter of fact, this place looks a lot like the fort in the old King-dom of Morocco where they filmed *March or Die* with Gene Hackman and Terrence Hill back in . . ."

Ashley bit her tongue. All she needed was to have to listen to two supposedly professional soldiers go on about imaginary wars in old movies.

"But," Rosemont cut in, "the fort in Morocco didn't have the Persian Gulf on one side, which is why I need to talk to you two. We've picked up In-tel indicating that we need to be on guard against frogmen coming in to hit the coastal installations. The word is that they've got a stealth sub and French osmosis breathing gear for the swimmers."

"Just exactly who in the hell are we fighting, sir?" Ashley asked. "This is supposed to be a fundamen-talist Islamic rebellion against Western technology, but these guys are using modern weapons against us, not flintlocks."

"I wish I could tell you, Wells," he answered. "In fact, I asked the colonel that very same question this morning, and his answer wasn't any better than mine. Nobody seems to know for sure. The Intelli-gence agencies of a dozen nations don't seem to know any more than we do. Until we can get a han-dle on who's really behind this, we're just going to have to stay frosty and be ready to deal with any-thing that shows up from tanks to swordsmen."

"In other words, sir," Sullivan said, "we're sup-posed to act as a ready reaction force."

"That's about it," Rosemont admitted. "And guard the facilities in your sector."

Ashley locked eyes with the company commander. "We're going to get a lot more of our people zeroed fighting that way."

"I know," Rosemont said. "But until we can identify who's behind this, we really don't have much choice, do we? We can't kill them if we don't know who they are."

Ashley hated to admit it, but Rosemont was right. Until she had a target to send her recon troops against, they were useless except in a defensive role. "No, sir, we don't. But this is a real waste of good people."

"I couldn't agree with your more," Rosemont admitted. "But those are the orders."

Sullivan saw an old familiar look come over Ashley's face. To keep her from opening her mouth and ending up on charges of insubordination, Sullivan changed the subject. "How about a bit of refreshment, sir?" he offered. "We just happen to have a small stock of a cold malt beverage."

Rosemont smiled. He, too, had heard the colonel's strict ruling against alcohol on the operation, but it seemed that armies were the same no matter what uniform they wore. He wished now that he had packed his usual field flask of his favorite brandy. "Just as long as it isn't beer. You know what the Old Man thinks about beer in Islamic countries."

"Oh no, sir," Sullivan said with a perfectly straight face as he handed him a cold can completely bare of labeling. "This is just a brewed malt beverage, an old German recipe, as I recall."

Rosemont popped the top and took a long sip. "That's really good."

It seemed that there was a little more to his XO than met the eye. Along with his mild manner and apparent mania for old movies, he had an old campaigner's appreciation for what really mattered in the field.

"It's made for us right outside Benning," Sullivan said as he handed a can to Ashley. "It's cheaper without the labeling."

"I understand." Rosemont took another long sip. "Put me down for a contribution to the beverage fund."

"It's been added to your mess bill, sir."

For several minutes, not much was said as the three officers enjoyed their drinks.

"What's the chance of any multinationals coming in to handle this guard duty for us and free us to do what we do best?" Sullivan asked, getting back to the topic foremost on his mind.

"Or even UN Eunuchs," Ashley added. Like all of the Peacekeepers, she had a low estimate of the value of the UN emergency troops, the "Eunuchs," as they were most often called. Even with the Russian and American Expeditionary Forces to deal with shooting wars, the UN still sent observers, mediating teams and sometimes even so-called emergency combat troops to potential world trouble spots. The number of actions the USEF and REF had fought in the past thirty years, however, showed that the UN was no more effective that it had ever been. And, since an Algerian Muslim of fundamentalist leanings was the current secretary general of the UN, no effective action was expected this time, either.

"The UN is still debating the nature of this emergency," Rosemont explained. "The Islamic bloc is claiming that this is a legitimate religious movement that falls beyond the UN mandate. They've got India on their side because if the UN acts in this religious conflict, it might act in India, as well, over the Punjab situation, and the Hindus can't afford to have that happen."

Ashley snorted. Typical UN bullshit. The Middle East was going up in flames again, and all they could do about it was jack their jaws. No wonder they were called UN Eunuchs. Anyone with any balls would get this shit stopped ASAP. But then, that was why the Peacekeepers had been formed in the first place.

"How about the multinationals, then?" Sullivan asked. Starting with the Gulf War of '91, various Western nations had become militarily involved in the Middle East over the past forty years. The nuke-weapons cleanup campaigns undertaken after the Arab-Israeli nuclear exchange of 2004 had been conducted by European and American multinational forces.

"They're coming," Rosemont said. "But they may become part of the problem rather than part of the solution. There has already been a clash between the French and the Russians along the Turkish border. The industrial nations are starting to panic about the potential loss of oil production. They are demanding that they be allowed to protect their treaty rights."

After the Palestinian Outrage, the industrial nations of the world had met outside the UN to decide who would get how much of the remaining Middle Eastern petroleum oil production. After much wrangling, an international treaty had been signed that guaranteed petroleum quotas to each nation. Every two years the quotas were reviewed and revised as agreed upon, but no nation could afford to lose out on its share of precious oil. The destruction of oil facilities had alarmed more than one nation, and it was not surprising that they were eager to get involved.

"So," Rosemont continued, "there's a good chance that we're going to find ourselves firing on multinationals, as well as Islamic religious fanatics, before too long."

"Sweet bleeding Jesus," Sullivan said softly.

"I agree," Rosemont said. "If that gets started, there won't be enough body bags in the world to handle the casualties."

"But I thought we're supposed to keep this kind of shit from getting started, sir," Sullivan said. "What the hell's going wrong?"

"As you know," Rosemont said, "the industrial nations were willing to see the USEF and the REF formed because they had abandoned war as a viable political policy. They knew that we would only be deployed against Third World nations, and only then to keep them from creating a serious problem. We were no danger to them, so they were willing to allow us to exist. But this time, the vital interests of the entire industrial world are at stake. No oil, no developed nations. They're scared shitless and they're not going to leave the fate of their national economies to the American and Russian Expeditionary Forces."

"If we get involved with the multinationals," Sullivan said, "we could be starting World War Three."

Rosemont's jaw was clenched. "That's why we have to prevent any further destruction of oil production targets. If we don't, the multinationals are going to say that we can't protect their interests and try to do it on their own."

Ashley spoke up. "If we can't find who's behind this and put a stop to it, what are they going to do? Shoot everyone in sight?"

"They might," Rosemont said. "That's what happened in Turkey. A mech battalion of French national forces chased some raiders back across the border and ran into a company of the Russians. When the French wouldn't back down, a major firefight broke out."

"Who won?" Leave it to Ashley to cut through the bullshit and get down to the only thing that really mattered.

Rosemont grinned. A woman after his own heart. "The Russians tore them a new asshole."

Ash grinned back. She had done an exchange with a recon company of the Russian Expeditionary Force and she had a great deal of respect for the way they operated. She wouldn't want to have to go up against them unless it was absolutely necessary.

"So," Rosemont concluded, "talk to your people and impress upon them the importance of this shit detail they've been handed. As soon as I can find someone for you to kill, I'll point them out to you. But for now, this is all we have and we're stuck with it."

"What about the rest of the company?" Sullivan asked. Even though he was playing platoon leader, he was still the company XO and had to keep track of them, as well.

"Second Platoon and the rest of the weapons platoon are parked in another little fort like this a few klicks down the coast, guarding one of the nuke plants, and I'm staying with them. Top Ward has the company rear co-located with force HQ. The colonel himself is talking with the Saudis right now and he'll be holding a company commanders meeting when he gets back.''

He glanced at his watch. ''Which means I'd better get back there. I'll flash you anything I pick up at the briefing.''

''What did you think of our little pep talk?'' Sullivan asked after Rosemont left.

Ashley looked out over the battlements of the fort at the darkness. After hearing the company commander spell out what was at stake here, she was taking the situation a little more seriously. ''I think I'm going to put two of my teams out in the skimmers tonight. I want my eyes out there so I can see 'em coming before they get in too close.''

''That's probably not a bad idea,'' he agreed. ''I'll alert Rivera so he doesn't shoot them up.''

''Do that,'' she said, ''because I'm going out there, too.''

12

Al Mish 'ab—13 June

The moon was in its waning phase when Ashley Wells led her two recon skimmers out of the fortress. Without the light of the moon, the drivers were totally dependent on their sensors and night-vision imagers to see, but that wasn't a problem. Most of their training had been conducted at night, and the drivers were as comfortable looking through the imagers as they were driving with sand goggles during the day.

Moving at a crawl, their driving fans muted, the recon vehicles separated a few klicks from the fort and went in opposite directions. Ashley's skimmer headed to the shoreline, and Kat's went east along the road to Kuwait. Once in their sectors, both skimmers stopped to let off the first pair of sentries, drove farther to drop off the second pair, then moved to their final positions. Both Ashley and Kat stayed with their vehicles at the last stop so they could use their skimmers as both a command post and a mobile gun platform if any of the sentry teams needed reinforcement.

After making her comlink checks and flashing their locations back to the fort, Ashley settled in for what promised to be a long night. Even though Rosemont had warned them about possible infiltrators, the latest report from force Intel didn't indicate an imminent attack. It was probably going to be another boring night, but at least she wouldn't be forced to watch one of Sullivan's old movies.

BACK AT THE FORT, Sullivan walked into the weapons platoon's fire direction center looking for First Lieutenant Hank Rivera, the platoon leader. "Hank, my man! What's happenin'?" Sullivan called out when he saw the slim, dark-haired gunnery officer bent over a rocket mortar plotting screen.

"Yo, Mick!" Rivera called back. "You've been watching those ancient movies of yours again."

Sullivan grinned. Any time Echo Company went to the field, Sullivan was the one man who could be counted on to use his entire personal weight allowance to pack a holoplayer and as many laser disks as possible. The fact that all of his disks were of old movies didn't bother the off-duty troops. They'd watch anything to break up the boredom of waiting to fight.

"Ash and Trash is out in the sand with two of her teams and she wanted me to make sure that your boys keep their fingers out tonight."

Rivera tapped the screen. "I know, she's sending in her defcons right now."

Sullivan glanced at the screen. Ashley's defensive fire concentrations were placed along the beach and covering the highway to the east. In light of Rosemont's warning, it was a good layout for preplanned fires, but it was not quite good enough. He picked up the light pen from the clip on the monitor. "Add a couple more, here, here and here." The pen touched the screen, creating defcon symbols on the west and north sides of the fort.

"You think they'll come out of the desert, like in one of your old movies?"

"Even though the CO said to watch out for frogmen, Arabs don't like the ocean very much."

"How about Sinbad?" Rivera asked, remembering one of Sullivan's old movies about a legendary Arab sailor.

"That's different, he was an old-time Arab. If these guys hit us tonight, they'll come overland."

"You're the boss," Rivera said, punching the additional defcons into his fire plan data bank. "Anything else going on tonight?"

"*Nada.*" Sullivan shook his head. "It looks like it's going to be nice and quiet again tonight. You want to stop by the comcenter for a movie later?"

"What're you going to watch?"

"The Magnificent Seven with Yul Brynner, James—"

"Pass," Rivera broke in. "I can't stand Westerns, particularly Mexican Westerns. My people were all city dwellers, not land owners or banditos."

"It's got a great musical score."

"Forget it."

ROSEMONT EXAMINED the printouts of the post-deployment equipment and stockage levels, signed them and reached for the next paper from the pile in front of him. Even on deployment, being a company commander meant an endless stream of paperwork. First Sergeant Ward took care of most logistical and administrative chores while he was in the sand with the grunts, but he still had to be aware of what had been said and done in his name.

The company CP had been set up with Jeb Stuart's Second Platoon and the other half of Rivera's weapons platoon in a wooded gully—or wadi, as it was called in the region—to the north of the nuclear desalinization plant on the Saudi coast. Stuart was rotating his squads in and out of the defensive positions around the plant, it was well within range of the rocket mortars at the CP.

Rosemont would have liked to have been a little closer to the desalinization unit so he could tie his defense in with the plant's. But a sizeable village had grown up around the plant, and he didn't want to be too close to the villagers. In a fluid situation like this, when the identity of the enemy was unknown, it was best to keep a safe distance from the local population.

Rosemont was not happy with the mission his company had been given. This static defensive posture robbed him of his two greatest strengths, initiative and mobility. As long as he had to sit and wait for the enemy to come to him, he couldn't use his people to their best advantage. So far, the situation reminded him of what he had read of the Vietnam War, where the American infantry battalions had sat in their jungle fire bases and waited for the North Vietnamese to attack.

As far as he was concerned, this was dumb thinking and certainly not what he had expected of the hard-hitting Peacekeepers. As a light infantry unit, Echo Company was designed to stay on the move, probing and reconning, trying to locate the enemy's concentrations. When they found them, the heavy infantry Hulks would go in and clean them up.

He also knew full well that until force Intel could come up with a target area for them to work, they might as well sit here instead of wearing the troops out searching empty sand dunes. It was almost as bad to work the troops unnecessarily as it was to keep them sitting on their asses. Another week, though, and he'd have to send them out just to keep them sane. They were good people, but like all infantry soldiers, they were quick to get bored. And in this business, being bored was a good way to find yourself dead at the most inopportune moment.

Suddenly an explosion shattered the night. It was immediately followed by the clatter of small-arms fire. As he snatched up his helmet, Rosemont heard both the light rattle of the grunts' 5 mm light assault rifles and the heavier bark of Han Type 98 assault rifles. The rifle fire was quickly joined by the hammering of his two 12.5 mm heavy machine guns. Whatever was happening out there, it was no probe.

Snapping down his visor, he called up his tac display and saw that they were being hit from two sides by large hostile forces. The early-warning sensors had detected them coming in. The explosion must have been one of the antiintrusion mines going off.

As he watched, he saw the hostiles throw themselves against the southern perimeter. His people were holding out so far and he heard the First Sergeant's voice shouting orders over the noise of the battle. But there were just too many hostiles, far too many. If he didn't get reinforcements, they would more than likely get wiped out.

After making a quick call to Sullivan at the fort, he flicked the selector switch of his LAR to burst fire and ran to join the grunts as just another rifleman. This was one of those times where the best thing he could do as a commander was to let his people do what they did best with no interference from him.

"THE CP IS BEING HIT!" the comtech yelled over to Sullivan, who was watching his movie. The XO jumped up and dashed to the monitor. "Get Ash and Trash moving," he snapped when he saw the situation. "And mount up two squads of First Platoon to go with them."

As the comtech was flashing the orders, an explosion rocked the room, shaking dust from the stone walls. "We're being hit, too!"

"Tell Ash she's got to do it on her own now. I need First Platoon to stay here!" Sullivan yelled as he snatched his helmet and LAR. "I'll be up on the walls!"

As Sullivan reached the door, a second rocket mortar round hit the parade ground in the open middle of the fort. A shower of dirt rained down on him, and frag sang past his head as he threw himself flat on the ground.

The explosion was answered by lesser explosions of outgoing rounds as Rivera's rocket mortars started their counter battery fire. Knowing that Rivera's hail of 90 mm rockets would quickly silence the hostile mortars, Sullivan raced across the open for the stone steps leading up to the walls.

By the time he reached the top of the battlements, the situation seemed to be pretty much under control. As in the old Foreign Legion movies, the sand crawled with hostiles and winked with muzzle-flashes. But unlike the movies, the grunts could see the enemy clearly through their night-vision gear as they approached. And unlike the hostiles encountered earlier at the pumping station, these men were not wearing stealth suits, so they made easy targets. The grunts were calmly picking off their targets as though they were on the firing range back at Benning.

Sullivan was thinking that it was almost too easy when a shot from behind him made him spin around. He had allowed himself to get sucked into concentrating on the obvious. Most of his troops had also been drawn into the battle along the south and east walls, leaving the north and west sides almost unguarded.

Seeing the matt black shape of a man in a stealth suit appear over the top of the northwest corner of the battlements, he fired off a short burst, dropping the man down inside the wall. "First squad!" he called out over the comlink. "Cover your right flank! Third squad form up on me!"

More black shapes appeared over that section of the battlements, weapons blazing. Sullivan thought they were going to be overrun before his grunts would reach him. Snatching a grenade from his ammo pouch, he thumbed the safety off and hurled it toward the far wall.

Before the grenade reached its target, he triggered off a long burst, raking the top of the wall. "Come on!" he yelled as the grenade detonated.

Shouting their battle cries, the dozen grunts followed their leader as he charged, his assault rifle blazing.

AT THE COM CENTER'S CALL, Ashley and Kat fired up their skimmers and raced back to retrieve the sentries they had posted. As the last man boarded and they turned around to join Sullivan's troops, the second call came in, telling Ash that the fort was under attack and she and Kat would have to go to Rosemont's rescue on their own.

Keying her tac display to link with Sullivan's, she saw the hostiles swarming over the north wall. Her first instinct was to help Mick, but his orders had been specific. She was to punch through to Rosemont and save the company CP at all costs.

The last thing she saw as she switched off her tac display was Mick's beacon as he led a charge against the north wall of the fort.

SULLIVAN'S CHARGE took the enemy by surprise, but they recovered quickly and fought furiously to keep their position atop the north wall. Bullets sang over his head and tugged at his uniform as he laid down a base of fire from his LAR. A round slammed into his Kevlar helmet, blanking his tac display. Another burst hit his armor and drove him to his knees, stunned.

One of the grunts threw himself between Sullivan and the hostiles to protect his fallen leader and took a wound in the legs. Hearing his cry, Sullivan dragged him to safety against the wall. Picking up the grunt's LAR in his left hand, he flicked the selector switches on both weapons down to full automatic.

Rising to his feet with LARs in both hands, he cradled the butts of the weapons against his hips and unleashed a full 800 rounds a minute. Both weapons emptied their 100-round magazines in seconds, but the storm of fire swept the battlements clear.

"Let's go!" he shouted over the comlink.

Screaming their war cries, the grunts of First Platoon charged again. This time the hostiles withered in the face of their combined fire. Several of them jumped back over the walls, and the rest were cut down.

Looking through a gap in the battlements, Sullivan saw that the hostiles were withdrawing. "Hank!" he called over the comlink. "Fire defcon four, they're getting away!"

In seconds, Rivera's rocket mortars were hurling toward their preplanned target, taking a heavy toll of the hostiles. As he shifted fire to keep up with the retreating enemy, the gunner remembered what Sullivan had said about an attack. The hostiles had come out of the sand, not the sea.

13

On the Coast Highway—13 June

Even though she was a recon grunt, Kat Wallenska rode the open hatch of her blacked-out skimmer as though she had been born in a ground-effects vehicle. She had learned the loose-hipped, rolling stance of a tanker long ago to keep from being beaten to death in the hatch as the skimmer drove forward at maximum speed. The ground-effects vehicle rode on a cushion of air instead of tracks or wheels, but at high speed it was still a rough ride.

One of her hands rested on the controls for the 30 mm chain-gun/grenade-launcher in the front of the turret and the other on the hatch controls, ready to dump the hatch at any moment. With the nav screen and terrain-following radar to guide her, Kat could have commanded the skimmer from inside the safety of the armor as well as she could standing in the open hatch. But no matter how good the electronics, she preferred her own eyes, particularly when she sensed she was riding into an ambush.

She hadn't seen anything on the threat sensors yet, but that old ache in the small of her back was more accurate than any electronic sensor. She forced herself to relax to keep from hunching her shoulders. They were going to get clobbered any moment now; she just knew it.

They had been able to escape the attack on the fort only because they had been outside the walls before it was hit. Ashley had wanted to go to Sullivan's rescue, but the XO had ordered them to reinforce Rosemont instead. You didn't have to be Napoleon to figure out that the two attacks had been coordinated and had been engineered to keep Sullivan bottled up so he couldn't go to Rosemont's rescue. If the attack had been that well planned, there was sure to be another unpleasant surprise coming up somewhere along the way.

The skirt of the vehicle slammed against an obstacle, throwing Kat against the side of the hatch. Her body armor saved her from any real damage, but she knew she'd be wearing a big bruise in the morning. "Watch where in the fuck you're going, malf!" she yelled to the driver over the intercom.

The driver glanced at her over his shoulder, his night-driving goggles making him look like a deep-space alien in a bad holoflick. He would have preferred to drive down inside the protection of the armor, but when Kat had her head out of the hatch, so did her driver, if he wanted to remain her driver. "Sorry, Kat."

IN THE FOLLOWING skimmer, Wells was monitoring the comlink transmissions from the Second Platoon grunts in contact. It was difficult to tell much from the jumble of orders, curses and shouts that she heard. All she could tell was that both the nuke plant and the CP were under heavy attack. From the readouts on her display, it looked as if the grunts at the plant were holding their own, but the CP was in trouble. With most of Stuart's Second Platoon at the nuke plant, only one grunt squad and the CP staff were left to defend their perimeter.

As she watched, another grunt's beacon started flashing yellow, indicating he was hit. Rosemont was surrounded and if he didn't get help real soon, he was going to be history.

She keyed her comlink, "Kat, make your run in from the south, along the road through that ville. I'm going to try to break away, cut north and come in from the east."

"Affirm," Kat sent back, her fingers clenched around the 30 mm firing controls.

FACEDOWN IN THE SAND, Rosemont rolled over to pull another magazine from his ammo pouch. Dropping the empty from the breech of his LAR, he clipped the loaded one into place and chambered the first round. Rolling back upright, he sighted in on a hostile muzzle-flash and triggered off a 3-round burst.

A stream of green tracers cut through the night from his left, and he twisted around to bring fire on it. Even with all the sensors and mark one eyeballs in the sand around his small perimeter, the hostiles had managed to sneak in fairly close to his position before they had been spotted. They had hit when Stuart was rotating the squads, so only one grunt squad and his handful of HQ people were holding the perimeter. The hostiles were too close for the mortars to fire support and if those recon vehicles didn't arrive ASAP, they were going to be in a world of hurt.

Several figures rose from the sand in Rosemont's night-vision imager, fifty meters to his right front. He focused his sights on the center of them and triggered off a long burst of 5 mm. A grunt to his right sent a 30 mm grenade into the middle of them, and Rosemont's visor blanked when the enhanced explosive detonated.

When his visor cleared, he saw the bunch of hostiles were down, but more kept popping up. Over the roar of battle, he heard Top Ward shouting as he dashed from one position to the other, coordinating the defense of the rapidly shrinking perimeter. Already two men were dead and at least three more were wounded. But there was no time to pull the wounded out of the line. They would live or die along with the rest.

"ASH, THIS IS KAT," Wallenska transmitted from the lead skimmer. "I've got a major concentration of hostiles converging on the nuke plant from the north. Grid three, nine, seven, two, six, four. Can you bring some fire on them as we pass? I'll cover the front."

"That's affirm," Ash answered as she swung the 30 mm chain gun around to bear and slaved it to her tac display. Kat had tagged the hostiles in red, and they were well within range. She punched in 3-round burst, slow fire, and dialed up both the EHE cannon and antipersonnel grenade ammo feed.

Aiming at the center of the target, she pressed the triggers. The 30 mm barked 3-round bursts of two EHE rounds and one grenade as it cycled back and forth between the two types of ammunition.

By the third burst, the target fragmented as the hostiles scattered for cover. She continued tracking the largest group and kept them under fire as the skimmer swept past, following Kat into the village. The way this was turning out, she had better forget her plan to swing around to the north. It was going to be hard enough for the two of them together to punch through as it was.

Swinging her turret to the front, Ash saw that her display showed a threat warning from the first house in the village. Firing a burst of 30 mm, she was rewarded by a small explosion. She saw Kat's vehicle slew to the side in the light of the explosion, the sergeant's chain gun hammering at yet another target. "Close in on them!" Ash called down to her driver.

The fans howled as the skimmer lurched forward, and Ash triggered her 30 mm again. Christ, she hated fighting from a vehicle in a built-up area! As long as she was in the skimmer, she was the primary target and there was no place she could hide.

Several fires had broken out, and the wavering light made her night imagers almost useless. Flipping them out of the way with a toss of her head, she searched the light and shadows with her naked gaze. Seeing movement between two small houses, she zeroed in on it and fired.

ABOVE THE CLOSE RATTLE of small-arms fire, Rosemont heard the authoritative bark of a 30 mm chain gun on slow fire. Wells was here with the cavalry. Bringing up his tac screen, he saw the two blue markers showing the recon skimmers approaching from the village to the south. With his display linked with the sensors in the speeding skimmers, he saw the identified enemy forces turn to face the onslaught from their rear. Suddenly a blinking threat symbol appeared behind and to the left of Kat's vehicle.

"Strider Alpha," Rosemont transmitted. "This is Bold Lancer. You have a Long Lash on your left flank, seven o'clock, and he's got his seeker on."

"Kat, affirm," the sergeant called back. "Thanks, Alex."

Rosemont chuckled as he watched Kat pivot her skimmer around on its rear fans to bring her chain gun to bear on the target. A short burst of 30 mm, and the threat blip disappeared from his screen.

He still wasn't used to the Peacekeepers' informality over the comlink. Although their transmissions were skip scrambled and next to impossible to unscramble even if they were intercepted, they refrained from using official call signs unless absolutely necessary. He was just going to have to get used to his sergeants calling him by his first name.

Trailing a plume of dust, Kat's skimmer raced up to Rosemont's shrinking CP perimeter, the big thirty Mike Mike hammering and the LARs of the troops inside spitting from the firing ports. Wells's skimmer was a few seconds behind Kat's. The cavalry had finally arrived!

Now that the skimmers were here, he had the hostiles right where he wanted them, caught between Stuart's Second Platoon at the nuke plant and the heavy guns of Wells's recon vehicles. Now he could get down to serious business.

"All Strider elements," he transmitted. "This is Alex. Let's do it to them. I want to get this shit over with."

His call was answered with a storm of fire from the two skimmers as they unloaded their infantry and spun around to face the enemy. The recon grunts quickly joined his people and formed fire teams. Under the cover of the 30 mm cannons, they started maneuvering against the hostiles. Faced with the heavy fire and fresh troops, the hostiles broke and ran.

Stopping only long enough to take on their recon grunts again, the two skimmers took off in hot pursuit of the retreating enemy. When they disappeared in the sand, Rosemont's few troops started policing up the immediate area around the CP.

While Top Ward supervised casualty collection, Rosemont got on the comlink with Stuart at the nuke plant and Sullivan at the coastal fort. Both lieutenants had their respective situations well under control. The fact that their attacks had been broken off at the same time that Rosemont's opponents had called it quits showed the attacks had been well coordinated. It was one more proof that there was more to this than a religious uprising.

ROSEMONT SET his camp stool back on its legs and started trying to make order out of chaos in the tattered remnants of his CP. A near miss by a mortar round had shredded the tent and sent shrapnel into his field desk. A comtech was in the corner replacing a damaged communications module while he sorted through his scattered paperwork.

He looked up and saw a dirty, smoke-stained Ashley Wells walk up. The platoon leader's LAR was slung over her right shoulder, the muzzle still smoking in the cool early-morning air. "We've mopped up the last of them, Major," she reported. "And secured the area. But no prisoners again."

He wasn't surprised. That seemed to be the pattern for their encounters so far. Christ, he hated fighting fanatics!

"Take a load off your feet and have a cup of coffee," he said, popping the heat tab on a canister and holding it out to her.

She took a deep drink. "Damn, it's hot."

"Yeah," he agreed. "They need to adjust the temperature on these things for the desert."

Ashley sat down on an ammunition crate, pulled off her helmet and fluffed her close-cropped blond hair. Her pale skin showed dark circles under her gray eyes, and she looked completely exhausted. Even so, she was still one of the most beautiful women Rosemont had ever known. She was certainly the most beautiful woman he had ever seen wearing a combat uniform.

"You and your people need to get as much rest as you can today," Rosemont said. "I don't think we're going to have any more trouble around here for a little while at least."

Ashley's eyes flicked over to the mangled hostile corpse lying in the sand outside. "They'll be back all right, sir."

"How're your people?"

She took another deep drink of the coffee. "I lost another one and had two more wounded, but only one seriously. If you hadn't warned Kat about that missile, we'd have lost even more.''

Rosemont caught the tone of her voice. "You're not used to taking casualties, are you?''

Her gray eyes locked on his. "No, sir. I'm not!'' she snapped. "We're supposed to be Peacekeepers, not some fucking Regular Army unit.''

Rosemont understood her anger. He had always felt enraged when he had lost men because of what he saw as stupid thinking in the chain of command. "The colonel's called a company commanders' meeting this morning. Maybe he'll have some new information about these people so we can see about putting an end to this.''

"I sure as hell hope so,'' she said. "So far, this entire operation has been a Saturday night dog fuck. How in the hell can we get this situation under control when we're sitting on our dead asses waiting for the hostiles to hit us at their convenience? Anybody with half a brain would see that we've got to get out there and...''

Rosemont let her get it out of her system. He had been a platoon leader a long time and knew the stresses that went with the job. Wells's frustration was being directed at the colonel and his staff because she couldn't identify the people she really was pissed at—whoever was behind this orgy of death and destruction. He knew that as soon as she was finished with her tirade, she would shut up and soldier, but until then she would bitch.

Wells was good at what she did, but Rosemont wondered if she wasn't a little too high-strung for this line of work. He hated to be sexist about it, but some women just weren't cut out to be combat leaders. He knew some male officers who flew off the handle every now and then, as well, but Ashley made a science of it and he was starting to get concerned about her.

He didn't have any complaints about her doing her job in combat, not at all. But when she was not killing hostiles, she contributed very little to the smooth running of the company. Before he asked the colonel to have her transferred out, however, he would have to see what he could do on his own to get her straightened out. Command counseling it was called, and, except for combat drops, it was the part of his job he hated most.

14

Force Headquarters, Saudi Arabia—14 June

Rosemont had his ID checked twice on the way into the CP. During the confusion of the battle at the nuke plant the night before, a hostile dressed in USEF-issue camouflage had attempted to infiltrate the Peacekeepers' headquarters. When he was finally challenged, he had set off a demolition charge he had been carrying rather than be captured. No Peacekeepers had been killed in the explosion, but security was tight today and would remain so.

The briefing tent was crowded with force staff officers, the company commanders and the combat support platoon leaders. Rosemont had not met half of them yet and nodded as he passed and took a chair next to Major Jim Collins, commander of the Bravo Company Bulls. Collins was a bull of a man himself, well suited to wearing the powered armored suit of a Hulk. In fact, even in fatigues, he looked as if he was wearing his armor.

"Heard you had some visitors last night," Collins greeted him.

Rosemont grinned. "They just stopped in to welcome us to the Middle East. Friendly folks around here."

Collins laughed. "Tell me about it. We've been picking them off our backs like fleas ever since we got here. They haven't figured out yet that a guy in a flowing robe is no match for a grunt in a Hulk suit."

Just then, the sergeant major entered the tent. "Ladies and gentlemen, the force commander."

Everyone stood as the colonel walked in. "Take your seats, please," he said as he laid his briefing folder on the podium.

"We have a new player in the game," he said. "Israeli Defense Forces armored units have been massing along the Jordanian and Syrian borders. Intel says that they are prepared to join the game any time they feel the situation has gotten too far out of control. Syria and Jordan have reacted to this buildup, and the United Nations is frantically trying to defuse the situation. The Israelis say they are only protecting their legitimate national interests and refuse to stand down until this situation is under control."

The colonel's eyes swept the room. "Our mission, therefore, is to get this thing shut down as soon as possible before the entire region blows up and we have World War Three on our hands. The question is, however, just exactly what are we dealing with here? I've had the Intel staff do an analysis of what has happened over the past week and I think you'll be interested in their findings."

The Intel officer who walked to the front of the tent was a tall, thin man with the look of an academic rather than a soldier. Actually he had been an academic before becoming a Peacekeeper and had never seen the need to acquire the mannerisms of a soldier. In his mind, his job in the USEF was the same as it had been in academia: to analyze data and arrive at a conclusion, and he didn't need to be a soldier to do that.

He flicked on the briefing monitor: "First off," he said, "I'd like to show you some stats on what has happened so far in this campaign. As you all know, the multinationals have reacted to the violence in the region and have sent troops to their regional allies to ensure that their treaty oil production continues to flow. The statistics, however, clearly show that this is not random violence, nor does it appear to be an attempt to curtail oil production."

He flashed some numbers on the screen. "For every attack on an oil facility, there has been seven-point-eight attacks on nuke power plants, electrical power distribution networks, desalinization units and irrigation projects. As far as the attacks on the oil facilities go, none of them has been very destructive. It's as if the hostiles are fully aware that without continued oil production as outlined in the multinational treaty, the Middle East has absolutely no value at all to the outside world. Whoever is behind this may be crazy, but they're not crazy enough to halt the flow of oil.

"What it all boils down to is this—regardless of what the multinationals think this is not a war about oil. Apparently the prime targets for hostile actions are, first, nuclear plants, particularly those that are powering the desalinization units, second, the desalinization units themselves and third, the irrigation networks and reforested areas. In other words, what we're seeing here is some kind of back-to-nature project that is attempting to turn the desert back into a desert again."

That got a chuckle. One of the ironies of the massive reforestation and irrigation projects that had been implemented in the Middle East over the past twenty years was that they had been violently opposed by the so-called Greens, the coalition of environmentalist groups throughout the world who claimed that greening the desert would upset the delicate balance of nature in the region. Their opposition had been so vehement and disruptive that the Middle Eastern government had been forced to ban them within their borders.

"We see the destruction of other technological targets in the cities as being mostly a side show," the scientist continued. "Something to distract the national forces of the region and keep them from guarding the primary targets."

"Who do you think's behind this?" one of the company commanders asked.

The Intel officer shrugged. "We haven't the slightest. We've had a hard enough time coming up with what they're doing and don't have a damned thing on who's doing it. Our best guess, however, is that it's being directed from outside the region, some non-Arabic source."

He held up his hand to forestall the next inevitable question. "As to why someone would want to destroy these irrigation projects, we haven't a clue. But now that we know what they're after, we can better guard against that specific threat."

"Where does this Twelfth Imam fit into all of this?" a different voice asked.

"Good question," the Intel officer said. He flicked on a replay of the original CNN holovee broadcast of the Imam and froze the frame on a full-length shot of him standing in front of the Karbala mosque.

"As I'm sure all of you know, we have been aware from the beginning that this so-called Twelfth Imam is no more than a hologram projection. A good one, that's true, but a projection nonetheless. The problem is that the locals aren't about to buy that explanation. People are now claiming that they have actually touched his hand or his robe."

There were a few snickers from the audience.

"Don't laugh," the Intel officer cautioned. "You have to understand that this is a significant cultural event for these people. As significant as the Second Coming of Christ would be for an orthodox Christian. Think of all the otherwise normal people who have seen the Virgin Mary's face in their pizza or in natural rock formations. We're dealing with an article of faith here, not fact, and there's no way that Western outsiders are going to convince the Islamic faithful with scientific explanations. Not even the moderate Islamic leaders have been able to convince their own people that this is a cruel, destructive hoax."

"Can't we intercept the holo transmission and trace it back?" the air officer asked.

"We could." The Intel officer nodded. "But to do that, we'd have to have our equipment in place beforehand. How do we know when or where the Imam is going to appear? Second, there's no way the Islamic faithful are going to allow Western technicians near their mystical Imam. They'd be torn to shreds the minute they showed up with their equipment. Along with the holovee crew that was killed in Karbala the day the Imam first appeared, two more CNN teams have been killed by the mobs."

He zoomed in on the Imam's face. "We are, however, trying to identify whoever it is who's playing the Imam. Every Intelligence service in the region is working on that right now, but so far, we have all drawn a blank. All that we know is that whoever he is, he knows medieval Arabic and speaks with what may be a Lebanese accent."

"Has anyone tried tracing him through the universities that teach Arabic studies?" a woman asked. "He looks young enough to be a college student somewhere."

"That's worth pursuing," the Intel officer admitted. "I'll have my people look into that. So far, though, we've been working on the premise that he's a terrorist or a Shiite commando from one of the Islamic Brotherhood units. Several of the hostile bodies we've recovered have been traced back to the Brotherhood. In fact, several have turned out to be Brotherhood leaders. If nothing else, when this operation is finished, the Islamic Brotherhood will be short of experienced leadership for a long time."

No one seemed to have any problem with that. Since the demise of the old PLO after the Palestinian Outrage of 2005, the Islamic Brotherhood had taken up the banner of international terrorism where the PLO had left off. While not as vicious as the old PLO had been, the Brotherhood had committed many senseless crimes against those whom they saw as the enemies of Islam. The only thing they didn't do was murder women and children like the old PLO had often done.

"In the same vein," the Intel officer continued, "I need to impress upon your field commanders the absolute necessity of capturing hostiles for interrogation. Until we can get our hands on one of these guys and put him through the wringer, we won't know who we are dealing with."

The "wringer" referred to was chemical interrogation. Developed from crude beginnings in the previous century using LSD and scopolamine, modern chemical interrogation employed a mixture of psychoactive drugs that rapidly and completely broke down a person's resistance to questioning. Even so, it was a time-consuming technique and a fine art. Regardless of what the subject knew, he would only answer the questions asked. The art of the technique was in asking the right questions.

When the interrogation was over, no permanent damage was done to the prisoner. Some even claimed that it served a useful purpose by resolving internal personality conflict. A modification of the technique was being used to treat sociopathic behavior in some civilian prisoners as a means of psychiatric rehabilitation.

Even though the Human Rightists screamed about using the technique on common criminals, they had backed down when it came to its military applications. Even the liberals realized that chemical interrogation of POWs could save lives in a combat situation.

"So you people get me some prisoners to work on, and I'll tell you what we can do to put an end to this situation." The Intel officer looked around. "Are there any questions? If not, the maintenance chief has some words of wisdom on keeping your machinery running in the desert."

"MAJOR ROSEMONT," the colonel called out as the meeting broke up.

"Sir?"

"Let's go into the operations room. I've got a mission for your company."

"Yes, sir."

Like all of the compact Peacekeepers headquarters, the operations room was small, crowded and busy. Everything in the room was also highly mobile and could be broken down in a matter of minutes and loaded into ground or air transport. Leading the company commander to a monitor, the colonel flashed onto the screen a large-scale map of the Middle East marked with the sites of the clashes over the last seven days.

"So far," he said, "we've been reacting instead of proacting, and I want to put an end to that ASAP. The Peacekeepers were not designed to operate that way." He smiled faintly. "It's time we got out there and started kicking ass."

"We'll have no problem with that, sir," Rosemont replied. "My people are getting a little tired of pulling garrison duty."

"I thought they might, which is why I picked them for this mission. I want you to put your recon in the field and have your line platoons standing by on ready reaction alert. I'll back them up with the Alpha Company Hulks and all the tactical air assets I can spare. Your mission is to find the roving Brotherhood units in our area of operations and zero them before they cause any more trouble. Also, like the Intel officer said, I want prisoners. As many as you can snatch."

"Where do you want us to go?"

The colonel handed him a hard copy. "Here's a list of likely Brotherhood targets the Intel staff came up with in Jordan, Kuwait, Iraq, Kurdistan and the Shiite Republic. You'll notice that Iran is still off-limits for our operations. They say that they can handle their own problems and have threatened to attack if we cross their borders. I want you to go down the list and check each of these locations out. Move fast but be thorough. When you find them, eliminate them and move on."

Rosemont smiled: this was his kind of operation. Move, shoot and communicate—the purest essence of mobile warfare and the perfect mission for his light infantry company. "We'll be more than happy to handle this for you, sir."

"I thought you might," the colonel said. "Check in with the operations officer before you leave, and he'll lay on your air assets."

"Yes, sir."

15

High over the Desert—15 June

The Second Platoon leader, First Lieutenant Jubal Early Butler Stuart, sat at the commander's console in the speeding AV-19 Tilt Wing assault transport and watched as the forward-looking radar and sensors gave him a panoramic view of the terrain they were approaching.

Although his first three names were different from the famous Confederate cavalry officer with the same initials and last name, he was still called Jeb and most of his friends thought he had been named after General Jeb Stuart. Being a son of the Old South, however, he didn't mind at all. In fact, his first two names were those of another less distinguished Confederate general from whom his family claimed descent. The Butler, however, was from his mother's family and had nothing to do with the American Civil War, or the War Between the States, as most Southerners still preferred to call it.

The situation that was unfolding on Stuart's tac screen display was right out of the exploits of his

UN-namesake—a cavalry raid deep into enemy territory. The difference was that he and his platoon were racing for their objective in Tilt Wings, not mounted on horseback. Which was a good thing, as this Jeb Stuart had never ridden a horse.

The tactics were much the same, however. Born of horse-and saber cavalry tactics by way of the Air Cav of the Vietnam War, the Tilt Wings would carry his people to their assault positions, drop them off and stick around to provide heavy-fire support as needed. When they had taken the objective, the assault transports would pick them up and carry them to the next target.

Quick in, kick ass and quick out. "Eagle Flights," they had been called back in the Vietnam War. Now it was just called doing business. And speaking of business, it was time for Second Platoon to go to work.

The tac screen showed a promising target, a small village at a road junction. Three military-type vehicles were parked close to some houses and covered with camouflage screens. They were all but invisible to the naked eye but the Tilt Wing's sensors picked up their heat signatures through the netting.

Stuart keyed the intercom connecting him to the two squads who were riding in the back compartment. "Okay, listen up, gang," he said. "We've got a ville coming up that looks like it might be hostile. SOP on the Lima Zulu. First squad, take 'em out, second squad, provide fire support. Remember now, the Old Man wants prisoners, so should you happen to come upon a hostile or two who aren't giving you too much trouble, snatch 'em.''

With a whine of electric motors, the Tilt Wing's copilot-gunner deployed his 30 mm chain-gun/grenade-launcher turret and his multiple rocket pods from their recesses in the fuselage. Any hostile who popped his head up to fire a burst would be instant dog meat.

He was disappointed that there was no activity from the ville on the final approach. With the Tilt Wing's rotors set on whisper mode, all that could be heard was a faint whine from the turbines as the assault transport touched down in a wadi five hundred meters from the ville. The rear ramp came down before the aircraft had all four wheels of her landing gear on the ground, and Stuart dashed out, leading his grunts.

Leading his first squad, Stuart moved up to take assault positions around the ville while second squad found a site overlooking the houses to fire support for the attack. Once everyone was in place, he keyed his mike and ordered the attack.

The assault went as smoothly as an exercise. Two men on guard duty were taken out silently. Since it was the heat of the day, most of the hostiles were inside the houses to stay cool, and were completely taken by surprise. There was some scattered resistance, but it was quickly overwhelmed.

No sooner had the last shots echoed away than the leader of Stuart's first squad, Alpha Battle Team, approached, raising his visor. "You wanted prisoners, LT? We got two of them."

Two Arab men were being led from one of the houses. One was holding his pants up as he was hurried along.

"The hostile we caught with his pants down had a pistol and map case. I think he's an officer."

"Outfuckingstanding."

Stuart immediately keyed his mike implant. "Bold Lancer," he transmitted. "This is Bold Cowboy."

"Lancer Xray," Mick Sullivan answered for Rosemont. "Go ahead, Jeb."

"Tell Bold Lancer that I've got him two prisoners. One's wounded, but the other's intact and he might be an officer."

"Bring 'em home ASAP."

"Affirm. On the way."

"Get 'em in the bus," Stuart said, pumping his arm up and down in the old visual signal to hurry. "We're going home."

To say that Ashley Wells was miffed when Jeb Stuart came sauntering into the mess hall at the small fort that was now First Platoon and recon's base camp would have been a serious understatement. She was thoroughly pissed because it should have been her recon teams who had captured the prisoners, not grunts from Stuart's line platoon. Not only was she pissed at Jeb, but she was also pissed at Rosemont for not having given her people his mission. While Stuart had had all the air assets, her people had been out busting sand dunes in their skimmers and hadn't found a thing.

"Well," she sneered, "if it isn't the cowboy himself."

"Miss Ashley," Stuart drawled, bowing from the waist like the Southern cavalier he fancied himself to be. "How nice to see you looking so well."

"Asshole."

"Miss Ashley!" Stuart raised his eyebrows in mock horror. "Such language! I'm shocked . . ."

"Stuff it, Stuart."

Jeb wisely shut his mouth. Like Mick, he, too, had come out on the wrong side of Ashley Wells more than once. When Ash and Trash was acting this way, it was better to keep out of her road.

Ashley got her meal and sat by herself at the end of the table and pretended not to listen as Stuart recounted his adventure to a flock of admiring listeners. She was going to have to have a long talk with the company commander about the proper use of her recon platoon. So far, this operation had been a complete dog fuck, and she wanted to get back to doing what she did best. And that did not mean picking up after the line platoon grunts.

ROSEMONT BLINKED and looked up from the monitor screen at the knock on the open door to his makeshift office in the coastal fort. *"Entrez, s'il vous plaît."*

"Oui, mon Commandant."

Spinning around in his chair, he saw Kat Wallenska standing in the doorway. "I didn't know you spoke French, Sergeant—is that on your 201 file?"

Kat grinned. "My family are Polish immigrants, sir, and we Poles still consider French to be the only true language of civilization. I took it in high school, but I'm told that I have a horrible accent."

Rosemont grinned. "So do I and I don't even speak the language. Have a seat."

As Kat sat beside Rosemont's desk, he noticed that she was wearing a clean uniform and a trace of makeup. Cleaned up and not wearing her body armor and helmet, he saw that she was a striking woman. A little muscular for his tastes, but still very interesting in an exotic, Slavic way. The silver skull dangling from her right ear, though, let him know that she was still all business.

"What can I do for you?"

"Well, sir—"

"You can drop the 'sirs' during office hours, Kat. I've noticed that the Peacekeepers are somewhat more informal than the Regular Army, so I guess I'd better start getting used to it."

He leaned over to the box lying on the sand beside his desk. "How about a cup?"

"I'd like that."

He grabbed a canister of coffee and handed it to her. "Watch it, it's hot."

She laughed. "I know. They need to adjust these for desert climates."

"I think I've heard that several times now over the last couple of days."

There was an awkward silence as she popped the tab on her coffee and took a tentative sip. "I wanted to thank you," she said hesitantly, "for warning me about that Long Lance the other night. That guy had me cold and would've zeroed me for sure if you hadn't told me that he was there."

"De nada," He shrugged. "You'd have done the same for me."

She continued as if she hadn't heard him, "I had my head up and locked, and I just wasn't keeping a close eye on my six."

Recon teams had adopted the fighter pilot's habit of referring to their environment in terms of the positions of the numbers on a clock. Twelve was dead ahead and six was their rear.

"Like I said, it was nothing. That's why I get to wear the helmet with all the readouts." Rosemont's command helmet had the ability to show anything that any of the troopers' sensors were picking up and combine the readouts into a comprehensive display of the battlefield. "It goes with the job. I'm just glad that I spotted him in time."

Kat drained off the last of her coffee and, getting to her feet, dropped the empty container in the open ration box.

"Thanks again, Alex." Her voice was husky as she leaned down and brushed her lips against his cheek before abruptly turning and walking out.

A smile formed slowly on Rosemont's face as he watched her leave. I'll be damned, he thought, I think I've got me an admirer. If that wasn't an invitation, he had been misusing his testosterone all these years.

Relationships between male and female personnel in the Peacekeepers were not outlawed, and it would have been stupid to even try. But they were not encouraged, either, particularly between officers and the enlisted ranks. It happened, though— Rosemont knew that, particularly in combat situations. There was something about being shot at that acted on a human's sense of survival at the deepest cellular level. In times of danger, the DNA screamed to live and, more often than not, those screams were translated into frantic sexual activity. After hard-fought battles, it was not uncommon to come upon male and female infantry troops answering the call of their frightened DNA.

But he was well aware that it was a risky business for any male officer or NCO to take up with one of his female troops. Not only was there a danger of jealousy raising its ugly head, but there was also the fact that few men could readily send their lovers out to face death in combat. And that was the primary job of an officer, to send his men and women out to die. Wellington had said that the only job of an officer was to show his men how to die properly, but he had forgotten to add that they also had to send them out to die.

He returned to the monitor. As flattered as he was, he really hadn't needed a reminder of his sexuality. It would be quite a while before he'd see any R-and-R time and, as the new guy on the block, he had to keep his pants zipped around the troops. It was too bad, because it had been a long time since he'd had an invitation like that.

If Alex Rosemont had any regrets about his chosen profession, it was that it would be a long time, if ever, before he would be able to live like other men and have a permanent lover. When he had been in the Regular Army, he'd had girlfriends while stationed in the States. Even though the RA offered a more settled life than the Peacekeepers, he was always on the move. If it wasn't a change of station, it was training maneuvers that took him away for months at a time. Few women wanted to live the life of an Army-camp follower.

Maybe when this mess was over, he would get away for a week or so at one of the Mediterranean hot spots. Perhaps he could talk his way into a bikini or two. Until then, however, he had a war to fight.

ASHLEY WELLS WAS surprised to see Kat Wallenska leave the company commander's CP tent. She was even more surprised to see the slight but unmistakable secret smile on her face. What in the hell was going on here?

Even though she steered clear of them, she was well aware of the sexual attachments within her platoon, both the permanent and the temporary ones. As long as they didn't affect anyone's duty performance, she kept her opinions about them to herself. But of all her people, Kat Wallenska was the last one she would have expected to see looking like that. And with Rosemont!

She had gone on R and R with Kat several times and she knew the tough recon sergeant wasn't a nun, but she had never brought her attachments back with her. And she had never known Kat to be interested in anyone in uniform, off duty or on.

Ashley herself kept an even tighter control on her hormones, pushing it almost to the point of being old-maid prudish about it. She knew the speculation in the force that she was a lesbian and didn't care what anyone thought. While not a virgin, her only sexual experience had been with an older man who had wanted to marry into her family's wealth.

She had been young, barely legal, and he had known how to play on her youthful insecurities. He had also known how to humiliate her in bed. The thing that had frightened her the most, however, was that a part of her had welcomed the humiliation. Being a sexual plaything had been both frightening and exciting at the same time.

She would have probably married him had not her father ordered a background check that revealed that he had already been married. When she confronted him with this, he had sneered and said that she was lucky to have a real man like him. He then attempted to throw her on the floor for a little more sexual humiliation. In the struggle, she snatched up a decorative art piece and beat him half to death with it.

Her father had been able to keep the incident out of the news, but it had still been a painful experience, both mentally and physically. That, combined with her father's well-publicized, frequent rutting, had shaped her outlook about the opposite sex.

She still thought that some day she would meet a man who would love her for who she was and not for being one of Winston Wells's many female offspring. Until then, though, she would not be used for anyone's pleasure or profit ever again. And if the men she worked with didn't like it—fuck 'em if they couldn't take a joke.

She had wanted to talk to Rosemont about the recon platoon tonight, but now she didn't think she could keep a civil tongue. Regardless of what she thought of him, he was still the company commander and she was under his military authority.

The biggest mystery about the fiercely independent Ashley Wells was not her sex life, or the lack thereof, it was why she had joined the Peacekeepers in the first place. Since her earliest childhood, she had never willingly submitted to authority of any kind. The main reason she had gotten into her only sexual relationship had been that her father had so strongly disapproved of the man. Her college career had been checkered because she was always in conflict with the authorities over campus rules. Had it not been for her last name, she probably would not have graduated. With the exception of the tight rein she kept on her sexuality and the fact that she never took drugs or got drunk, she almost went out of her way to break the rules and resented authority in any form.

Why had she chosen one of the most disciplined professions in the world and had subjected herself to the rigors of military discipline, no one knew. Least of all USEF First Lieutenant Ashley Wells.

16

Force Headquarters—16 June

The Peacekeepers' briefing tent was crowded to
overflowing the next day as every officer in the force
gathered to hear what the Intel officer had learned
from interrogating Jeb Stuart's two prisoners. Jeb
leaned back and grinned broadly as he accepted
congratulations from his fellow platoon leaders.
Usually it was Ashley's recon people who came up
with coups like this, so it was nice to be on the receiving end for a change.

He knew that Ashley was pissed at him for steal-
ing her thunder, so he had been careful to keep out
of her way. Once they got back out in the sand and
started doing it again, however, he knew she would
calm down. At least he hoped she would. Having
Ash and Trash on his case got real old, real quick.

The shop talk ceased abruptly when the sergeant
major walked up to the front of the tent and introduced the force commander.

Colonel Jacobson smiled as he walked up to the
podium. ''My thanks to Lieutenant Jeb Stuart for a

job well done,'' he said, nodding to Jeb. ''Now we
have a somewhat better idea of what we're dealing
with here. We still don't know all the answers, but
we're getting closer.''

''Our main informant is a high-ranking officer of
the Islamic Brotherhood. It seems that the love of
his life lives in the ville where he was captured and
he was taking a little R and R with her when Jeb and
his gang dropped in. In fact, I understand they had
to help him back into his pants before they could
load him into the Tilt Wing.''

Everyone laughed at the thought of an officer of
the feared Islamic Brotherhood being caught with
his pants down.

''Anyway,'' the colonel continued, ''let that be a
lesson to all of you to double-check your three, six,
nine and twelve before dropping your pants.''

Laughter broke out again and as it faded, Jacobson asked the Intel officer to come forward.

The Intel officer stepped up to the podium with a
thick folder in his hand. ''First off, our man con-
firms what the stats showed you three days ago.
Their primary targets are associated with water, not
oil. While our man is an officer, he is only the
equivalent of a company commander. Like all company commanders, he does what he is told.''

Broad grins appeared on the faces of the company commanders in the audience.

''And he hasn't been told much. Apparently the
Brotherhood isn't big on in-depth command brief-

ings. So far, he's only been told to hit certain targets, not why they need to be hit. But this information should calm some fears among the multinationals and get them to back down a little.

"Second, there definitely appears to be a European connection involved. Our informant is a very observant lad. He has seen things that he doesn't even know he has seen, and that is where we are getting most of our information."

He flicked on the briefing screen. "For instance, he saw a huge shipment of weapons that had French markings on them. These crates contained Long Lance antitank missiles."

"How the hell did he know they were French?" Rosemont whispered to the officer beside him.

"I heard that, Major," the Intel officer said, looking over at him. "And it's a fair question. How I know is that I had our man draw the letters he saw on the crates, and the words he wrote out were French. When a subject's mind is locked on whatever I'm asking him, he can see the scene as if he is there again. And he can describe it in detail, as well as map it out for me."

Rosemont nodded his understanding.

"He also played back a conversation he had with one of his higher command about a vacation the other man took in Italy. A quick vacation, it is true, but what was a Shiite terrorist leader doing in Italy? Apparently the man described a countryside that we think is in northern Italy, and we're checking that out now."

He looked over at Stuart. "If you'd have captured his man's boss instead, we'd have everything we need."

"Sorry, sir," Jeb replied with a grin. "We'll try harder next time."

"I sure as hell hope so, LT." The Intel officer grinned. "This isn't some RA unit."

That got a laugh from nearly everyone in the room.

"So we have the targets tied down and have an Italian and French connection. The next question is who in the hell is running this operation and why? As to who, we haven't come up with much yet, but we're still digging. And as to why they're doing it, we haven't a clue yet.

"We are, however, picking up some interesting information from our intelligence counterparts in the multinationals. The other day someone here suggested that I try to track down our mysterious Twelfth Imam by checking out universities that have Arabic Studies programs.

"Well, I passed this on to the multis, and the French may have come up with our man. They have a Hassain Fadal, a French citizen of Lebanese descent, who is not where he should be—that is to say, in the Arabic Studies program at the Sorbonne in Paris. His family hasn't seen him in several weeks, and he was purposefully vague about his plans before he disappeared.

"Even though the French made a good match from family photos of him, his father says that the Imam can't be his son. He says that he raised his family away from Islam and claims that even though his son studies ancient Arabic, he isn't religious.

"Even so, this Hassain has apparently vanished. As you may know, the French have a fetish for individual identity documents and have installed a nation-wide system that logs the ID data every time one of their citizens leaves the country. According to their official records, Hassain didn't leave by any legitimate route and appears to have been smuggled out of the country. We now have all the governments in the region on the lookout. If he is our mysterious Imam, I don't expect them to find him lying on the beach working on his tan. He'll be holed up somewhere quiet so he can play his little charade out in peace and quiet.

"As to how we're going to find him, I will be followed by the operations officer."

The operations officer stepped up to the podium and looked around the room. This was one staff officer who didn't look like an academic. The authoritative way he wore his uniform with the combat infantry badge, jump wings and Ranger tab showed that he had been on the sharp end of the stick more than once. His dark black skin, shaved head and dead cigar clamped between his teeth only added to his kick-ass image.

"Okay, people," he said around the cigar. "Listen up! So far, we have been flogging our logs here and it's time we got back to doing business the way it should be done. Commencing tomorrow morning, we are turning over the defense of the installations we've been guarding to the Saudis. Now that we know what the hostiles are targeting, we think they can hold them on their own."

A slow smile built on his face. "After the turnover is complete, we're going on a little rampage. It's about time we stopped keeping the peace and got back to the reason we came here in the first place—making war."

Cheers and shouts broke out as the operations officer's smile widened. A "rampage" was an all-out operation where Peacekeeper units ranged far and wide to seek out and destroy the enemy. Once the Peacekeepers had been loosed to do what they did best, they wouldn't stop until the last hostile was facedown in the sand and they had their boot on the back of his neck.

"Rosemont." The operations officer locked eyes with the company commander.

"Yes, sir."

"Your unit will conduct a search-and-destroy operation commencing 0600 hours tomorrow." He flicked a map on the screen that covered the southern half of Iraq, Kuwait and the borders of Iran.

"You will have enough Tilt Wing assets and Bubble Tops to completely cover your area of operations. You'll be backed up by the Bulls. And as soon as you find someone who needs it done to them, pin 'em down and call in the Hulks to kick the shit out of 'em. Any questions?"

Rosemont took a deep breath. Finally he was being ordered to do what he had expected from the United States Expeditionary Force. "No, sir!"

"Hermann." The operations officer addressed the Delta Company commander. "You will do the same as Echo Company, but to their north. It's about time that you light infantry grunts got a little sand in your boots. Your Hulk backup will be Alpha Company."

Major Hermann nodded.

"Fire support company will deploy AT sections with the grunts."

Major Santino, the fire support company commander, nodded. Sitting to his right, Lieutenant Rhonda Lashette, the antitank platoon leader, grinned broadly. So far, all the hostile armor had been taken out by the Hulks and her people had had very little to do.

"We don't expect to have to deal with hostile aircraft, but I want the antiaircraft platoon to be on standby for immediate deployment.

"Are there any questions?"

There were none.

"The mission packets will be at the S-3 shop, so pick them up on your way out."

The operations officer looked around the tent. Everyone was on the edge of their chairs waiting to do what they did best. "Okay, people," he concluded. "Let's get out there and make war!"

"War! War!" The officers started a low chant that slowly built in intensity. "War! War! War!"

To his surprise, Rosemont found himself chanting along with the others. "War! War!"

The sergeant major had to shout to dismiss the briefing.

BACK AT THE Echo Company CP, Mick Sullivan was deeply involved with his mission preparation chores. The routine work was part of his mental preparation for combat, a form of military Zen, and helped him get over his premission jitters. Over his years with the Peacekeepers, he had learned that the more excited he was about the mission, the more time he took to prepare for it.

As he got started this time, Sullivan realized that he was really excited about this mission when he found himself disassembling the plastic cylindrical magazines for his M-25 LAR and checking the spring tension and feed slots on each one of them.

A rampage mission could be good or bad, depending on a lot of variables. The good part was that they would have the initiative and not be in a reactive situation. They would be taking the war to the enemy instead of sitting and waiting for the war to come to them. The flip side was that since they would be moving so fast and covering so much territory, they would be light on the ground. If they came upon a major enemy force, they would have to handle it on their own until they could get help. And that could get hairy. But that's what a light infantry recon was all about. Haul ass, bypass and call for gas.

He forced his mind back to his preparations and quickly reassembled his magazines. Then he carefully wiped the dirt and sand off every round of 5 mm caseless ammunition before reloading the magazines, a hundred rounds into each. As each magazine was reloaded, he carefully tightened the spring tension so it would feed properly. Only then did he put it back into his magazine pouches.

Next he broke down his rifle. The M-25 light assault rifle was a simple yet sophisticated weapon, rugged and reliable. With the built-in targeting scope, it could reach out to a thousand meters with accurate 3-round bursts. But, with its full cycle rate of 800 rounds a minute on fast fire, it was also equally effective at short ranges when massive fire power was called for. The hundred-round cylindrical magazine, fitted at the rear of the breech, insured that even on fast fire he had an ample supply of high velocity, 5 mm caseless ammo on hand.

Once the LAR was spotless, the lieutenant stripped his M-19 10 mm semiautomatic pistol,

cleaned it and checked its magazines. When he was
finished with that, he pulled the pistol's accessory
laser sight and silencer from the holster and checked
them over as well. With the laser and silencer fitted
to the pistol, he had a long-range, quiet-kill capa-
bility that he just might need before the operation
was over.

Then he inspected the hand grenades, six frags,
two smoke and two thermite, checking their pins
and fuzes to make sure that they were tightly
screwed into the body. Then he clipped the thumb
release, safety catches over the spoons. That way,
even if the pin snagged on something and pulled off,
the spoon wouldn't fly off. It was considered un-
healthy to have a grenade spoon fly off before you
wanted it to.

Last he pulled his double-edged, teflon fighting
knife from its boot sheath and gave the blade a
couple of passes with his sharpening pad. He wasn't
an edged-weapon freak like Wallenska, but he had
to admit that a good knife was a grunt's best friend.
It never ran out of ammo and never malfunctioned
and, while you might never use it for anything other
than opening a ration pack, if you did need it and
didn't have it, you were dead.

When his weapons were ready, he turned to the
rest of his personal gear. First he chose his Readi-
Heat field ration meals. Since they would be operating out of the Tilt Wings, he went short on rations. And since he was able to resupply daily from

the aircraft, there was no sense having to hump the extra weight. But he did pack enough to keep him going for two days just in case, as well as extra coffee. He also packed several small rolls of ration-issue toilet paper in a sealable plastic bag with two pairs of extra socks. If there was anything he hated, it was to run out of ass wipe or fresh socks.

All of this went into his tactical pack with his poncho liner, a bag of replacement blood, two sticks of plastic explosive, a replacement power pack for his comgear and sensors and his extra ammunition. His optical compass, penlight, salt tablets, hardcopy map and grease pencils were already packed in the side pouches of his pack, but he checked them anyway. Then he put fresh water in all three of his two-liter canteens. Now he was ready to go to work.

Sullivan laid his gear aside and, getting out his writing pad, started a letter to his father back home. He was not the first soldier in his family since his ancestors had come over from Ireland right before the Civil War. His people had enlisted in almost every war the United States had ever fought and his younger brother was a Brown Bar in an RA tank outfit back in the States.

But, even though his father was a combat veteran of the Middle East himself, he still worried about him. Sullivan tried to reassure him that he was all right by keeping him informed about what he was doing. From the letters he was receiving, that didn't seem to have helped much, but he tried to write home once a week, anyway.

As he tried to find something to tell his father about the operation that wasn't classified, he couldn't help but think about where he was headed again. There were at least a hundred and one things that could go wrong on a mission like this. All he could do was to put his faith in his fellow Peacekeepers and hope that he didn't run into a Golden BB.

17

Al Mish'ab—16 June

Like Sullivan, Kat Wallenska was also taking great care with her mission preparation. While she didn't make a ritual of it, she, too, was extracareful as she checked off each item of her weapons and equipment. She also knew that even the slightest oversight on her part could mean her death or the deaths of the other people in her recon team.

She had just run the function checks on her helmet sensors and comgear when Ashley Wells walked up. "Sergeant Wallenska," she said, "I want you to make sure your people are standing tall tomorrow morning. I don't want anyone out there half-assed prepared."

Kat got to her feet, but held her tongue. Her team was always prepared for every mission and the comment was uncalled-for. Kat didn't have the slightest idea what had crawled up Ash's ass, but she had been a superbitch ever since Jeb Stuart had pulled the prisoner coup. But Kat knew how to deal with Ashley Wells when she had her tits in a knot.

"No problem, Lieutenant," she answered formally. "Will there be anything else?"

Ash stared at her coldly. "No, that will be all, Sergeant."

"Thank you, Lieutenant."

As Ashley walked away, Kat went back to her gear. She could tell that this was not going to be a fun operation.

ROSEMONT FINISHED keying the last of the operation plan into his tac display and flashed it to force HQ. With the exception of picking a recon team to accompany him on the sweep, his mission preparation was finished. Like Sullivan, he had gone over his weapons and equipment carefully. Even though he would be directing the sweep units from an aerial command post in one of the Tilt Wings, he had to be ready to get sand in his boots, too. On an operation like this, things developed so fast that he was sure he would get a chance to get his buckle in the dust along with the troops.

Rosemont was not a "sit back, watch the screen and tell 'em where to go" kind of officer. He was happiest when he was leading an attack in person, not waiting somewhere in the rear for reports from the units in contact. That was why he had been picked to join the Peacekeepers. In Operation Pershing on the Mexican border, he had been decorated for leading a night attack against a mountain fortress.

Ashley Wells knocked on the open door of his CP. "Wells," he said looking up. "Come in. I was just about to send for you. I need your opinion. I want to borrow one of your recon teams to accompany me in the CP Tilt Wing as a reaction force and I was thinking that Kat's—"

"Sergeant Wallenska, you mean, sir?"

Rosemont was surprised. From everything he had observed, the Peacekeepers operated on a very informal basis. Their internal comlink chatter was almost always on a first-name basis and the "sirs" between the NCOs and officers were kept to a bare parade ground minimum.

"You have something against informality?"

"Only when it affects the combat efficiency of my platoon," she snapped.

Rosemont had about all he could take of his moody recon platoon leader. He didn't care what her problem was. It was time that she got her act together and soldiered or packed up and cleared out of the company area. Right now he really didn't care which. He had a war to fight and didn't have time for this shit.

"I assure you, Lieutenant—" Rosemont's voice was cold and controlled as he stood up "—that anytime I do anything to compromise the combat efficiency of this unit, I will hand in my resignation. Is that clear?"

She nodded stiffly.

"And until such time as that occurs, I highly recommend that you watch your mouth."

Wells blinked under Rosemont's verbal lashing and took a deep breath as if to answer him.

But he beat her to it. "Now, I am not unaware that you appear to be unhappy with my assignment as your new commanding officer. I think it only fair to inform you that I am also not completely happy with your performance as my recon platoon leader. Therefore, I am ready to accept your request for transfer at this time and will forward it to the colonel with my highest recommendation. However, should you choose to remain under my command, you don't have to like me, but I expect you to soldier. Should it become necessary, however, for me to transfer you at some later date, I will not do it with a positive recommendation. You will either do your job or get out now while you still can."

Ashley was stunned. No one had ever talked to her this way since basic training, not even her military superiors. Her record was so outstanding that no one had ever questioned her leadership before. She was considered the outstanding platoon leader in the force and was on the early promotion list to captain.

"Which will it be, Lieutenant?" Rosemont snapped. "I'm busy planning an operation and I want to get this taken care of immediately."

"I'll stay, sir." She bit off the "sir" as though it killed her to say it.

Rosemont sat down. "Now that that's settled, have a seat. Maybe I should spend a few minutes with you and..."

Ashley remained standing.

"Sit down!"

Ashley sat.

"I was going to tell you a little more about the way I operate, but maybe I should ask a few questions instead. I know we got off to a bad start but, if you are going to continue running *my* recon platoon, we need to get a few things cleared up right now."

Ashley was silent.

"First, do you have any military objection to my taking Kat's recon team with me in the Tilt Wing?"

"No, sir."

"Do you have any reason to believe that she is not capable of running her team in a professional manner?"

"No, sir."

"Then exactly what is your problem?"

"Nothing, sir," she snapped.

Rosemont studied her for a moment. Back in garrison, he would have the time to try to find out what the problem was and work on resolving it. Right now, however, time was something he had very little of.

"Okay," he said. "Have it your way, Wells. Be advised, however, that I expect you to do your job

in a professional manner and that includes following orders. Do you have any questions?''

"No, sir."

"You are dismissed."

Ashley stood up, snapped to attention and rendered a crisp salute. Military rituals allowed a soldier to distance himself or herself from issues of
personality and get on with the job. In this case, had
it not been for the rigid military formality, she knew
that her mouth would get the better of her, and she
wasn't about to give Rosemont the pleasure of firing her.

Rosemont returned her salute and watched as she
did an about-face and marched out of the CP. As he
watched her stiff, retreating back, he fervently
hoped that he wouldn't come to regret his decision
to allow her to continue with Echo Company. The
recon platoon was a vital part of a light infantry
unit, and having a problem in recon could get
someone killed. Maybe a lot of someones.

Maybe it was time that he got an insider's view on
what in the hell was going on here. He quickly
tapped in Sullivan's com code.

"Mick here," the XO answered.

"This is Alex, how about coming over here for a
minute?"

"On the way, sir."

SULLIVAN HAD SEEN Ashley leave the CP and from
the stiff way she had walked, looking neither to the

right nor the left, he knew that Rosemont had taken her ass off about something again. And, obviously, the company commander's call was about her. Dammit anyway, why did she have to be so goddamned difficult so much of the time?

Ash had saved Sullivan's butt more than once, and he felt that he owed her, but there were limits to what he could do for her. Since he wasn't sleeping with her, he was duty bound to give the CO an honest appraisal if he was asked. He wasn't about to volunteer anything, but he was a professional soldier and the unit was more important than any of the individuals in it. Even Ash and Trash.

"You wanted to see me, sir?"

"Have a seat." Rosemont reached into the cooler and produced two of the unmarked beer cans Sullivan had so thoughtfully provided him. "Here, have a cold malt beverage."

"Don't mind if I do, sir."

"Hold the 'sirs' down to one a minute or less," Rosemont growled. "This is social."

Mick popped the top on his can and took a deep drink.

"Great stuff, this malt beverage."

"Yes, it is," Rosemount agreed. "It's an old German recipe or so I've been told."

"What would you like to talk about this afternoon, Alex?"

"Women."

Sullivan grinned. "That's something I like to think I'm a minor expert on."

"Okay, then, what's the story on Miss Ashley Wells?"

"Well, sir..." Sullivan began.

"Can the 'sirs' for now. I need to know what's going on here, and anything you say will be kept strictly confidential, so give."

"To paraphrase somebody famous whose name I've forgotten," Sullivan said, "Miss Ashley is an enigma wrapped in a mystery." He rolled the cool can between his hands. "I've known her for several years now, and I know as little about her as I did the first day I met her."

"But you know something about how she thinks."

"I know how she has thought in the past," Mick corrected him. "But that has nothing to do with what she will think tomorrow. Or is thinking today, for that matter."

"I didn't need to hear that, Sullivan."

Mick shrugged. "What seems to be the problem, sir, if I might ask?"

"It seems that she has taken an active dislike to me," Rosemont admitted. "And I'm afraid that it's beginning to affect my ability to command this company. I'm seriously considering asking the colonel to transfer her to another company."

Sullivan was shocked. "She would never do anything to affect the unit. The Peacekeepers are her family."

"What is it, then?"

"Well, sir." Sullivan hesitated. "I'm afraid that it may be something completely different. Something a little more personal instead of military."

"How's that?"

"As I'm sure you noticed, Ashley Wells is an extremely beautiful woman."

Rosemont nodded his agreement; he wasn't blind.

"And as with many beautiful women," Sullivan continued, "this can both a blessing and a curse. With her, it seems to be more of a curse. She resents the fact that even though she's one of the best junior officers in the force, she is praised more for her beauty than for her military accomplishments."

"I can understand that," Rosemont said.

"At the same time, she knows that she's beautiful and is very proud of it. I think the problem may be that you didn't react to her the way she expected."

Rosemont frowned. "What do you mean?"

"If you'll excuse me, sir. You seem to be the only man I've ever met who wasn't instantly smitten with Ashley Wells. I've even seen generals come completely unglued and drool on their chins when they meet her."

Rosemont laughed. He could understand that.

"And when men do that, she knows how to handle them. But then you come along and treat her like one of the boys, and she doesn't know how to deal with it."

"But she is one of the 'boys,' damn it," Rosemont growled. "She's my recon platoon leader and she'd better be the best boy I've got or I'm going to can her young ass and replace her with someone I can work with."

That statement chilled Sullivan. The thought of Echo Company without Ashley Wells wasn't something he wanted to contemplate. She could be a real bitch when she wanted to, but she added something to the spirit of the unit that would be impossible to replace.

"You've told her this?"

"Yes, just now."

"And how did she react?"

"Like I had offended her dignity."

Sullivan took a deep breath. "I'll have a little talk with her if you'd like, sir."

"Please do."

SULLIVAN FOUND ASHLEY alone in her room, lying on her bunk. "Ash?" He tapped on the open door. "Can I have a word with you?"

She looked up, a scowl on her face. "What do you want?"

"Ah..." He hesitated. "Ash, I'm here in a semiofficial capacity. We have to talk."

One of the reasons that Mick was the company executive officer instead of Ash was that he had a few days' rank on her. The other reason was that Ashley wouldn't have taken his job for a spot promotion to Captain with a date of rank back to the turn of the century. She was a field officer and would have resigned rather than put up with all the bullshit that went with the XO's job.

"Okay, you're official, so what's going on?"

He took a seat on the bunk next to her. "Ash, it's pretty obvious that you've got a real problem with Rosemont, but I'm not sure that you're aware of how serious it's gotten to be."

"What the hell are you babbling about, Mick? If you've got something to say, spit it out. If not, shut the fuck up and kindly get your ass outta here. I'm trying to get my beauty rest."

He took a deep breath. Why did she always go out of her way to be difficult? "Rosemont's about ready to ship your 'young ass' out, as he put it."

That got her fullest attention. "You're shitting me," she hissed as she sat up on her bunk. "He wouldn't dare."

"He's pissed, Ash." He shook his head. "I don't know what you've been on his case about, but he's not going to put up with it anymore."

"That son of a bitch!" She bit off each word. "That sorry motherless bastard! He said he'd give me a chance to soldier for him."

"He is," Mick said. "I talked him into giving you another chance. But . . ." He raised a hand to forestall her next outburst. "You're going to have to show him something other than the back side of your hand every time you're around him. Alexander the Great is all too human and . . ."

"I wish you'd stop calling him that stupid name," she snapped.

"Why?" he asked sincerely. "Everyone's got a nickname here. What's wrong with it?"

She dropped her eyes to her boots and took a deep breath. "I don't know what it is, but every time I get around that guy I want to punch him right in the mouth."

He grinned. "You've got to learn to curb your gentler instincts."

Ash was not amused at his attempt at humor. "What can I do, Mick?" she asked, her voice soft. "I can't let him get rid of me. I've been in Echo Company since I joined the force."

For an instant, Mick saw a frightened little girl under the Ash and Trash image she usually wore. He wanted to reach out and give her a hug, but was afraid that she'd revert to type and break both his arms.

"I don't know, Ash," he said. "All you can do is give it your best shot. But you've got to be frosty with that guy. I think he may be a little tougher than you are."

That brought a half smile to her face. "Bullshit. I can take him three falls out of three any day of the week."

"But he's the boss and that counts for a lot."

"I'll try, Mick."

He stood and clapped her on the shoulder as if she was one of the male lieutenants. "See you on the PZ tomorrow morning."

"Right."

18

Al Mish 'ab—17 June

The morning broke cool and clear over the desert as the men and women of Echo Company waited at the PZ outside the coastal fort for their transport. Kat Wallenska sat on the sand with her recon team gathered around. They all had their body armor loosened, and their helmets lying loose in their laps, to enjoy the cool morning air. This would be their last chance to feel the wind in their faces for a long time. They had all been on rampage missions before and knew that they would live, fight and die in their war suits till it was over.

The term *rampage* had first been applied to describe USEF search-and-destroy operations by a reporter from the *New Berkeley Voice,* the last of the left-wing newsfaxes in the United States. The reporter's liberal sensibilities had been aroused to a fever pitch when he had toured a combat zone in Pakistan after the Peacekeepers had gone through eliminating Pakistani nuclear weapons.

It was true that the area was a mess as only a war-ravaged land could be. The Pakistanis had fought hard to save their outlawed nukes, and the Peace-keepers had fought even harder. Crops were torn up by vehicles and blasted by artillery as always happens in a combat zone. Bodies lay in the streets and fields where they had fallen. But they had been combatants, not women and children. The facilities and buildings that had been destroyed all had military significance.

But the reporter had chosen to see only the horrors of war, the death and the destruction. He had not wanted to see that the nuclear weapons, which had once been aimed at India, had been rendered into so much radioactive scrap by the USEF. He had hysterically used the word *rampage* in his completely biased reports to describe the Peacekeepers' campaign, hoping to arouse a storm of protest from the far left. But it failed. Instead, the entire world had praised their efforts to make the planet a safer place to live, and the word had been adopted by the USEF as a term of pride.

Sergeant John Ironstone, Wallenska's assistant team leader, lay stretched out on his back, letting the early-morning sun bathe his dark copper-colored skin and blue-black hair. A Comanche from outside Oklahoma City, Ironstone considered himself to be a modern Indian warrior following a long proud Comanche tradition. He didn't ride a horse to war anymore, but the skimmers and Tilt Wings carried him to battle far faster.

He did, however, follow the Comanche tradition of wearing war paint. Three broad black stripes adorned each of his cheeks, slanting upward. No one could see the war paint when his helmet visor was down, but he knew it was there and that was what mattered. The paint was his honor and strength, and he would no more go into battle without it than he would leave his assault rifle behind.

Kat looked over at him. "You ready for this shit, Ironman?"

"I'm frosty, Kat." A slow smile stretched the stripes painted on his cheeks as he patted the LAR at his side. "It's about time we got this situation zeroed. I've got a fresh squeeze back at Benning I need to be with."

"I thought you liked this stuff." Kat grinned. "Going on the warpath in the desert, lots of hostiles to shoot at you."

Ironstone shrugged. "That's only when I don't have anything to squeeze. It's different right now, but check in with me in a month. I may be available for this shit."

Kat laughed. Ironstone's amorous adventures, if they could be called that, were legendary in the USEF. No matter where they were deployed or what they did while they were there, the handsome Indian warrior always seemed to find himself a new squeeze. He called it spreading the message of peace, love and brotherhood among all the people of the earth.

"If you're not careful," she said, "you're going to find yourself getting married someday, and your fighting days will be over."

Ironstone made a sign of aversion against evil words. "Watch what you say, woman," he growled.

Kat grinned. "Is the 'Chief with Many Feathers' afraid of living under a woman's roof?"

He thumped his chest. "With my people, a woman lives under a man's roof."

Kat laughed and slapped his leg. "You know what the Chinese say—'Every man is a king *outside* his own house.'"

"What do they know about being warriors anyway?" he shot back. "They're the guys who send a hundred men to do the job of five good recon grunts."

Kat laughed. The Chinese Han Empire was still famous for using the tactics of overwhelming numbers on the battlefield. Even though they were the only non-Western nation in the world that didn't have a population growth problem, old habits died hard. Particularly old military habits that had worked so well in the past.

At the other end of the PZ, Rosemont saw the black specks low in the sky rapidly approaching and glanced at his watch. The Tilt Wings were right on time. "Okay, people," he transmitted over the comlink. "Our ride's here. Suit up!"

At his command, the men and women of Echo Company snapped their body armor closed, put on their helmets, checked their comlinks and flicked on their tac displays. It was time to make peace by going to war.

Kicking up swirling dust storms as they flared out for a landing in the sand, the AV-19 Tilt Wing assault transports dropped their rear ramps. IR-shielded exhausts of their turbines blew hotter than the cool morning air, wavering their crouching outlines. In an hour or so, however, the ambient air temperature in the sun would be so close to that of the turbine exhausts that they would hardly show on an IR sensor.

It took very little time for the nine Tilt Wings to take on their loads of infantrymen. With another swirl of sand blown up by their rotors, the assault transports lifted off and turned east toward southern Iraq and Kuwait. The Bubble Top scout ships were already on station and waiting for them to show.

IN THE LEAD SHIP, Rosemont watched the readouts from the ship's sensors displayed on the commander's monitor. By keying in the other aircrafts' tail numbers, he could also see what any other Tilt Wing or Bubble Top in the company was picking up as well. But right now, he was running a free-for-all and each assault transport was on its own.

In the back of the Tilt Wing, Kat Wallenska watched the same image on her tac screen that Rosemont saw on his command monitor. On a mission like this, her helmet was slaved to the commander's readouts as he conducted his search for a target. Suddenly her display came alive with multiple blips indicating a small group of vehicles clustered in a column in a narrow wadi just ahead.

The vehicles were not transmitting a friendly signal and had been camouflaged. Nothing short of the most sophisticated jammers, however, could camouflage them from the MAD—Magnetic Anomaly Detector—sensors that homed in on their magnetic fields, the IR sensors that detected the heat from a command car or the radar that plotted their outlines under the camouflage nets. For all practical purposes, they might as well have put up a giant sign saying, Here I Am! Come Blow Me Up!

And that was exactly the first thing that came to Rosemont's mind when he saw the target blips appear. Before he did that, though, he wanted to dismount the recon team and cordon off the area. The minute the Tilt Wing opened up on the parked vehicles, the hostiles would scatter into the desert, and he wanted to kill or capture them before they could escape.

He tongued his mike. "Wallenska?"

"Sir?"

"Do you have the target?"

"I have it and it looks good."

"Alert your people. I'm going to have the pilot set us down well out of sight so we can cordon off the area before he goes in. I don't want any of those little bastards getting away from us."

Kat chuckled. "That's most affirm."

"Get 'em ready, we're going in."

As soon as the Tilt Wing touched down, Kat was the first one down the rear ramp with John Ironstone following close on her heels. Regardless of the Indian's rather cavalier approach to women, he had no trouble working under Kat's command. She could take him three falls out of three, and he knew it. In his mind, that put her in the category of being an honorary man, a woman warrior, and he could serve under her with no loss of pride.

Also, any woman who wore a silver skull in her ear was a person to be respected. Despite his war paint, Ironstone was a completely modern American in most respects, but he still had great regard for the old ways of his people. And among the Comanche, skulls were a source of ancient, arcane knowledge. Who knew what secrets the silver skull whispered into Kat's ear when she went into combat? He, for one, didn't want to find out. He wanted to take his own chances on the battlefield without foreknowledge from the spirit world.

The last one out, Rosemont quickly joined up with Wallenska's team as they spread out along the high ground covering the wadi. Since there were so few of them, each grunt had to cover well over a hundred meters of ground, but with the sensors and commo built into the recon helmets, they could stay in touch while they were out of sight of each other.

Rosemont stayed with Wallenska. As soon as she gave a thumbs-up that everyone was in place, he keyed his mike implant. "Bold Lightning," he called up to the Tilt Wing. "This is Bold Lancer, target uplink now. Do it to them."

"Lightning, affirm." the pilot answered. "We've got it and it's on the way."

With the Tilt Wing's rotors set on whisper mode, Rosemont could barely hear it as it came in low on its gun run. All he could hear on his helmet audio pickup was a thin whine from the two wingtip-mounted turbines. Without audio gear, the hostiles probably wouldn't even be able to hear that much. They wouldn't know they were under attack until the first rounds hit them.

Using the uplink from Rosemont's sensors as a guide, the Tilt Wing hugged the ground as it approached the target. At the last moment, it popped up over the ridge looking down onto the wadi. An alert hostile on guard in one of the trucks spotted the gunship. Giving the alarm, he started to swing a heavy machine gun around to bear upon it, but he was far too late. The target coordinates had already been set in the Tilt Wing's weapons computer, and the instant the weapons pods were in the clear, they automatically fired.

For his opening shot, the copilot/gunner had selected a brace of Long Lash antiarmor missiles with fire and forget guidance systems. As soon as the rockets cleared the pods and were on their way, the pilot racked his machine around and ducked back behind the cover of the ridge. The missiles flew on unerringly to their targets.

Still linked with Rosemont's target acquisition system, the Tilt Wing's gunner could see his rounds when they hit. One of the missiles impacted in the middle of the rear wheel of the truck at the end of the column. The explosion of the warhead ripped the truck in half and sent the rear axle tumbling through the air. Another missile impacted in the center of the lead vehicle, a military skimmer.

Startled men poured out of the other vehicles, their weapons ready, but the gunship was back before they had even half a chance to reach cover. For its second gun run, the Tilt Wing's gunner selected the 30 mm chain gun, dialing in the EHE grenade ammo feed. Setting the gun on slow-burst fire, he locked the weapon to his helmet target display and wrapped his fingers around the firing controls.

"Do it!" he told the pilot.

The pilot eased his machine up, exposing the 30 mm turret in the nose of the ship. To aim, the gunner merely had to look at his target and center the diamond pip in his target display where he wanted the rounds to hit; the gun automatically tracked. Even if the aircraft was throwing itself around in the sky to evade enemy fire, the stabilized gun stayed where it was aimed.

As soon as the muzzle of the chain gun was clear, it started spitting grenades in slow bursts. Each squeeze on the gunner's trigger sent three more enhanced high-explosive grenades on their way. The hostiles went down like wheat before a windstorm. Most of them never even got a shot off at the attacking Tilt Wing.

From their position on the ridge overlooking the wadi, Rosemont and Kat watched as the devastating EHE grenades walked through the hostiles. When there was no one left on their feet, the gunner switched his sights to the remaining vehicles. Although the 30 mm grenades had been designed as antipersonnel rounds, they still packed enough explosive punch to tear up soft-skinned vehicles. The skimmers, light trucks and jeeps went up in flames as the grenades set off their gas tanks and detonated the ammunition they carried. After one last pass over the wadi, the Tilt Wing pulled out of its gun run and took up a low orbit over the area.

The recon team moved into the wadi to mop up, smoke from the burning vehicles rose into the air carrying the characteristic odors of the battlefield: the sharp sweet smell of fresh blood, the stench of blasted bodies, the acrid smell of explosive residue.

The Tilt Wing had done a good job, not only had it smashed all of the hostile vehicles, the Brotherhood commandos had been smashed as well. Broken bodies littered the area leaking blood into the sand. As the grunts moved in, several muffled shots rang out, but none of the rounds was aimed at them. As before, the wounded Islamic commandos would not allow themselves to be captured.

"Sorry we couldn't have captured a couple of them, sir," Kat said to Rosemont as she turned a black-clad body over with her boot before kneeling down to strip the ammo carrier and assault rifle from the corpse.

"There'll be more later," he answered, scanning the destruction. "Have your people finish getting the weapons policed up here and let's get back to it."

"Yes, sir."

Leaving the hostile dead where they had fallen, the recon team carried the captured weapons as they walked out of the mouth of the wadi. Once they were in the open, the Tilt Wing made one last pass overhead to make sure that the area was clear of further hostiles before landing and dropping the rear ramp. In seconds Rosemont and the grunts were lifting off to find another target.

19

In the Iraqi Desert—17 June

Night fell suddenly over the stark landscape. One minute it was light, the next dark. The moon would not come up this night, and only the twinkling of countless stars in the clear sky kept the night from being pitch-black. The light-intensifying imagers of the grunts' helmets took that faint stellar glimmer, however, and made it light enough for them to see clearly out to five hundred meters—more than enough to detect and accurately target any would-be intruders.

Earlier that afternoon, Rosemont had instructed his Tilt Wing pilot to make some dummy insertions, setting down in several locations, rotors still turning, and waiting several minutes before flying on. He knew that the desert had unseen eyes hiding in the rocks, and he didn't want to fly directly to the spot where he planned to spend the night. The dummy insertions were insurance that if his Tilt Wing had been spotted by hostiles, they wouldn't know where the aircraft had dropped its troops.

While this was going on, Rosemont and the team refilled their canteens and drew rations for their dinner and breakfast from the supplies stockpiled in the Tilt Wing. When they finally exited the aircraft, Rosemont instructed the pilot to make a couple more dummy insertions in the area before flying back to its base. In the morning it would return to pick up the team so they could continue the operation.

The small hill Rosemont had chosen to occupy was a perfect RON, remain overnight, ambush site. With the help of their night-vision devices and the strategically placed remote sensors around the RON site, they could keep close watch on the surrounding area during the night without needing the Tilt Wing's fire support. If the sensors picked up anything too big for them to handle, they could have the gunships back within twenty minutes.

After setting up the sensors and digging their fighting positions, Rosemont linked into force HQ to get a tactical update on the day's activities. Beyond a couple more small actions like the aerial ambush he had sprung in the wadi, the only major fighting had been when Delta Company had come upon a column of hostile armor to the north flying the green banners of jihad.

When the tanks smashed their way past the light infantry, the Delta grunts had been forced to call in the Alpha Hulks to deal with them. The Hell's Angels Hulks had done a damned good job of it. Once more the long-range weaponry and protection of the powered fighting suits had proven adequate to handle the heavy armored vehicles.

Other than that, the day had been relatively quiet. The long-range Intel forecast, however, promised that tomorrow would be more interesting. Mobs were gathering in several cities on the rumor that the Mahdi would make another appearance at noon. The force Intel officer was predicting that the Brotherhood units would use the inevitable civilian rioting to cover their movements and planned to move the Peacekeepers into position to counter that threat. New mission orders would be issued in the morning.

Rosemont keyed his comlink and called Kat up to his position to fill her in on the Intel update. After keying the day's activities into her data bank, Kat slid her visor open and looked up at the stars. "It's sure beautiful here at night," she said wistfully. "I can see why the locals think they're so close to God. He blesses them at night and punishes them by day."

Rosemont wasn't surprised to hear poetic observation coming from the battle-hardened recon sergeant. One of the biggest misconceptions the public had about professional soldiers was that they were all hard-hearted killers with steel trap minds. They were hard-hearted when it came to business, that was true, and they had steel-trap military minds, as well, but that was not the complete picture. Living so close to death gave most of them a far greater appreciation for life than the average civilian who had never had a round fired at him would ever have.

Rosemont's grandfather had brought back a cigarette lighter from his tour as an infantryman in the Vietnam War that had been inscribed with the motto To Those Who Have Fought For It, Life Has A Flavor The Protected Will Never Know.

He hadn't completely understood those words until he had survived his first intense firefight. When it was over, he had sat on the ground, removed his helmet and reveled in the simple pleasure of the breeze blowing through his hair as he savored the taste of warm stale water from his canteen. Now he felt those words were the best way he knew to describe the life of the professional soldier.

He looked skyward, as well. "It is beautiful here at night," he agreed. "And that's why we have to keep on our toes tonight. This serene beauty just might attract gentlemen callers packing Type 98s."

Kat grinned, the starlight showing her teeth. "We've got this area blanketed with sensors, and not even a field mouse will be able to sneak up on us without setting them off. But even if they do, I like to fight at night. It's nice and cool for a change."

Rosemont chuckled quietly. Kat Wallenska was the pure professional. Day or night, it was all the same to her—close with and destroy the enemy and, if she wasn't fighting, enjoy wherever she was.

"But I need my beauty rest," he said. "Riding around all day in that damned plane has worn me out, and when the colonel calls me in the morning, I want to be bright and shining."

She laughed. "I'll do what I can do so you can get some sleep, Major."

"Please, but have me called for the last guard shift." Although he was their company commander, Rosemont planned to take his turn on watch that night along with the rest of the team. As far as he was concerned, when he was in the field he was just another grunt and pulled the shit details right along with everyone else. He was not above using his rank, however, to pick what shift he wanted to pull.

"Will do, sir," she said as she got to her feet. "See you in the morning."

AT THE RUINED FORTRESS in the foothills of the Zagros Mountains of Iran, Colonel Jean-Claude Francillion also looked over the combat reports of the past twenty-four hours. He clenched his jaw as he read of the Brotherhood units that had been wiped out by the Americans and of the nuclear power plants that were still standing.

The carefully thought-out plan was falling badly behind schedule, and the jihad was in danger of crumbling. Already the region's governments had managed to regain shaky control of several key cities and the Peacekeepers had done considerable damage to his Brotherhood forces. He hated to admit it, but it looked as if he had seriously underestimated the ability of the United States Expeditionary Force to swiftly and violently counter his moves. Nothing incites violence like violence, and the Peacekeepers had more than answered his forces round for round.

He had known that, sooner or later, some kind of civil order would be restored. Even with repeated appearances of the Imam spurring on the faithful, the religious frenzy couldn't be maintained forever. Sooner or later even the most fanatic Shiite would look up from his most recent piece of butchery and wonder why he was laying waste to his country. But hopefully, by then it would be too late.

His plan, though, was designed to have all the nuke plants and desalinization units destroyed long before that happened as well as seeing to it that the new forests of the Middle East burned back to sand. The damage to the social and political infrastructure was to be so great as to literally put the Middle East back a thousand years.

Francillion was one of those Europeans who fully believed that without oil and the Western technology that the oil revenues bought, the entire Arabic world would be right back where it had been when Muhammad's followers had ridden out of the desert screaming *"Allah Akbar!"* as they slaughtered everyone in sight.

The only three commodities that the Arabic world was self-sufficient in were camels, horses and oil. And of the three, only oil was of value anywhere outside the region. Were it not for Israel and the

Russians trading their excess foodstuffs for Arabic oil, they couldn't even feed themselves, which was why they had built the desalinization plants to purify seawater for irrigation.

While the Middle East still had enough uncontaminated oil to survive another twenty years or so before it all ran out, gone were the days when endless petro dollars ensured that some oil-producing nations had the highest per-capita incomes on earth. The days when expensive automobiles had lain abandoned in the desert because they had a flat tire and the driver hadn't wanted to bother himself with changing it were over. Back then it had been easier to buy a new car, but those days had come to a crashing end with the Palestinian Outrage.

Most of the oil-producing states still had enough oil income to enjoy a comfortable standard of living, but the days of being unable to spend all of their money for fear of disrupting the world economy were long gone. There was nothing to replace the contaminated oil, and that was why the nuclear power plants and the desalinization units they had powered were so important. They were the last chance for the Middle East to at least be able to feed itself.

The way Francillion and his employers saw it, this would be the final war that was ever fought over this worthless tract of barren wasteland. The locals would most assuredly go back to raiding each other's tents and livestock, but there would never again be anything really worth fighting for with modern military forces in the region. In an attempt to rebuild from the jihad, the remaining oil would flow as fast as the Arabs could pump it out of the ground. The treaty nations would buy it as fast as it came on the market, pump it back into their own storage areas in the ground and that would be the end of it.

The money from the last of the oil would not be enough to build new nuke plants and desalinization units, so no forests and fields would be watered from the sea. The desert would revert to desert, and the weather over southern Europe would go back to what it had been for all time. The vines would grow once again at Château Francillion, and no European would mourn the new conditions in the Middle East. Europe and the rest of the Western World had suffered the problems of the Middle East more than long enough.

But for this to happen as it had been so carefully planned, Francillion had to revitalize the jihad before the Peacekeepers tore the guts out of it and it collapsed. The Twelfth Imam had to drive his followers on to even greater religious frenzy. The cities had to be taken over again and, if needs be, human-wave attacks launched at the remaining nuke plants. It was essential that they be destroyed while there was still time.

"Get that kid in here," Francillion told Caproni. "I have to talk to him."

"About what?" the Italian scientist asked.

"About his next appearance to the faithful," the mercenary said.

"But we already have the script prepared for his next appearance," Caproni protested.

Francillion tapped a hard copy of the script. "I've read it and it's not forceful enough."

"But it was approved by the board of directors," Caproni said. The Italian lived in an orderly world where orders came down from shadowy figures at the top, and all important decisions were made there. He wasn't comfortable around men like the mercenary colonel who hatched wild plots on the spur of the moment, and then changed them whenever he felt like it. It offended his sense of order in the grand scheme of things.

This was the moment that Francillion had known would come sooner or later. The directors of the EuroAgCombine were in overall command of this operation, but they had given him sole authority regarding the military aspects. He had insisted on that clause in his contract. All too often in his career as a mercenary, fainthearted civilian employers had tried to snatch defeat from the jaws of victory on an operation, and he would not allow that to happen this time.

Francillion locked eyes with the scientist. "This is a military emergency," he said, his voice low but firm. "As military commander, I insist that the

Imam's text tomorrow be changed. Also, I want to see that kid before he goes on stage.''

"As you say, Colonel."

"Now!''

IN HIS MAKESHIFT underground quarters in the old cistern, Hassain Fadal flipped through a rack of holodisks to see if there was something that he hadn't watched a hundred times already. Had he known that he was going to be cut off from the world this way, he would have packed more than a few dozen of his favorite holos.

He had been warned that he would be isolated, but, since he had never been out of Europe before, he thought that it would be like going into the country outside Paris on vacation. He had never imaged it possible to be cut off completely from all civilized life in the twenty-first century. Francillion had told him that they didn't even have a satellite link, which he found hard to believe. Even the poorest nomads of the desert had personal satellite links, or so he had heard.

Actually Hassain had never seen a Middle Eastern Arab in the flesh who wasn't a tourist in Paris. Sure, he had seen Arabs on the CNN holovee newscasts every now and then whenever a new problem erupted in the volatile area. But until he had flown into this ruin, he had never set foot in an Arab country. But since he didn't really know where this hidden facility was, for all he knew, he might not even be in the Middle East.

Wherever he was, though, Hassain Fadal was bored to death. At first, playing the Mahdi had been fun, but it had grown old fast. He would have gladly given half of his promised pay if he could just spend a weekend somewhere even halfway civilized. He had heard that Cairo had interesting nightclubs, and even some casinos now. He knew that Beirut was the classiest hot spot in the Mediterranean. The only way Lebanon had been able to rebuild after decades of civil war had been to turn the city into a wide-open playground for Europe's elite. Every vice known to mankind was available in Beirut at bargain-basement prices.

He was surprised when he heard the knock on his door. "Fadal," the Italian scientist called out to him. "The colonel wants to see you."

That was even more surprising. Usually the tall, scar-faced mercenary wouldn't give him the right time of day, and the feeling was more than mutual. Hassain didn't like the way the colonel looked at him or how he spoke to him. It had to be something unpleasant for Francillion to want to see him. Whatever it was, it would be better than staring at the bare rock walls of what he had come to think of as his monk's cell.

Rising from his bed, Hassain slipped on his shoes and ran his fingers through his long hair. The first thing he would do when he reached civilization would be to get a decent haircut. He was tired of looking like something out of an ancient history book. Before that could happen, though, he had to put this Mahdi bullshit behind him once and for all.

Caproni knocked on the door again. "Hassain, he's waiting."

"Hold your water!" Hassain snapped. "I'm coming."

20

In the Iraqi Desert—18 June

Just as the night had come swiftly to the desert, so did the dawn. Rosemont's small unit was awake long before sunrise. Dawn was a popular time for desert people to attack their sleeping enemies, and Rosemont was much too smart to fall prey to that old trick.

As soon as the sun was up, Rosemont's team ate a cold breakfast while he popped the tab on a coffee container and got a tac update from his widely scattered units. For most of Echo Company, the night had passed uneventfully. Except, of course, for Jeb Stuart's Second Platoon. Their RON site had been situated on a small hill overlooking a road that led into an irrigation pumping station. Right before midnight, a remote sensor had alerted him to a convoy moving toward the irrigation station.

A hasty ambush had stopped the lead vehicle, but dozens of well-armed troops poured out of the other vehicles, and a brisk firefight had erupted. He'd had his hands full for a time before force headquarters could send additional fire support in the form of a pair of Tilt Wing gunships, the tac air support fighter version of the assault transport. They made short work of the hostiles, chasing them into the desert. Even though the fight had been close, only two of Stuart's troops had been wounded and neither one of them seriously.

The other Peacekeeper companies had had a relatively quiet night of it. So quiet, in fact, that the force commander decided to change his tactics for the coming day. Rather than send his units out again to range free and hit targets of opportunity, he decided to send their Tilt Wings to them, but keep the troops on their scattered RON sites as reaction forces until worthwhile targets were spotted.

The Imam was reported to be making an appearance today and, if the Brotherhood decided to use the disruption that would surely follow Imam's appearance to mask their movements, the colonel wanted to be ready for them. While the grunts and Hulks sat, he would put all of his Bubble Top recon choppers in the air to scout out the hostiles.

Upon transmitting the change in his orders, Rosemont called Wallenska over. "Kat," he said, "I'm going to send you away on detached duty today. Force is sending a Bubble Top out with the Tilt Wing. We are to remain here and let the scout ships find targets for us."

"No problem, sir," Kat said. "I'll leave Ironman in charge of the rest of the team."

"Good. Their ETA is twenty minutes."
"I'll be ready."

ISLAMIC BROTHERHOOD commando Hamadi Abu
Ali carefully checked the guidance system readouts
on his Broad Arrow antiaircraft missile. The LIRS
missile was the latest development in the missiles-
versus-aircraft counter-measures battle. Unlike a
conventional heat seeker, its guidance system
couldn't be diverted from its target by the tactic of
firing decoy flares that were hotter than the heat
source it was locked onto. Once the LIRS seeker
head had identified its target, it would reject any
other heat sources that were more than a hundred
degrees hotter than the one it was locked onto. And
it could pick up a target that was only a hundred
degrees hotter than ambient air temperature. Neither shield turbine exhausts nor IR countermeasures would protect an aircraft from being shot
down by this new missile.

The most recent product of British Aerospace In-
dustry Ltd., the Broad Arrow was so highly classified that the USEF had no data on the system's
capabilities. The British hadn't bothered to divulge
that sixty of the potent missiles had been stolen from
a test center in the Caribbean. A team of Irish Re-
publican Army commandos had raided the site,
stolen the weapons and disappeared into the night.

The British Secret Service and Scotland Yard were
investigating the theft. But beyond turning up the

fact that the college-age son of the Labor prime minister was a secret supporter of the outlawed IRA terrorists, no trace of the missiles had been found. Since disclosure of the loss would be sure to bring down the government, nothing had been said about the affair. The prime minister was desperately hoping to recover the missiles intact and keep their loss a secret.

But that was going to be difficult. The IRA had given two dozen of the missiles to the EuroAg-Combine for their assistance with making the theft possible. And most of them were now in the hands of Francillion's Islamic Brotherhood commando units.

Hamadi's group, a raiding party of several skimmers and trucks trying to hide during the day, was one of the units that had one of the Broad Arrow missiles.

USEF FIRST LIEUTENANT "Speedy" Gonzales dropped the nose of his Bubble Top and twisted the throttle up hard as he nudged the cyclic control stick forward at the same time that he slammed it all the way over to the right. The small scout ship went up on one side as it nosed even closer to the ground at well over two hundred and fifty miles an hour.

"You drop this fucking thing any lower and I can get out and do the recon on foot," Kat Wallenska growled.

Gonzales grinned broadly behind his helmet visor. Speedy was his name, and high-speed, low-altitude recon was his game. The OH-39 NOTAR— no tail rotor—Bubble Top scout ship was the most maneuverable helicopter ever built. The combination of the rigid main rotor and jet-thrust directional control design allowed the chopper to perform like a small fixed-wing aerobatic aircraft.

And along with the scout ship's high speed and high maneuverability went a full package of both recon sensors and ground-attack weapons. If Speedy detected anything on his flight, he didn't have to run for cover and call the big boys in to knock it out; he could do it himself.

Speedy particularly liked taking out armored vehicles. There was something about the David-and-Goliath aspect of killing tanks that appealed to him. So far on this mission, he hadn't yet had a chance to pull the trigger on a tank. Maybe he'd get lucky today. He had a full pod of Long Lash antiarmor missiles and even some high density, depleted uranium AP rounds loaded in his 20 mm chain gun ammunition bays. He was ready to go to work, all he needed was a target.

Seeing a ridge line approaching, the pilot chopped his throttle and, leveling out, deployed his MADDS, rotor mast acquisition and detection system. Extending one meter above the rotor disk when it was fully deployed, this sensor system allowed him to look over a hill without exposing the scout ship to enemy observation and fire.

"Bingo!" he called out when he saw the readout. "We've got customers, Kat. There's several military skimmers hiding in a wadi about half a klick in front of us. Check your harness. We're going in."

THOUGH THE BUBBLE TOP had a low-noise-signature rotor system, it wasn't completely silent. As Speedy racked the ship into a good firing position, the rotor tips hit a hot-air pocket and made the unmistakable, characteristic *wop-wop-wop* sound of a helicopter. Echoing off the wadi walls, the noise alerted the commando on air guard duty with the Broad Arrow missile.

Swinging the missile launcher toward the noise, Hamadi locked the image of the approaching Bubble Top in the launcher's optical acquisition sight and pressed the track button. The missile dumped its pressurized nitrogen coolant to the seeker head and spun up its internal gyro. In less than a second Hamadi heard the launch-lock tone in his headset and pulled the firing trigger.

The booster charge kicked the missile out of the launcher, accelerating it to supersonic speed. Twenty meters out of the launch tube, the second-stage rocket motor kicked in as the thrust-vectoring nozzles swiveled to make a course correction to follow the speeding chopper as it started its gun run.

"LOCK ON!" Speedy yelled, racking his ship around in a brutal snap turn. Thrown against the harness with the violent G force loads, Kat braced her hands against the crash pad in front of her. "We've got a heat seeker on us!"

As he snapped out of the hard-banked turn, the pilot hit the flare launch sequence button on his cyclic control stick. Decoy flares dropped out of the belly of the chopper and ignited to burn at well over two thousand degrees. With the shielded turbine exhaust running at only about five hundred degrees, the higher heat of the flares should pull the missile's heat seeker head off them and onto the flares.

"*¡Madre!*" he yelled. "It's not tracking the flares!"

"Do something!" Kat yelled back.

In a desperate maneuver, Speedy hauled back on the cyclic control, jerking the nose of the ship up almost vertically, aiming it at the sun. If the IR trace of the blazing desert sun couldn't break the lock, nothing could. Holding his course for thirty seconds, he slammed the control stick over to the right and shoved it all the way forward.

The Bubble Top made a high G force snap turn to bank away from the sun and dive toward the ground below. But the missile followed him instead of continuing on to try to reach the sun.

"*¡Tu madre!*"

The Broad Arrow missile hit right under the chopper's turbine exhaust. The warhead was also an advanced design, a semi-shaped charge that fired a cluster of diamond-shaped steel pellets out of a sixty-degree cone. Traveling as fast as machine-gun bullets, the tempered steel pellets tore the guts out of the small recon ship, smashing the transmission and rotor controls. Speedy just had time to cut the fuel feed to the turbine when it declutched and screamed on over-rev as it self-destructed.

"We're going down!"

The pilot frantically tried to establish autorotation with the plunging ship, but he was too low for the rotor blades to come back up to speed and establish life. At the last possible second he pulled full pitch to the blades with his collective, but it barely cushioned the crash.

The Bubble Top hit a glancing blow against the ridge line and rolled onto its side, its five main rotor blades snapping off and flying away. The 20 mm cannon barrel in the nose turret dug into the ground, stopping the ship, but sent the tail boom careening over the canopy. Snapping off, the tail section continued while the shattered remains of the crew compartment came to a rest right-side up only a hundred meters from the hostiles in the wadi.

KAT WOKE to the feeling of hands roughly jerking her out of the wreckage. She glanced to her left and saw Speedy jammed up against the instrument panel. His eyes were open and dull behind his smashed visor, and his head was cocked at an impossible angle. He was dead, but she had no time to mourn him now.

Her hand flashed down to her boot top, only to find that her teflon fighting knife wasn't in its sheath. A stunning blow to her shoulder numbed her arm. A grinning Arab wearing a black commando suit stood before her, his Han assault rifle raised for another blow if she resisted. She went limp and allowed the hostiles to drag her out.

The hostiles were talking in rapid Arabic, but even though Kat had had the standard Peacekeepers hypno-briefing on the language, they were speaking too fast for her to follow it. All she could pick out were the words *bint* and *askari*. Those two words she recognized because *bint* meant woman and *askari* was soldier.

Facing a dozen assault rifle muzzles, Kat stood stock-still as hands ripped her body armor open and snatched the helmet from her head. She stiffened when another pair of hands went for her waist. She held her breath as the man undid the clasp holding her tac belt and pistol holder. Pulling it free, he reached for the belt to her field pants.

Here it is, she thought. Rape was always the fate of a captured female soldier, but why did there have to be so many of them?

Ripping her field pants down to her boots, the men grinned broadly as they forced her down onto her back on the ground. Hard hands held her shoulders down, while others grabbed her ankles and savagely jerked her legs far apart.

The thought flashed through her mind that she didn't need to allow herself to go through this; she could resist and force them to kill her easily enough. But if she was dead, she wouldn't be able to avenge Speedy's death or her rape. It was better to let them do whatever they wanted to, in the hope that they would leave her alive at the end of it. And if she did somehow survive, this bunch of bastards would wish that their fathers had cut their mothers' throats before they had been conceived.

The man who had undressed her grinned obscenely as he kneeled between her outstretched legs and reached for his own belt buckle. Kat involuntarily closed her eyes as the man lowered his weight onto her. She was going to be raped, but she sure as hell didn't have to look at the son of a bitch while he was doing it.

His penetration took her by surprise, and a gasp escaped her lips. She forced herself to relax, but the pain defeated her. Fortunately for her, the man didn't last long. But no sooner was he finished than another hostile took his place. With the leavings of the first man inside her, the pain lessened, but not the humiliation. Her only salvation was to run through her mind all the ways she knew to kill a man with her bare hands, particularly those methods that involved ripping his testicles off.

A third Arab was moving into position between her legs when a shout caused him to look up. The would-be rapist scrambled to his feet and, holding his pants up with one hand, stood at attention as an officer approached the group. At least it looked to Kat as if he was an officer. The man wore no rank badges that she could see, but he was wearing a clean desert camouflage uniform and looked to be several degrees more intelligent than the leering thugs clustered around her.

"Get up," he told her in heavily accented English.

Shaking all over, Kat shook her arms free from her captors, quickly pulled her field pants back up and fastened her belt before even trying to stand. Taking a deep breath, she forced herself to stop shaking as she rose and stood at attention in front of the officer. These bastards had raped her, but she wasn't going to give them the pleasure of seeing her fear.

The officer met her gaze. "You are a Peacekeeper?" he asked.

"Sergeant Katrina T. Wallenska, 465-51-5150," she answered, giving her name, rank and service number.

The man looked at her, his eyes hard above the sand mask over his nose and mouth. "You are a Peacekeeper, no?"

"Yes," she replied, meeting his eyes and instantly deciding that she had better play ball with this guy before he gave her back to his goons to finish off. "I am a member of the United States Expeditionary Force."

He nodded slightly. "You come with me."

21

In the Wadi—18 June

Two Brotherhood commandos grabbed Kat Wallenska's arms and marched her to a sand-colored, open-top skimmer parked at the end of the column. Pressing her face-first against the armored side of the scout car, they jerked her arms behind her back and bound her wrists tightly with what felt like a braided leather rope. After double-checking the knots, they lifted her into the back of the open car and dropped her on the metal deck. The officer mounted the vehicle, and they drove off, heading east.

As she lay with her face against the steel decking, Kat tested her bonds, but they were tight and the rough rope cut into her wrists. Even so, she continued to work against it, feeling the blood start to flow as her skin tore. If the rope was braided leather, like she thought it was, it should stretch slightly when it got wet and her blood was all she had to wet it with.

Entering a state of Zen meditation, Kat moved the pain from her wrists into a small corner of her mind and shielded it from her conscious awareness. Right now she had to concentrate on what she was doing and didn't have time to experience the pain. There would be time for that after she freed herself.

ROSEMONT'S TILT WING, it's rotors shut down, was sitting on the small hill where he had spent the night. He was inside the sunbaked fuselage, sitting at his command monitor. The assault transport was still on the ground because there was a distinct lack of targets this morning. He was waiting in the sweltering heat for the far-ranging Bubble Top scout ships to stir up some business when a call came in over his comlink.

"Bold Lancer," Ashley Wells's voice sounded in his earphones. "This is Bold Strider." As the recon platoon leader, Wells was coordinating the aerial recon from a site several klicks to the north.

"Lancer, go," Rosemont answered, surprised at the urgency in her voice.

"This is Strider. Be advised that as of fifteen minutes ago, Strider Alpha went missing in a Bubble Top."

Rosemont flicked on his nav screen. "Do you have a fix on the beacons yet?"

"That's a negative," Wells answered. "Both of the personnel locators are out, as well as the Bubble Top's crash beacon."

"What is their last reported location?"

"We have them at three, seven, niner, five, niner, eight."

Rosemont keyed in the numbers and saw the locator blip over the representation of a hilly area close to the base of the Zagros Mountains in Iran. The site was not in Iran, which was good, but it wasn't too many klicks from the border, and that could be trouble.

"Divert your assets to that location and start searching for them."

"I have two Bubble Tops on the way there now."

Rosemont checked his screen. "Good. I'll be lifting off immediately and I'll vector some of Stuart's people there, too."

"Affirm. Bold Strider out."

Seconds after Rosemont sent the assembly call over the comlink, the troops were on board and the Tilt Wing lifted off in a flurry of dust.

THE ASSAULT TRANSPORT carrying two squads of Jeb Stuart's platoon arrived at the crash site as Rosemont's ship touched down. While Kat's recon team rushed out, Rosemont waited for Stuart to deplane, then started with him toward the wreckage. As they approached the downed Bubble Top, they saw what looked like one body still in the cockpit, but as they got closer, they saw that the body had no head.

The pilot's head had been cut off and placed faceup between his legs. His contorted face was battered and bloodied from slamming into the instrument panel, and his eyes were open and staring dully in death.

"Ah, shit!" Stuart said, wincing as he turned away. "Not Speedy. Goddammit, anyway, he was the best fucking pilot we had."

Now Rosemont remembered why he hated war so much, particularly warring against Third World cultures. He hadn't known the pilot personally, but that didn't matter. He had been a comrade and there had been no need to mutilate his dead body. To try to kill or wound an enemy was simply part of doing business, but to abuse the dead served absolutely no purpose to a professional soldier. Only fanatics committed atrocities on corpses, and they did it more to pump themselves up than to terrorize the enemy.

The pilot's mutilation didn't cause Rosemont to fear for his own fate. It only made him even more determined to bring some serious smoke down on the people responsible.

"Get him out of there," he called out to two grunts.

As Speedy's remains were sealed into a body bag, the rest of the grunts fanned out to look for Kat or her body. From what they found in the chopper, however, Rosemont had little hope of finding her alive. Men who would mutilate a dead enemy would rape and kill a captured female without a second thought.

When a quick look around the area showed that Kat wasn't anywhere in the immediate vicinity, Rosemont sent the grunts farther afield. While they spread out, Rosemont examined the downed Bubble Top for some sign of what had gone wrong. It took no more than a few minutes before he realized what had happened; the evidence couldn't have been any clearer.

From the faint marks left on the hard-packed ground, he could see that at least half a dozen heavy vehicles had been parked in the wadi, and there was no sign that any aerial ordnance had been delivered anywhere in the vicinity. Apparently Speedy hadn't spotted them in time and they had shot him down before he could fire a shot. How the chopper pilot had missed seeing them he had no idea, but Rosemont was certain that he had been taken by surprise and hadn't even gotten a shot off in his defence.

The smashed chopper showed signs of having suffered an external explosion in the turbine area, the sheet metal skin and formers were all bent inwards, so it must have been shot down with an antiaircraft missile. Rosemont knew that the scout ships were equipped with the best IR shielding and decoy systems that money could buy to prevent that very thing from happening. But he also knew that countermeasures didn't work all the time. Sometimes the bad guys just got lucky or you ran into a

Golden BB. And this looked like it had been one of these times.

It was bad luck for the pilot, but even worse luck for Kat Wallenska.

"We can't find Sergeant Wallenska's body anywhere," Stuart reported back over the comlink. "But there's vehicle tracks heading east, so they might have taken her with them."

Rosemont's blue eyes flicked over to the faint tire tracks showing in the hard packed wadi. If they had taken her away, she might still be alive. He had to try to find her.

Rosemont was no stranger to losing both men and women in combat. That went with the job of being an infantry company commander. The casualties Echo Company had sustained in the assault on the oil-pumping station and the night attack on the company CP hadn't affected him too much because he hadn't known any of the dead. In fact, that was one of the great advantages of being a stranger to a unit when you took it to combat. The deaths didn't hurt as much that way.

So far, he hadn't had the time to get to know more than a few of his people other than the officers and key NCOs he worked with. But one of those people he had come to know well was recon Sergeant Kat Wallenska.

He remembered the night she had come to see him in his office and her subtle invitation to accept his hero's reward for having saved her life. Damn it anyway, this was one of the biggest reasons he hadn't taken her up on her interesting offer.

He had gone into combat with female troops before and he had carried women's broken bodies off more than one battlefield. He knew that a woman's blood was as red as the blood of any man and that their pain and fear were the same. But there was still something in his DNA that screamed each time a female soldier was hurt or killed. The caveman buried deep in his psyche told him that women were designed for tending the hearth fire and raising children, not for facing death on the battlefield.

"What are we going to do now, sir?" Stuart asked.

Rosemont's jaw was clenched tight. "We're going to find her or her body," he said, the tension showing in his voice. "Tell your people to start checking along the back trail where the vehicles went."

"Affirm."

ROSEMONT WAITED at the crash site until the recovery Tilt Wing could fly in from Saudi and retrieve the wreckage. Even though the Bubble Top was little more than a shattered hulk, it hadn't burned, and parts salvaged from it could help keep the others in the air. Also, it was considered bad form to leave the battlefield littered with the wreckage of Peacekeeper equipment. Blasted hostile equipment was left where it had been destroyed as a warning to others who wouldn't keep the peace, but no one would ever display a Peacekeeper wreck as a war trophy.

The recovery ship showed up quickly, and as soon as the wreckage was slingloaded under the Tilt Wing, it lifted off. Once he was back in the air, Rosemont comlinked with the two Bubble Tops flying search patterns to the east to receive their readouts. One of the scout ships was flying a ground-hugging profile, trying to follow the faint track the vehicles had made, but the hard, rocky terrain left few tracks even when crossed by heavy-wheeled vehicles. Spotting the trace of a skimmer or a light truck was next to impossible.

Nonetheless, the Bubble Top's pilot had found some fresh tracks and had plotted their direction. Calling up his nav display, Rosemont superimposed the Bubble Top's search path on it and saw that the trail the pilot had found indicated the vehicles were heading toward a sizable village right outside the Iranian border.

Reporting these findings to the force operations officer, he requested and received permission to check out the village. He was also told to keep a sharp lookout for any potential targets along the way.

WHEN THE BROTHERHOOD skimmer carrying Kat Wallenska pulled into a village, the recon sergeant was grateful for the relief from the pounding she was taking in the back of the vehicle. No matter how she had tried to brace herself with her hands and shoulders, the skimmer was beating her half to death. So far, though, she had worked her bonds enough that she thought the leather rope felt a little looser. But her hands and wrists were now so numb that it just might have been loss of sensation instead of slack in the rope.

As soon as the skimmer stopped, the officer dismounted and she caught the Arabic word *bint* again in what he said to his driver. The driver walked back, leaned over the side of the rear compartment and, grabbing Kat by the collar, jerked her upright into a sitting position. Slowly drawing the canteen from his field belt, he unscrewed the cap and extended it toward her.

Kat's mouth and throat were more than dry and caked with dust. She was parched and could almost taste the water he was offering. She knew it would be hot, stale and metallic tasting from the canteen, but it would be wet and welcome. Kat was thirsty, but she wasn't dehydrated yet and she had a better use in mind for the water.

Leaning forward awkwardly with her mouth open, she slammed her chin against the canteen and knocked it from the Arab's hand. The water spilled onto the metal floor plates. The driver cursed, then laughed when he saw the carefully staged expression of horror on her face.

"Lick it up from the floorboards, bitch," he spit in Arabic as he snatched up the canteen and fastened it back on his belt before walking away.

As soon as the driver was out of sight around the corner of a building, Kat twisted around and leaned back until her bound wrists were resting in the spilled water. She could feel the moisture on her skin as she twisted her hands against the rope. Slowly, as she tugged against her bonds, she felt the leather soften and stretch. The question now was, would the rope shrink tight again when it dried? She hoped that she would be able to keep enough pressure against the rope as the water evaporated so it wouldn't tighten up again and she could keep the precious slack she had gained.

She had just sat back up again when the officer and his driver returned. With a single glance back to make sure that she was where she should be, the officer climbed into his seat and ordered the driver to start the engine. In seconds, fans whining, the skimmer pulled out on the road leading east out of the village, quickly picking up speed.

With the muscles in her arms tensed to keep the tension on the loosened bonds, Kat watched as she was driven toward the mountains of Iran. She knew that Iran was off-limits for the Peacekeepers who would come looking for her and they wouldn't be able to cross into the mountains. But if she could free herself, she could always walk out.

Kat wasn't about to give up until she had been killed nine times.

COLONEL FRANCILLION smiled when he got the report from the commando unit that they had captured a female Peacekeeper sergeant. He would have rather had an officer, but it was rare that a Peacekeeper was captured and even a sergeant would know something of the Expeditionary Force's operational plans. He'd had the foresight to bring a chemical interrogation kit with him, and under the chemicals, this Peacekeeper would spill her guts to him in short order. Since she was female, she might have some hostage value, as well.

He knew that the Peacekeepers made a fetish out of recovering their own, dead or alive, and what went for the male personnel should go twice for a captured female. The outcome of this operation was still seriously in doubt, so a female prisoner might come in very handy if things went bad. He knew of instances where USEF units had taken further needless casualties simply trying to recover the bodies of their dead.

To him, this didn't make good military sense. Being loyal to your troops was only good military leadership, but spending men to recover corpses was a fool's game. The French Foreign Legion had taken very good care of their people, but not even the legion had gone to those lengths.

The skimmer bringing her to the mountain hideout was due in just a couple of hours and he planned to devote his complete attention to her when she arrived. Until then, however, there was the matter of the Mahdi's next appearance.

"Get that kid in here!" he ordered. "It's almost time for him to go on."

22

In the Village—18 June

Rosemont walked down the main street of the Iraqi village, his LAR held at the ready, his finger on the trigger. The battle was over, but that was no reason to take chances, particularly not with these people.

Although Stuart's troops and Rosemont's recon team had achieved complete tactical surprise and had had gunship support, the Brotherhood commandos had reacted violently to the attack. The resulting firefight had been brief but savage. Several of the small houses were shattered by explosives and bore bullet marks on their walls. Torn and smoke-stained green banners of the jihad hung limply from their poles. Black-clad bodies lay sprawled in the streets and shattered buildings. But this time, the grunts had taken a few Brotherhood commandos prisoner.

In the shade of a tree by the old communal well, John Ironstone squatted on his heels while he talked to one of the Brotherhood prisoners. The company's recognized Arabic language expert, he was conducting the interrogations.

"What do you have so far?" Rosemont asked as he walked up to him.

"If I've got this right, sir," the Indian replied, "this guy says that there was a skimmer in the village earlier today with a Ferengi woman in the back."

"What's a Ferengi?"

"A foreigner. Specifically, a Westerner."

"Was she a soldier?"

"He thinks she was, but he says he didn't see her too clearly."

"Anyone else here see this skimmer?"

The Comanche shrugged. "I'm sure there are, but none of them will own up to it. Apparently the skimmer belonged to a high-ranking officer who stopped in here to use the secure comgear."

"Who'd he call?"

Ironstone shrugged. "That's what I can't find out, and the equipment was destroyed in the fighting."

"Keep talking to this guy." Rosemont snapped his helmet visor down. "I'll be right back."

Rosemont walked over to his small clutch of prisoners held apart from their civilian captives. Even though none of the men wore officer's rank badges or sergeant's stripes, it shouldn't be too difficult for him to figure out who the senior man was here. It was natural for a soldier to look to his leader for guidance, particularly in a tense situation like this. He would simply raise the tension a couple of notches and see what they did.

Huddled in a small group on the bare ground, the prisoners were guarded by four of Stuart's grunts. When Rosemont walked toward them, his rifle slung over his shoulder, the prisoners looked up, their apprehension plain on their faces. He knew the picture he presented to their eyes with his visor hiding his face and his chameleon suit slowly shifting colors as he walked in front of different backgrounds. To them he was a faceless man of war in a magic uniform that changed colors like a genie's cloak in a fairy tale from the *Thousand and One Nights*.

He halted a few steps from the hostiles and undid the flap of his pistol holster. Drawing the weapon, he took the silencer from the holster pocket and slowly screwed it onto the pistol's muzzle, all the while studying the faces in front of him. He soon noticed the two men whom the others nervously looked at as he chambered a round in the weapon.

"Those two," he said, pointing them out with the pistol. "Take them over to Ironstone."

Two of the grunts grabbed the commandos and marched them over to the tree. Holding one of the men back out of earshot, Ironstone started questioning the other one. Since Rosemont hadn't undergone hypno-training in the language, the Arabic sounded both flowing and harsh to his ears and he didn't understand a word of it. The Arab looked up at him and spit a long string of what Rosemont knew could only be curses. Some things always transcended the barrier of language.

"He said that your father screwed male camels and your mother took it up the ass like a boy," the Indian reported without cracking a smile. "I told him that at least you had a father."

"See if you can get him past the cheap shots and find out about that skimmer and where it was going."

Ironstone tried again, but all he got in return was more of the same as the Arab tried to spit on Rosemont's boots.

"All he wants to do is talk about your ancestors." Ironstone shrugged.

Rosemont was frustrated. If he had a chemical interrogation team from the S-2 shop with him, they could plug their chemical IV drips into these guys and get the formation out of them in a minute. But the Intel officer couldn't promise a POW team until tomorrow morning at the earliest. The problem was that he couldn't wait until tomorrow. He needed whatever information they had sooner than right now. The longer Kat was held prisoner, the greater the chances were of her being killed.

"Keep talking to them," he told Ironstone.

The Indian was frustrated, as well. Having his team leader held captive by the Brotherhood was something he didn't want to contemplate. He knew how these people treated women who fell into their hands. Kat was strong, but there was only so much a woman could endure, even a woman warrior who spoke with the ancient spirits.

"Sir?" he said. "If I can borrow a Bubble Top for a few minutes, I may be able to get what we need from at least one of these guys."

"How's that?"

Ironstone grinned. "I've found that it helps sometimes if the guy you're talking to thinks that you're about ready to drop him on his head from two thousand feet."

Rosemont shook his head. "We can't do that. It's against the London conventions, as well as force regulations regarding the treatment of prisoners of war."

When nuclear weapons had been outlawed in the aftermath of the Arab-Israeli war of 2004, the rules of war had also been revised. The old Geneva conventions regarding the treatment of POWs had been honored more in the absence than they had been followed. The nation that had most closely honored the code, the United States, hadn't even been a signatory to the old pact. The new London conventions had teeth in them, but took a more realistic view of the conduct of modern war than the old treaty, which had been put together in 1929.

While allowing chemical interrogation of POWs, physical interrogation was still outlawed. Even though Rosemont knew that the Brotherhood wasn't concerned about the niceties of the rules of war, he was a Peacekeeper and he had to play the game by the rules.

"As much as I'd like to let you at them," Rosemont admitted, "we just can't do it. We're supposed to be the good guys here."

"Okay, sir," Ironstone said. "Then how about letting me borrow one of the female grunts for a moment and you take a long walk down to the other end of the ville?"

"Now what?"

"I won't hurt them, sir," Ironstone promised. "And I'll give them back to you completely intact except perhaps for their sense of masculine dignity."

Rosemont smiled thinly. He knew that Arabs, like all Semitic peoples, had strict prohibitions about men being contaminated by certain kinds of intimate contact with women. Since Ironstone came from a people who had similar cultural inhibitions and knew the Arabic mind through his language training, he might be able to get immediate results with whatever he had in mind.

"Just as long as they aren't physically damaged," he cautioned.

The Indian grinned. "They won't be, sir."

As Rosemont left to find Stuart, he saw one of the female troopers walk toward the prisoners with a big smirk on her face. A few minutes later he heard a loud shout of indignation followed by feminine laughter and a long argument.

A few minutes after that, Ironstone walked up to him. "I think we've got it, sir," he said, his face grim. "They've taken her into Iran."

THE UAV-15C BAT, an unmanned aerial vehicle, soared a thousand feet above the desert floor. The Mirror Skin on the belly of the remote-controlled recon flyer was set to light blue to match the cloudless, brilliant sky it silently flew through. Measuring only two meters across its curved, Manta Ray-like wings, the UAV was almost impossible to see from the ground, but it had a better than bird's-eye view of the terrain it silently passed over.

The flyer could be equipped with various sensor packages, but today it was loaded with a belly full of optical enhancement gear and the sensitive receivers tuned to pick up the signal of a Peacekeeper personal location beacon.

Upon receiving Rosemont's information that Kat Wallenska had been captured and was presumed to be in Iran, the force commander had ordered the aerial recon platoon to launch as many Bats as they could spare into the air to search for her. With a Tilt Wing mother ship on station to handle the incoming data and to refuel the flyers, the four Bats could stay in the air indefinitely. If Kat's beacon was still intact, they would find her sooner or later. The only question was, would it be in time?

THE SUN WAS GOING DOWN behind them as the skimmer carrying Kat Wallenska sped into the eastern foothills of the Zagros Mountains. The driver and officer had kept up a steady chatter for most of the trip, but it had meant little to Kat. She had recognized a few words of their conversation including one or two that she thought might be names, but they were European names. They sure as hell weren't Arabic.

All the way up from the village, Kat had kept her wrists tensed against the leather rope. The rope had dried, but the hard-won slack she had gained was still there. Seeing the driver was occupied trying to keep the speeding skimmer on the unpaved mountain road, Kat started twisting the rope against her wrists. Now that she had the slack, she needed a lubricant to help ease her hands through. Again her blood would do nicely.

She winced as the rope cut into her bruised flesh again and reopened the dried scabs, but she forced the pain back and persisted. Struggle and tug as hard as she could, however, her hands simply wouldn't slip through the rope. Her mother had always told her that she had a man's hands, but this was the first time that Kat had ever minded. Her hands were just the right size for operating weapons or for tearing a man's throat out, but they were too big to pull through the slack in the rope.

Slumping back against the side of the skimmer, Kat searched her mind for an alternative. She refused to accept that there was no way for her to get free, because she knew that as soon as she did that, she would be as good as dead.

Suddenly she remembered a holoflick she had seen, an action-adventure thing about IRA terrorists. The hero had had his hands tied behind his back, but he had been able to slide his bound wrists down over his feet and bring them around in front of him. It had looked easy in the holo, but then the hero always had it easy in the flicks.

Kat was stocky, but her size was all muscle and her endless hours of unarmed-combat practice had made her as limber as an acrobat. She had long arms, as well as big hands, so maybe she could do it. The thing was, she didn't know if it was possible to do it while wearing combat boots. The molded cleats on the bottoms of the soles might catch and hold the rope, but she had to give it a try.

Rolling onto her side, Kat extended her arms behind her back as far as she could. Pointing the toes of her boots until her feet ached, she drew her heels up until they were pressed tightly against her buttocks and brought her bound wrists down over them.

Her hands slipped down over the heels of the boot, but the rope caught when she tried dragging it up onto the sole. Rocking her wrists from side to side, she worked them halfway up the soles, but the rope caught in between the mud cleats. She arched her back and strained to pull one of her boots through. The rope cut deeper into her wrists as she tugged and twisted, but she felt the rope ride up over one of the boots. Pushing as hard as she could and giving it a final jerk, the one foot was free. The other followed immediately.

Not waiting an instant in case one of her captors turned around, she rose to her knees, clasped her still-bound hands together and swung them against the side of the officer's head as though they were a sledgehammer. The blow carried with it her outrage at everything that had been done to her that day, as well as her last hope of regaining freedom.

Her clenched fists struck right above the officer's left ear. She was rewarded by hearing a dull crack over the whine of the vehicle's fans as his skull was crushed in. His head lolled on his neck as he slumped forward in his seat, dead.

Recovering before the driver could go for his weapon, she turned and, opening her arms wide, slid her hands down over his head and around his neck. With her bound wrists on each side of his throat, she hugged the driver to her in a deadly embrace, squeezing his windpipe.

His hands frantically tearing at hers as he fought to breathe, the driver lost control of the skimmer. The ground-effects car edged off the side of the road and lost lift on that side. The driver made a wild grab with one hand to try to correct the slip, but was too late. The skimmer headed down the side of the mountain.

Gathering her feet under her, Kat tried to throw herself clear as the skimmer rolled over. The side came up and slammed her in the back as she jumped clear, knocking the wind out of her. She crashed into the rocks as the skimmer went end over end into the chasm.

Stunned by the fall, Kat twisted around and raised her bound wrists up to her mouth. Her sharp teeth made short work of the leather rope. Ignoring the pain in her wrists and the battering she had taken in her fall, she headed downhill for the wreck of the skimmer. She had to make sure that the two commandos were dead. But even more importantly, she needed to strip the bodies if she was going to survive.

Both the driver and the officer had been thrown out of the skimmer in its wild ride down the mountain. She found the officer first. He didn't have a canteen on his field belt, but he was armed with a Russian Makarov 9 mm pistol which she took along with the pistol belt, holster and extra magazines. Farther down she came upon the driver lying next to his wrecked vehicle and he had a Han Type 98 assault rifle clipped to the back of his seat. She appropriated it as well and stuffed the extra loaded magazines into the side pockets of her field pants.

His canteen was less than half-full. He hadn't had a chance to refill it after she had dumped it in the back of the skimmer. It wasn't much water for this kind of heat or this kind of journey, but it would have to do. Neither of the Arabs had any rations, but she knew she could last a hell of a lot longer without food than she could without water.

Now that she was armed and had some water at least, it was high time that she got the hell out of the area before someone spotted the wreck.

Kat cut across the valley to pick up a switchback on the road farther down the mountainside. Without her helmet and nav display, she had no idea where she was. From what she remembered of the hard-copy maps, she figured she was pretty deep into Iran by now, and Iran was hostile territory.

By her rough calculations, she had to be at least two hundred klicks from the nearest Peacekeeper base camp, and that would be a good hump even in friendly territory. As it was, she'd have to stay well under cover to keep from being seen by the locals, and that would make it harder for the searchers to spot her.

She had no way of telling if her personal locator beacon was still transmitting. If it was, all she needed to do was to follow the sinking sun, try to stay out of sight and someone would find her sooner or later. Until then, though, she had to stay alive.

23

Along the Iraqi-Iranian Border—18 June

High above the desert, the Tilt Wing UAV mother ship flew a wide, high orbit, keeping well clear of the Iranian border. Since it could control its unmanned aerial vehicles from a thousand klicks away, it didn't have to risk flying into hostile airspace to conduct the search for the missing Kat Wallenska.

Inside the ship a UAV controller studied the readouts of the four recon flyers he had in the air. All four UAVs were well inside Iran, but there was no way that the Iranians would ever detect them. The Bats were well stealthed against radar, IR and EM emission detection. Even if they were somehow detected, the Iranians would never be able to bring them down. The Bats were also equipped with a miniaturized, full ECM package and, when coupled with their small size and extreme maneuverability, they were an almost impossible target for anything but the most sophisticated anti-UAV weapons.

The lack of risk, however, did not mean that the UAV controllers had a dull job. Quite to the contrary. The art of gathering useful information from the recon flyers lay with the controller's ability to properly interpret the sensor readouts he received on his monitors. Like a man on a ground recon, the value of the information he gathered depended on his interpretation of what he saw. But right now, he wasn't seeing much of anything.

"Willie," the mother ship pilot called back to the controller over the intercom. "What's your status?"

"I don't have dick," the controller answered. "As soon as they're finished with the sector they're working on now, I'm going to vector them north and try there for a while before I go deeper into Iranian territory."

"Affirm," the pilot replied. "But I hope to Christ you find something pretty soon. My ass is going to sleep up here."

Willie chuckled. "Affirm. Mine, too."

KAT STOPPED WALKING when it became too dark to see. The moon was down, and even with the thousands of stars burning in the sky, she couldn't see clearly enough to make her way across the rocky terrain. To a fully equipped recon grunt, the night was the same as day, moon or no moon. But without her night-vision system to guide her, there was too great a chance of her stumbling in the dark and breaking something in a hard fall.

Since she was still all in one piece, more or less, she decided that she had better use her head and stay that way. Her chances of being found were slim anyway, but if she was down somewhere with a broken leg or twisted ankle, she would be as good as dead.

Though it was difficult to judge distances accurately in the dark, she figured that she had walked at least eight klicks since leaving the wrecked skimmer. Since she didn't know exactly where the border ran, she would continue heading west at daybreak. She did know that as soon as she reached the westernmost of the two big rivers, the Tigris and the Euphrates, she would be home free in Iraq.

Groping in the dark, she found shelter beside a cluster of large boulders that offered good cover and concealment, and settled in for the night. The rocks still held the heat of the sun and would protect her from the chilly night wind. As high up in the mountains as she was, it grew cold as soon as the blazing sun went down and the winds came up. The last thing in the world she needed right now was to come down with pneumonia.

She took only a small sip of the warm water in the canteen. Strict water rationing would be in effect until she reached a stream or a river. Even though she was armed, she would have to stay away from village wells if she wanted to keep her hard-won freedom. As far as being hungry, she simply ignored the message being sent from her empty stomach and didn't even regret not having eaten a bigger breakfast. She'd been hungry before and, as long as she remained a soldier, she would be hungry again.

Switching the safety of her Han rifle over to full auto, she laid it across her lap with her right hand wrapped around the pistol grip. Pressing her back against the warmth of the rock, she drifted off into a light sleep.

TEN THOUSAND FEET above the ground, a UAV-15C Bat sensed a weak, intermittent signal on the frequency it was monitoring. This tripped a preplanned program in its data bank that sent it into a slow, banked circle, its sensors probing the darkness. When the craft determined where the signal was the strongest, it sent a message to the controller in the mother ship.

The controller had noticed when the Bat went into its signal search pattern. He saw that while its signal was weak and was not reading out the missing sergeant's IFF code, it was the right frequency. "Randy!" he called up to the pilot. "I think we've got something. It's not squawking IFF, but it looks good."

"About fucking time."

"I'm going in to take a closer look."

"Affirm."

"SIR," the voice of the comtech in Rosemont's jump CP came in over the company commander's headphones. "The flyers have picked up a signal."

"Is it Sergeant Wallenska?" he asked.

"They don't know. The beacon isn't flashing her IFF code but it's on the recon platoon frequency, and she's the only recon grunt who's missing."

"That's good enough for me," Rosemont said, sitting up. "Where is she?"

The comtech flashed the grid to Rosemont's helmet display, and he immediately saw that the beacon was quite a few klicks outside his area of operations—and inside the Iranian border. Iran was strictly off-limits, but Echo Company looked after its own.

"Get me a Bubble Top," he ordered as he tapped an alert to John Ironstone. "I'm going in after her."

The Indian recon grunt showed up as Rosemont finished grabbing the gear he was taking.

"Where we going, sir?"

"Your canteen full?" Rosemont asked.

"Yes, sir."

"We're going after Kat," Rosemont explained. "The recon flyers say that she's down in the border region of Iran and her signal's not moving. She may be hurt, so I'm not going to waste time trying to get permission to go in after her. You with me?"

Ironstone nodded. "Let's do it, Major."

The Bubble Top pilot showed up a few minutes later and found Rosemont and Ironstone waiting for him. Though it was designed as a two-man scout ship, the Bubble Top had room behind the pilot's and observer's seats for two passengers in fold-out jump seats. Ironstone pulled out one of the jump seats and climbed in the back as Rosemont took the right hand observer's seat beside the pilot and plugged his helmet into the chopper's com system.

"Wind her up," he ordered the pilot as he fastened his shoulder harness.

"Where we going, sir?" the pilot asked as he pulled pitch to his main rotor and nudged forward on his cyclic control.

Rosemont sent the grid for the signal to the chopper's nav screen.

"That's off-limits, sir, in hostile territory," the pilot said as he saw the location on his nav screen. As a second lieutenant, he was used to obeying orders from majors, but he wanted to double-check this one. The last thing he needed was to have the force commander on his ass for violating the border.

"I know, Lieutenant," Rosemont answered. "That's why I ordered a Bubble Top for this mission and not a Tilt Wing. One of my sergeants is down there, so we're going in there low and fast to get her out. You just keep the wick turned up all the way on this thing and stay flat on the deck until we get there."

"Who is it we're going after, sir?" The pilot was still not convinced.

"Kat Wallenska."

"On the way, Major." He pushed the throttle all the way forward and punched the over-rev switch on the turbine-governor control. He had worked with Wallenska before and wanted her back as much as anyone in Echo Company. The turbine screamed as the small scout ship gained speed.

On the way into Iranian airspace, Rosemont linked with the Bat mother ship for an update on hostiles in the area. The recon birds still showed that the area around the signal was clear. But since it was so close to the mountain road, Rosemont knew that situation could change at any moment. After ordering the mother ship to keep two of her birds over the site, he had the pilot bring the speeding scout ship down even lower.

The mother ship vectored the Bubble Top directly to where its flyer had picked up the faint signal. The pilot pulled up to gain a little altitude and started searching with his IR sensors and night imager. In the back of the scout ship, Ironstone slid the side door back and looked out into the night using his helmet sensors and night-vision gear. The terrain below was a broken jumble of rocks, and there were hundreds of places where Kat could be hiding. With her location beacon out, it was going to be difficult to spot her.

The scout ship pilot knew his business, however, and picked up a reading on his second pass. "There she is, sir," he said, flashing the IR sensor reading. "She's moving slightly, so she's still alive."

"Any hostiles in the area?"

"None that I can see, sir. It looks clean."

"Then let's get down there and get her."

"Affirm."

THE FAINT SOUND of a whining turbine broke through Kat's light sleep and brought her fully alert. A turbine could only mean a chopper, and a chopper meant that she had been found. Knowing that whoever was in the Bubble Top would have their weapons trained on her, she stood and slowly slung her captured Han assault rifle upside down over her shoulder.

In seconds the Bubble Top touched down in the clearing next to the rocks. Ironstone was off the ship, his LAR at the ready, before it even came to a stop.

"Kat," he called into the dark, his night-vision imager turned all the way up. "Kat!"

"Over here," she said softly as she walked out into the open.

"Jesus, woman," the Indian said as he lowered his rifle and reached for the canteen on his field belt. "I thought you were dead."

"No such fucking luck." She reached for the canteen. "You're just going to have to get promoted the hard way, Ironman. Work for it."

Kat took a long drink, paused and drank deeply again. "Jesus, that tastes good."

"Come on," he said, taking her arm and leading her to the Bubble Top. "The major's waiting."

"He came for me himself?"

"He insisted on it."

Once they were inside the ship, the pilot pulled pitch and the chopper jumped up into the air. Doing a hard-banked turn, he pointed west, hit over-rev again and dropped down as low as he could go. He planned to stay in over-rev until they were well clear of Iranian airspace.

"You okay?" Rosemont twisted around against the shoulder harness.

"I'm fine, sir," Kat replied hesitantly.

"I'm taking you to the field hospital anyway," he said.

"Please, sir," She leaned forward. "I don't need any of those damned medics messing around with me right now. Just let me take a shower and get into a fresh uniform and I'll be ready for duty again."

"Forget it, Sergeant," Rosemont said. "You're going to the field hospital and you're not coming back to the company until you have full medical clearance to return to duty."

She slumped back against the jump seat. "Yes, sir."

Kat knew that beyond a few bruises and the torn skin on her wrists, she was okay. Her contraceptive implant was good for several more months, so she didn't have to worry about being pregnant. She also knew that she could sneak a broad-spectrum antibiotic from the company medic's aid bag to take care of any disease that might have been passed to her.

She needed to have her wrists cleaned and bandaged, but she sure as hell didn't want the medics sniffing around her crotch. It was bad enough that she had been raped, but she didn't want it to become everyone's business. She knew that if she said anything to the medics about it, it would be entered on her medical records and such entries had a way of becoming common knowledge in a military unit.

It was better that she keep it to herself and take care of it in her own way. She knew that there was no way that she'd ever be able to get her hands on those particular hostiles again, except by sheer luck. But she would take a certain pleasure in dealing with any Arab men she did see through the sights of her rifle. Or even better yet, at the point of the blade of her fighting knife. As soon as she got a replacement for the one she'd lost, that was.

As for the rest of it, she'd take care of erasing that incident from her memory with something she knew for certain would work, taking another man into her body. But with love and respect this time. And she had a pretty good idea who the man was who would do that little thing for her. This was the second time that he had rescued her from danger, but the third rescue that she had in mind would be the most important of the three.

Lulled by the low drone of the chopper's turbine, Kat fixed the image of Rosemont's face in her mind and fell right to sleep.

24

In the Iraqi Desert—18 June

Mick Sullivan's platoon had set up at a RON site overlooking a bridge crossing one of the tributaries in southern Iraq feeding into the Tigris River. Ashley Wells and one of her recon teams were sharing the site for the night. Like everyone else in Echo Company, they were anxiously awaiting word of Rosemont's rescue mission.

"Ash!" Sullivan called over to her. "The major's picked up Kat!"

"Is she okay?"

"Except for dehydration, a few bruises and a little sunburn, he says she's okay."

Even though Ash was still a little pissed at what she saw as Kat's sucking up to Rosemont, she was relieved to hear that her sergeant was alive. A small, nagging voice in the back of her mind, however, couldn't help but wonder if Rosemont's dramatic rescue had been motivated by something other than what he would do for any other member of his command. But she quickly put those thoughts aside.

The Kat was back, and that was all that really mattered.

Since Kat was a member of her platoon, Ash would have to thank Rosemont for having put himself at risk to rescue her. The thought of doing that stuck in her craw, but she knew she could do it if she had to, and it looked as if she was going to have to. Damn it, anyway, why did everything connected with that major have to be a problem for her? Life had been so much easier before he took over the company.

AFTER DROPPING Kat Wallenska off at the field hospital, Rosemont had the Bubble Top pilot fly him out to Sullivan's camp before delivering Ironstone back to his team. Now that Kat was back, the company could devote all of their attention to the matter at hand and Sullivan's First Platoon was out on the point.

A small delegation met him as he stepped out of the chopper, and he spent a few minutes reporting on Kat's condition. After accepting their congratulations for the rescue, he turned to go.

"Major Rosemont."

Rosemont turned back and saw Ashley Wells standing not quite at a position of attention. "Yes?"

"I would like to thank you, sir," she said stiffly. "For going after Sergeant Wallenska. I should have done that myself."

"No thanks are needed," Rosemont replied. "I was closer to her, and it's something that goes with the job." He grinned slowly. "I'd even go after you if you were down."

Ash stiffened slightly, not knowing exactly how to take his comment. A dozen different explanations raced through her mind. Did he mean what he said on the surface? Or was he hinting at something else? Why did she have such a difficult time with this man?

"Yes, sir," she said, not knowing what else to say.

Rosemont caught the puzzled look on her face and the defensive tone in her voice. Now what the hell had he said? He remembered why he had never married. It hadn't been because of his profession; he had always been too afraid that a marriage would end up like this.

"You'd better learn to lighten up a little, Lieutenant," he said. "You take life much too seriously."

"Yes, sir."

FORCE HEADQUARTERS was humming with activity when Rosemont arrived the next morning. An early call had ordered him in for a special mission briefing. He found Colonel Jacobson, the ops officer and the Intel officer huddled in front of a holoscreen displaying a large-scale map.

"There you are, Rosemont," the colonel said, looking up. "Come over here, you need to see this."

When Rosemont stepped up to the screen, he saw that it was displaying a section of mountainous terrain in northern Iran. Someone had circled a large section of it, some fifty klicks across, in red.

"We put your Sergeant Wallenska under chemical interrogation last night," the Intel officer said. "And she gave us most of the Arabic conversation that she'd overheard during her captivity."

"I didn't know you could do that, sir. Make a person speak a foreign language, I mean."

The Intel officer smiled. "Actually it isn't all that difficult if you're dealing with a subject who has undergone hypno-training for the language like Wallenska has. Once the brain has been trained to recognize the particular sounds that make up a language, it remembers the words even if the person doesn't understand what was said. We can even do it with a person who hasn't heard the language before. But we don't always get the right intonation or phrasing and have to run it through the linguistic computers to unscramble it."

"Anyway," said the colonel, breaking in on the Intel officer's lecture. "From what we can tell, Wallenska was real fortunate to get away from those two men. They were taking her to the hostile headquarters for questioning."

"So you've found their headquarters?"

"Not exactly," the Intel officer said. "All we know is that it's somewhere in this area." He tapped the red-circled area on the map. "They didn't mention any place names we can identify. In fact, they only called it the 'fortress' in Arabic. That can be a real fort as we know it, or merely a camp somewhere in the desert. They did mention, however, how long it would take them to reach this place, and we know what direction they were traveling. Therefore, we've got a good handle on the area we need to search."

"But that territory's in Iran," Rosemont said. "And I understood that the Iranians have threatened to move their entire army against us if we cross their borders."

In the last decade, the Iranian army had been the largest in the area. Even though their weapons were outmoded, they were still a force to be reckoned with.

"They have," the colonel confirmed. "But I'm not going to let that stop us now that we have something solid to go on. The Imam made appearances in several more towns yesterday and there has been renewed violence in the cities. Some of the areas that had been brought back under control have been lost again, and we have to get this guy shut down as soon as possible."

"I've been in contact with my opposite number in the Russian Peacekeepers, and they're going to create a diversion for us along their border with Iran to draw attention away while we go in and search this area."

"What does the satellite recon coverage show?"

"We've been running satellite recon over this entire region since this started and we haven't found anything, yet. Apparently our opposition is well dug in and it's going to take low-level-aerial and ground recon to find them. And this is where you come in. Echo Company's been doing a good job, so I'm tapping you to handle this mission."

Now that he had a mission, Rosemont slipped into his commander's tactical mode. "What exactly do you want us to look for, sir?"

The colonel turned back to face the holomap. "That's what we don't know at this point. I want you to cover this area in detail and look for anything that might indicate where these people are hiding. Obviously you'll be looking for any kind of holo transmission setup, satellite antennae and that sort of thing, hidden away. But any kind of military camp is suspect.

"Now, we know that the Iranians are sheltering Islamic Brotherhood commando units inside their borders, and we're going to target them, as well. If this operation works as we've planned it, we should be able to put those people out of business for good.

"You'll have the entire resources of the Expeditionary Force backing you up this time. I'm moving everything to the border so when you do find something, we'll be able to react almost instantly. Air support, fire support, it'll all be standing by. Get out there and find the target so we can get this thing finished."

"Yes, sir."

"The ops officer has your mission packet," the colonel said as he turned to go. "And he'll brief you on the fire and air support plan."

"Yes, sir."

"Oh, Rosemont." The colonel turned around. "When this operation is over, you and I are going to have a little chat about your unauthorized flight into Iran."

Rosemont stiffened. He had expected to have his ass taken off, but it had almost looked as if the colonel had forgotten it. He should have known better.

"Yes, sir."

"Carry on."

COLONEL FRANCILLION read over the latest Intelligence report he had received from his agents in the field. Damn that Brotherhood officer to hell! He should have known better than to leave a Peace-keeper prisoner unguarded, even a woman. *Merde!* Particularly a woman. From what he had heard of the female troops in the USEF, they were Amazons. There was something about American women when they set out to prove that they were as good as any man that made them particularly tough. This one had been tough enough to free herself, kill two men and wreck a skimmer.

From the reports of a Peacekeeper Bubble Top violating Iranian airspace last night, it was obvious that she had been rescued and wasn't wandering around lost in the hills. If so, the Peacekeepers now had their first clue as to where he was. If he knew anything about the USEF, they would be swarming all over the Zagros before long. It was time for him to pull out all the stops and push his operation to its swift and violent conclusion.

The appearance of the holographic Twelfth Imam yesterday had been very successful. He had rewritten the kid's script, and the Islamic mobs had gone crazy. Only the swift reaction of a Peacekeeper unit had prevented them from destroying the last desalinization unit in Saudi Arabia. Once again the Americans had countered his plans, but as good as the Peacekeepers were, they couldn't be everywhere at the same time. Now that he had recaptured the lost momentum of the jihad, it was time to finish the job once and for all.

Francillion wasn't concerned, however, about anyone learning who had been behind the jihad. He had taken steps to ensure that his pivotal role in the affair would never be discovered. When converting the ancient cistern into his headquarters, he had included three items of which his fellow conspirators were completely unaware. One was a huge liquid-propane tank, one an equally large oxygen supply and the third a sophisticated timing device and detonator. When put together, they became the ingredients for a powerful fuel-air explosive device that would level the mountain and destroy all traces of their occupancy in the fortress.

Short of a small tactical nuclear explosion, nothing else would do as good a job of eradicating any evidence of what they had been doing there.

The devastation would be blamed on the Peacekeepers, and no connection would ever be made between him and the jihad. To further cover his tracks, an old comrade vaguely resembling him had used his passport to take a flight to the island of Grenada in the Caribbean. Until the operation was over, he was staying in seclusion on the island where Francillion would join him and assume his own identity again.

The weak link in the plan was the kid who played the Imam and the Italian technical staff who knew who he was. The explosion would erase all traces of them, as well. Francillion's concern was to complete the job so he would be paid the second half of his fee and return to his vineyards. Everyone and everything else was expendable.

But all of that would happen later. Right now, he focused on the matter at hand. He wanted the Imam to make a few more appearances at certain selected cities to keep the Peacekeepers busy while he pulled the Brotherhood forces back to protect the fortress. He particularly needed to get the rest of his stock of Broad Arrow antiaircraft missiles deployed around the fortress. When the Peacekeepers came, they would arrive in their Tilt Wing assault transports and a gunship escort, and he wanted to be ready for them.

BY THE TIME ROSEMONT returned to Sullivan's RON site, the rest of the company had closed on the area, as well. The small hill was abuzz with activity as weapons techs, sensor techs and supply people from force HQ helped the grunts prepare for the search mission.

The first thing he saw when he stepped out of the Bubble Top was the stocky form of recon Sergeant Kat Wallenska in a clean uniform. "Kat," he said, smiling. "I'm glad to see you back. I take it you got your medical clearance?"

Kat grinned and handed him a hard copy of the form releasing her to full duty. It had been no problem for her to coerce one of the medtechs to key out this version of the medical release. The man had enjoyed being able to walk on both legs and hadn't wanted to take a chance of pissing Kat off over something that didn't make any difference to him. Keeping his legs unbroken did, however.

The original medical release had specified that she be assigned to noncombat duties for the duration of the operation as was customarily done with all returned POWs. But she was not about to go along with that program. The only R and R she needed was an opportunity to kill a few hostiles. She'd lie in the sun and take it easy when this was all over.

"Great," Rosemont said, pleased when he read the release. "I really do need you on this operation. How are your wrists and hands?"

"I just took Ironstone two out of three falls." She grinned. "I'm ready."

"Good." Rosemont smiled back. "Oh, by the way, I'll be going in with your team when we move out again."

"You're always welcome on my team, Major."

ROSEMONT'S OFFICERS' and NCOs' meeting fifteen minutes later was well attended. Rumors of the mission had swept through the ranks, and everyone was anxious to get the word. He quickly outlined the colonel's plant to blanket the target area and delineated the fire support and logistical plans.

"I'll be making the drop with Strider Alpha," Rosemont said in conclusion. "And I'll be with them as long as we're in the field."

He didn't notice the tightening of Ashley's jaw at that announcement or the almost imperceptible smile that swiftly flashed across Kat's face.

"Any questions?"

It was a straightforward assignment, so there were none. All they had to do was make a detailed search of several thousand square kilometers of mountainous desert, looking for some unspecified something out of the ordinary. Nothing to it.

Rosemont quickly dismissed the briefing, and everyone got busy preparing for the mission. Kat noticed that Ashley kept well away from her as the recon platoon went through their mission prep, saying only what was absolutely necessary in the strict line of duty. Obviously, whatever was biting her still had its teeth clamped tightly in her ass. But Kat didn't care. She didn't have time to play nursemaid to a childish platoon leader.

25

High over Iran — 20 June

Major Alex Rosemont sat huddled in his drop capsule as the C-36B Valkyrie droned through the night sky. Once more a cold sweat soaked his skin. He had just gone through this a few days ago and he thought it would have been a little easier this time, but no such luck. The same old barely controllable fears were back in full force.

Kat Wallenska sat across the aisle from him, her deep green eyes fixed on his face. He couldn't tell if she could see his fear, but having her watching him didn't make him nervous as he would be if it were Ashley Wells who was sitting there.

It was ironic that the one woman in his command he felt closest to wasn't an officer and his only female officer seemed to go out of her way to be disagreeable and hard to get along with. It was supposed to work the other way around. Since there was no way in hell that he was ever going to get either one of them into bed. However, the point was purely academic.

It was nice to know that he could drop some of the command facade bullshit around Kat. Instinctively he knew that even if she were to find out that he was scared half to death, she wouldn't see it as a fatal weakness. Ashley would openly sneer at him for it, but Kat wouldn't think less of him.

He forced his mind back to the mission at hand. The colonel's plan was audacious and dangerous. Both of Echo Company's line platoons had been broken up into recon teams and, combined with the four teams from Wells's recon platoon, he would have sixteen separate recon units on the ground. Once dropped in a precise grid pattern in the target area, the teams would thoroughly search their sectors inch by inch while a full complement of UAV recon flyers would be aloft to provide early warning of hostile movements in the area. The rest of the Peacekeepers would be standing by to reinforce the teams if they got into trouble, or to move in and exploit any lead they found.

While the entire resources of the Expeditionary Force would be entirely at Rosemont's disposal, his people would still be scattered deep inside hostile territory and basically on their own. If they ran into something they couldn't handle immediately by themselves, no matter how fast the colonel reacted, someone was going to get hurt. So far in this operation, the major hurting had all been done by the Peacekeepers, rather than being done to them, and he wanted to keep it that way.

That was why he had chosen to make the drop with one of the teams rather than remain behind and run the operation from a jump CP location. At least if he was on the ground with his people, he would be able to make the "on the spot" decisions that might help keep them alive.

The flight was short and the "suit up" signal sounded in Rosemont's earphones all too soon. Since the trip from the assembly area had been so short, the jumpers were already buttoned up and ready to drop. Rising, Rosemont closed his visor, checked the helmet seals and turned on the oxygen supply for the drop.

After running a final functional check on his capsule, he moved to the head of the drop stick. At the capsule launchers, he stepped back into the launch cradle and felt the clamps secure him as the magnoelastic joints of his capsule stiffened, locking his legs together and his arms tightly to his sides.

He was dropping at the head of the stick this time. As soon as the drop tone sounded in his earphones, he felt the slam of the launch as his capsule was ejected into the cold night air. His stomach lurched, he clamped his jaws tightly together and he sucked in the stale bottled oxygen as the capsule bounced in the drop ship's turbulence before the stabilizers snapped into position. Once in the clear air, he flicked on his visor display and watched the altimeter numbers swiftly wind down.

As on his earlier drop, his drop speed was high, but he didn't worry too much about it this time. Dropping at night, he wanted to get on the ground as soon as he could. He took up the slack on the trigger for the speed brakes, however, just in case the numbers crept up a little too high.

As the altimeter's digits ticked off too fast for his eyes to follow, he watched the other five capsules on his screen. In a tightly grouped pattern, they were following closely behind him. When they landed, they should have no trouble linking up in the dark.

He tried to relax and enjoy the ride down, but he made the mistake of glancing at the airspeed indicator and saw that he was falling at close to three hundred miles per hour. He felt his testicles suck up into his belly again, and his hand tightened on the retard trigger of its own accord. He forced himself to refrain from using it, however, and suffered the rest of the way down.

Since he was the lead capsule, he popped his main chute first. The opening shock slammed him against the capsule shell as the breaking chute fully deployed. An instant later he hit the ground hard, knocking the breath out of him.

He wasn't even out of his capsule before the other five grunts were on the ground in a small circle around him. Once free of their drop capsules, the team quickly set up a small defensive perimeter and took a closer look around them. As soon as the area proved to be clear of hostiles, they settled in for the night.

Since there was no place to hide the empty capsules, they were stacked in a pile in the center of the perimeter and their self-destruct, booby-trap mechanisms were set. If the mission went as planned, they would be recovered by force maintenance personnel later. If, however, they were discovered by hostiles, the first man to disturb them would set off the demolition charges, destroying both them and himself.

Once that was done, Rosemont received the reports over his comlink that the rest of his teams had made it down without mishap. All they had to do now was to wait the coming of dawn.

THE MORNING SUN ROSE over a desolate landscape. The terrain around the clearing the team had dropped into was mountainous and rugged, and offered little vegetation for cover and concealment. What few low trees and shrubs were there were scattered and far apart. Even with their chameleon suits set to muted shades of brown, tan and light green, they were going to be totally exposed as they moved across country. The only good thing was that any hostiles in the area would be equally obvious to them.

The team had been awake since before dawn, eating breakfast and giving their weapons and equipment a final going over in the dark as they waited for the sun. As soon as it was light enough to see without the use of the night-vision gear, Rosemont called out over the comlink. "Okay people, let's do it."

Taking up an extended diamond formation, Rosemont and the five recon grunts moved out with Ironstone up on the point and Kat walking his slack. Wanting to stay out of the way of the more experienced troopers, Rosemont took the drag position, covering their back trail. That way, he could also let the younger men and women move out as fast as they could, thereby forcing him to have to keep up with them.

He knew that he was still a young man by anyone's standards and in good physical condition, but being a twenty-nine-year-old grunt trying to keep up with people even a few years younger than he was could tax him. The infantry was a young man's game and he was more than feeling his age today. While they had been in the field for quite some time now, he had spent most of it on his ass sitting in static positions or riding around in aircraft and he was out of shape for an extended hump. He knew that after a couple days of this, however, he'd have his legs back and be able to keep up with the best of them. Until then, though, he'd suffer.

By 1000 hours Rosemont was starting to regret his decision to join the search teams instead of staying in the CP and simply coordinating their efforts. The sun baked down on the barren, rock-strewn land, and there wasn't even a wisp of a breeze. Wiping the sweat from his face, he downed a couple of electrolyte tablets and took a sip of water. Even though he had been in the desert for almost two weeks now, he still hadn't completely acclimatized to the blistering heat and needed to keep a close watch on his salt and water intake. The ultimate embarrassment would be for him to become a heat casualty.

So far, his team had covered several square kilometers, but they had found nothing of interest. The frequent sitreps from the other search units told him that no one else had found anything, either, but he wasn't really concerned. He knew that it would have stretched the bounds of luck for them to have found something on their first morning out. If this mission went the way this sort of thing usually did, they wouldn't find the hostile headquarters until the absolute last hour of the scheduled search. Then, when everyone was worn-out from humping the mountains for days, they would get thrown into a desperate firefight.

"Lancer," came Kat's controlled voice over the team's internal frequency. "This is One Zero, we got company."

For the past half hour Kat had been up on point with Ironman in her slack position. Right now, they were on a ridge line several hundred meters ahead waiting for the others to join them before leapfrogging on ahead.

"Where are they?"

Rosemont's screen lit up with locator pips showing the hostiles' location. Kat's relayed imager showed a small group of military vehicles flying green jihad banners with some twenty men in desert-camouflaged uniforms clustered around them. He couldn't see that they had any heavy weapons with them, but he wanted to check that out for himself before committing to battle.

"I'm coming up."

"Affirm," she answered. "But stay frosty. They're in position to bring fire on us if they spot you."

Keeping to the rocks, Rosemont climbed the reverse slope of the ridge and joined Kat. As the relayed image had shown, the hostiles below seemed to be taking a break or awaiting orders to move. Their six vehicles were parked close together, and he couldn't see heavy weaponry on any of them.

"Let's zero 'em," Kat growled.

Rosemont hesitated, scanning the high ground surrounding the draw. "I want to check in with the recon flyers first. They may have some friends in the area we can't see. We don't need any interruptions when we start in on these guys."

Kat saw the wisdom in that and settled down to wait a few more minutes before getting her payback. Like the animal she was nicknamed after, patience had always been Kat's strong point. She didn't mind waiting, as long as she knew that she was going to get hers in the end.

By now the entire team was deployed along the back side of the ridge and was ready to go to work as soon as Kat gave the signal. Ironstone had taken up a well-concealed firing position on the far left flank, covering the hostile's only avenue of retreat. With a ranging scope fitting to his assault rifle, he could bring accurate single-shot fire out to a range of eight to nine hundred meters.

"Okay," Rosemont said. "The Bats say they're alone, so let's do it to them."

Kat flashed the attack signal, and Ironstone's finger took up the slack on his trigger. His first shot took out the commando seated in the command vehicle who looked to be giving the orders. The high-velocity 5 mm round took the man high in his chest and knocked him backward out of his seat.

The echo of Ironstone's shot hadn't even died away before the recon grunts opened up on the rest of the commandos.

For the next several seconds, the Peacekeepers had things all their way. With their LARs on full auto, they sent a rain of deadly 5 mm fire down into the draw, taking the hostile unit completely by surprise. The 30 mm grenade launchers on two of the team members' assault rifles added to the carnage. Though not packing the range of the aircraft 30 mm rounds, they had the same enhanced high-explosive warhead and did the same kind of damage.

The commandos scrambled for their weapons and returned fire as quickly as they could. But most of them were too late and completely exposed to the ambush. The commandos who were able to make it to cover behind their vehicles fared no better. Ironstone's carefully aimed shots and the high-arching grenades took them out. It was over in seconds, and almost two dozen men lay scattered between the vehicles.

"Cease fire!" Rosemont called out.

The gunfire echoed into silence and for a second all was quiet again.

"Let's clear the kill zone," Rosemont ordered.

Their weapons at the ready, the team cautiously moved down into the draw. Kat, however, ran on ahead of the rest, eager to get closer to her enemies. The first commando she came to was dead, his chest torn open by grenade frag. The second one wore several bullet holes in his upper body. The third one, however, had only a grazing head wound and moaned when Kat rolled him over.

Reaching down, she grabbed the front of his camouflage jacket and pulled him to his feet. Rosemont saw her left arm around the commando's neck and the fighting knife poised in her other hand.

"Kat!" he yelled. "Don't! We need him!"

But his warning came too late.

The knife blade flashed. Burying it to the hilt in the commando's lower belly, Kat gave it a savage twist in his guts, severing his aorta. But she wasn't content to release the man and let him die. In those few brief seconds before his brain shut down from lack of blood, she looked deep into his dark, panicked eyes.

"Die, motherfucker," she hissed as she ripped the knife upward. The blade tore through his intestines, stomach and lungs, separating the ends of his ribs from his sternum, as she drove for her objective, his heart. When the blade bit into his still-pumping heart, his pupils dilated completely and his eyes faded into a dull glaze as he went limp in her grasp.

When Rosemont reached her, Kat had withdrawn the knife and was poised to stab him again. "Kat!" he said sharply, grabbing her shoulder. "That's enough, he's dead."

She turned toward her commander and seemed to blink back into focus. The pupils of her deep green eyes were wide and glittering, and her face was pale and her lips drawn back from her teeth.

"Kat! Are you okay?"

She forced her mouth into a terrible caricature of a smile. "Yeah," she said softly as if she was coming out of a deep sleep. "I'm fine, Alex." She nodded slowly.

Rosemont studied her face for a moment before flicking his eyes down to the front of her uniform. The browns and tans of her camouflage suit were soaked in bright blood, but she didn't seem to notice. When he reached down and carefully pried her bloodied fingers from the hilt of her knife, the expression on her face didn't change.

"Ironstone!" he called out.

"Yo!"

"Over here."

26

In the Mountains—21 June

The Indian grunt ran up to Rosemont and Kat, his scoped rifle in his hands. "Yes, sir?"

"Something's wrong with Sergeant Wallenska," Rosemont said curtly. "Move her into the shade and check her over for wounds."

Ironstone's eyes flicked over to Kat. "Yes, sir."

Slinging his rifle over his shoulder, Ironstone took her arm, led her to the only tree in the area and helped her sit. He knelt at her side and offered her his canteen. She took it and drank deeply.

"Thanks, Ironman."

The Indian studied her for a long moment. The color was back in her face, and her eyes were losing their adrenaline glitter. "What happened, Kat?"

She shook herself and took a deep breath. "I just got a little carried away," she said.

His eyes took in the commando's blood now turning dark as it dried on her chameleon suit. "I hope to shit you did." He chuckled. "Usually you don't gut 'em, you just cut 'em. What happened?"

"I thought that I recognized him," she said softly. "I thought he was one of them."

"One of who?"

Her hand flashed up, locking her fingers in the front of his armor, and her glittering green eyes fixed on his. "Not a word about that to anyone, got that?"

Ironstone didn't move. "Sure, Kat," he said as nonchalantly as he could.

"I mean it, Ironman." Her voice was as hard and as sharp as the blade of her knife. "Not one fucking word."

He forced himself to smile. "I'm frosty, Kat."

WHEN ROSEMONT and the rest of the team had cleared the kill zone, he joined Kat and Ironstone under the tree. She still looked a little pale, but she seemed to have completely recovered her composure.

"How are you feeling?" he asked.

"I'm fine, Major." She got to her feet.

"I can get a Dustoff in here for you if you need it," he said.

She shook her head. "Don't do that, sir. Really, I'm okay. You bring a chopper in here, and you'll blow the whole recon."

He realized she was right about that, but he still wasn't convinced that she should continue the mission. He also realized that he was the one who bore the blame for this incident. He should have insisted that she take the mandatory released-prisoner leave whether she wanted it or not. For the first time in his military career, he had let his personal feelings get in the way of exercising sound command judgment, and now he was hung on the horns of a dilemma of his own making.

"Ironstone," he said, "come over here a minute."

Rosemont led the Indian well out of Kat's earshot before speaking. "I need your best advice."

"Yes, sir."

"You've worked with Sergeant Wallenska a long time, right?"

Ironstone nodded.

"What do you think happened here today?"

Ironstone hesitated. While he felt that he knew Kat Wallenska better than anyone in the company, even Lieutenant Wells, he knew her only as a warrior and a comrade-in-arms, not as a woman. They had fought side by side, but never had they lain side by side. He knew her warrior's strengths, not her woman's vulnerabilities.

Were he to answer Rosemont's question with only what he knew of her as a Peacekeeper, he would have to say that she had slipped out of her warrior role into a mission of personal vengeance. Since he knew how seriously she took her role as a warrior, that would mean that she'd had an overpowering reason to let her iron discipline slip. And since she was a woman, as well as a warrior, that could only mean that she had been mistreated while in captivity, probably raped.

"I don't know exactly what happened to her out there today, sir." Ironstone chose his words as carefully as he would his steps through a mine field. "But may I ask a question?"

"Sure."

"Did the medics check to see if she'd been raped when we took her in?"

Rosemont clenched his teeth. Damn it, he thought, he should have foreseen this. He should have known better than to accept at face value her assurances that night that she was all right. He also remembered her reluctance to be taken to the field hospital after she had been rescued. At the time he had thought that she was just being recon tough, but maybe Ironstone was right. If she had been raped and had kept it to herself, that could be the reason she had lost control here today.

"I'm going to call a Dustoff in here to take her back and I want you to take over the team till this thing is finished up."

Ironstone reflexively grabbed Rosemont's arm. "Please, Major," he pleaded, "don't do that to her. If you do, it'll destroy her." The company commander studied him closely. "Why do you say that?"

The Indian hesitated just a second before answering. He had already said far too much, but it was too late to stop now. He had to do what he could to help her. "Kat's a warrior, sir. And if she was abused when the hostiles had her, she has to regain her honor as a warrior. If you send her back like this, defeated by this thing, whatever it was, it'll completely destroy her.

"Please, sir." His voice pleaded more than his words. "Give her another chance. She just let it get away from her for a minute, but she's okay now, I'm sure she is. Give her back the team, and I promise that I'll keep a close eye on her for the rest of the mission."

Rosemont thought fast. Sending her back would be the safest thing for him to do if this incident was ever investigated. But if Ironstone was right, it wouldn't necessarily be the best thing for Kat Wallenska. And sometimes a company commander had to stick out his neck for his people.

"She can stay," he said. "But it's on your head, Ironstone. If she loses it again, I'll have no choice but to relieve her and send her to the rear for a psych evaluation."

Ironstone swallowed hard. "I understand, sir."

COLONEL FRANCILLION called up his computer map of the area around the ruined fortress and studied the terrain carefully. The abruptly cut-off report from the Brotherhood commandos who had stumbled onto a Peacekeeper unit in the mountains indicated that the curtain had gone up on the final act of this drama.

He had known that sooner or later the Americans would come looking for him. He hadn't expected that it would be this soon. But this was not the time to wail and bemoan the fact, this was the time for him to put his military skills to the test of battle once again. And that was something the mercenary welcomed.

While it had been fun to use the phony Twelfth Imam to play puppet master with the population of the Middle East, it had quickly grown stale. Francillion was a soldier because he was addicted to the adrenaline rush of combat as he pitted his skills against those of his enemies. His fondest memories were of desperate battles, furious jungle ambushes and overwhelming night attacks where he had tested his courage and determination against worthy opponents. This might prove to be his biggest test yet, as there was no more worthy opponent than the United States Expeditionary Force.

He knew full well that his Brotherhood commandos were not half the soldiers that his Foreign Legion comrades had been. They weren't even up to the standards of the international mercenaries he had led on so many battlefields. Being Islamic fanatics, they were almost complete strangers to Western-style military discipline. Worst of all, they were far too eager to join Allah in his Islamic paradise when it wasn't absolutely necessary. But they were all he had to work with and they would have to do. It would be up to him to ensure that when they threw their lives away, they at least took some of the Peacekeepers with them.

Hopefully they would kill enough Americans to buy Francillion the time he needed to complete the destruction of the targeted facilities for his employers. Regardless of the outcome of a battle in the mountains, he still had to complete the primary mission if he was to be paid.

Not for the first time since this operation had begun, Francillion wished for a small cadre of his old, experienced soldiers of fortune—the battle-tested French, Irish and South African mercenaries who had seen him through a hundred battles. Now that the operation was going into its final phase, he sorely missed their combat savvy and common sense. But the EuroAgCombine directors had specifically forbidden him from bringing any outsiders into the operation. Their need for the strictest security had made them more than a little paranoid. Were any word of their involvement to leak out, the least they could expect was to spend the rest of their lives in prison for crimes against humanity.

He keyed in the location of the first reported contact with the USEF fighters. The interrupted transmission hadn't told him how many Peacekeepers had been spotted. He had no idea if the Americans had dropped several small recon teams into the area or were doing a reconnaissance in force with full companies. Before he could maneuver his units to effectively counter the Peacekeepers, it was

essential that he know where they were and what
they were doing. As always, success on the battlefield depended on timely information, and the win-
ning commander was most often the man who had
the most information at his command, not the one
with the most troops and guns.

Until he had more information, he would concentrate his troop strength in the hills around the
fortress and send out the commandos. He switched
his comlink over to the Brotherhood commander's
secure channel and reached for the microphone.

ALEX ROSEMONT took the sitreps from his other
search teams while he was on the move. With the
exception of one other brief firefight like the one he
had initiated, there was nothing to report. The teams
had covered a quarter of the search area and were
closing in on their preselected RON sites to hole up
for the night. They would continue their search in
the morning.

Rosemont had kept a close watch on Kat all afternoon, and it looked as though Ironstone had been
right. She had pulled herself together and was leading the team as well as she had done before. He
briefly wondered if the two of them had ever shared
more than a foxhole during a lull in a battle somewhere. He knew it happened all the time in mixed-
sex units, and the Indian had seemed a little more
protective of her than mere comradeship would call
for.

For some reason, the thought of the two of them releasing the fear and tension of combat in the age-old dance of the hormones made him feel a slight twinge of jealousy. He immediately recognized that thought for what it was, however, and brushed it aside. It had been a long time since he had been to bed with a woman, and combat always raised his level of sexual tension. No matter how this operation turned out, he knew that he had better get his young ass to an R-and-R center and get himself thoroughly laid so he could get his mind off sex for a month or two.

The last thing in the world he needed right now was to get involved with one of his troops. Particularly one who was apparently trying to recover from a sexual trauma.

ROSEMONT WAS PART of an extended line formation when Kat's team entered the mouth of a high mountain pass. They had been climbing uphill all afternoon, and according to his nav display, this small valley was the last good place to stop for the night before they started down the other side of the mountain. The mountain peaks on either side were too rugged to contain the hostile headquarters they were looking for, so the area should be as safe as anywhere this deep in hostile territory. He was bone weary from the all-day trek and would welcome the halt.

The late-afternoon sun was throwing golden highlights and deep shadows on the rugged rocks when the cliffs exploded in gunfire.

"Ambush!" Kat shouted over the comlink.

Rosemont made it safely behind a huge boulder at the north side of the pass. Carefully peering around the rock, he saw that the pointman lay crumpled on the trail. From the rapidly spreading pool of blood under him, there was no use trying to get him under cover, he was dead. Even so, the Gods of War had been with them again.

Had the Brotherhood commandos held their fire just a few minutes longer, they could have taken out most of the team. As it was, only the one man had fallen in the initial burst. The others scrambled for cover in the rocks on the north side of the pass and no one was reporting an injury.

Most of the team was holding their fire as the hostiles raked the area. But, at the far end of the team, Rosemont saw Ironstone unlimber his sniper rifle and sight in on the hostile positions. After his second shot, the hostiles concentrated their fire on him and Kat was able to race over to join Rosemont behind the safety of his boulder.

"I'd say that we're pretty much Victor Sierra Foxtrot, Major," she panted as she edged the muzzle of her LAR around the side of the rock.

"Victor Sierra Foxtrot?"

"Very severely fucked."

Rosemont had to chuckle in spite of himself. "I'd say that you have an accurate grasp of the situation, Sergeant. I'd better get on the horn to see if we can get bailed out of this mess."

Rosemont quickly reported their situation to force HQ and requested fire support ASAP. The colonel had promised them the world if they got in trouble, and now they needed it badly.

There was little Kat could do to counter the ambush while Rosemont tried to get help. They had located the enemy, as a recon team was supposed to, but this time the enemy had seen them first. With the enemy commanding the opposite high ground, all they could do was keep their heads down and wait for reinforcements. Kat cursed silently as hostile rounds whined overhead; this wasn't the way she usually did business. She knew it was one of those things that could happen to anyone, but it wasn't supposed to have happened to her.

"What'd they say?" Kat asked when Rosemont ended his report.

"They've got a couple of Tilt Wings orbiting over the border that they can send ASAP and they're going to suit up a Hulk Company to get this sorted out."

Kat looked up at the setting sun. "They'd better get those bastards in here soon. We have only half an hour or so before the sun goes down, and with the targets hiding in the rocks, the gunships are going to need light to spot them."

27

In the Mountains—21 June

The promised pair of Tilt Wing gunships were over Rosemont's position within fifteen minutes. "Bold Lancer," the lead pilot radioed as he orbited right outside small-arms fire range. "This is Hawk Eye Lead, on station and ready to go to work."

"Affirm, Hawk Eye Lead," Rosemont replied, ducking his head as he keyed his comset for a tac link with the gunship. "Flashing target data now."

"Affirm, Lancer, we have it and we're rolling in now. Keep your heads down."

The Tilt Wing gunship had no sooner started her gun run through the pass when a commando hiding in the jumbled rocks jumped up with a Broad Arrow antiaircraft missile launcher on his shoulder. The missile's Low IR seeker head easily picked up the faint heat signature from the Tilt Wing's shielded turbine exhausts in the cool mountain air and sent a lock-on tone to the gunner's earphones. He pulled the trigger, and the missile leapt from the launcher.

When the missile's seeker head picked him up, the gunship pilot got the lock on warning from his threat sensors in his earphones. "Lock on!" he yelled to his gunner as he desperately fired decoy flares and tried to maneuver his gunship out of the way of the incoming missile. But the Broad Arrow didn't swerve from its target.

Within seconds the missile flew up the tailpipe of the starboard turbine and detonated. The explosion ripped the wing from the fuselage and sent the gunship careening into an uncontrollable dive that ended with its impact at the western end of the pass. The valley rang with the explosion as debris of both men and machine rained down upon the rocks.

The second gunship was still well away from the pass, and the pilot dropped out of sight behind the mountain peaks before the missile gunners could get a lock on him, too.

"I'm sorry, Lancer." The pilot's voice was quavering when he called. "But I've got to get the fuck out of here before they shove one up my tailpipe, too. I don't know what they're shooting at us, but we can't deal with it. We'll try to get help for you as soon as we can."

"Affirm, Hawk Eye," Rosemont called back. "I understand your situation. If force can send some help, you know where they can find us."

"That's affirm. Good luck, Lancer."

DEEP UNDER the ruined fortress, Colonel Francillion watched his tactical screens closely as the surviving Tilt Wing left the area. The deadly Broad Arrow missiles had prevented the Peacekeepers from using their tac air support to rescue the recon team that had stumbled into the valley. But he knew they'd be back. They had troops pinned down and would not abandon them to be destroyed.

He briefly considered ordering the Brotherhood to cease fire and allow what was left of the American recon team to escape. Since his underground facility hadn't been discovered yet, the Peacekeepers might back off and search for him elsewhere.

But, while that might be the prudent thing to do, Francillion just couldn't bring himself to stop the battle he knew was coming. He had a reinforced battalion in the area now, over six hundred men, and would have another three hundred in position before dawn. He had wanted to fight the Peacekeepers on ground of his own choosing, and this was the best place he could think of.

As long as he could keep the combat confined to the mountains, his Brotherhood commandos could hold their own against the better-disciplined Peacekeepers. The rugged terrain reduced the fighting to a man-to-man level and negated the advantages of the Americans' superior tactics and communications. It even rendered most of their sophisticated sensors and imagers useless, as well.

They hadn't started firing supporting artillery yet, but even when they did, it too would be rendered almost impotent. With the commandos hiding in the jagged rocks, a shell could detonate a few meters away from them, but leave them completely unhurt because the rocks would protect them from anything other than a direct hit. Also, the American artillery could not damage his facility buried in the ancient cistern. It was so far underground that only a tactical nuke could blast through the rock to reach them.

The best thing about the developing situation was that it looked like he was sucking the Peacekeepers in. And if they concentrated their forces here trying to win the mountain battle, they wouldn't be able to prevent the destruction of the last of the designated targets in the gulf region. All it should take was one more appearance of the Twelfth Imam, and his mission would be completed. Then he could set the timer for his fuel-air explosive device and make his escape.

"Caproni," he called out. "There's been a change in plans. Get that kid ready to go on stage again. I have one last message for the faithful."

KAT WATCHED GRIMLY as a thick column of greasy black smoke rose from the burning wreckage of the gunship. "There's no doubt in my mind that we're Victor Sierra Foxtrot now."

Rosemont could only agree with Kat's blunt assessment. He had seen aircraft shot down by missiles before, but only when they had been caught by surprise or bad luck. That hadn't been the case this time. The gunship pilot had known that there were active hostiles in this area and surely had approached with his full set of jammers and shields activated. Rosemont had also seen him launch his IR decoy flares and go into evasive maneuvering designed to break the lock on.

But, as he had seen, the missile had not deviated one millimeter from its intercept path on its way to shooting down the Tilt Wing. He remembered how he had thought that the scout ship pilot, Speedy Gonzales, had run into a Golden BB when his Bubble Top had been shot down. Now, however, he was certain that it had not been bad luck but an unknown, superior missile that had killed him and had put Kat on the ground to be captured.

Obviously, as long as the hostiles had a supply of those missiles, tac air support couldn't help them. Since he didn't know the range of those deadly missiles, air reinforcements, even with stealthed drop capsules, was also out of the question. Advanced military technology wasn't the solution this time. The only way that he and the surviving recon grunts were going to get out of this mess was as infantry, on their own feet. And even that was going to be iffy.

From what he could see, the hostiles controlled the high ground on both sides of the pass and the valley floor completely exposed to their fire. Trying to go west, back the way they had come, was out of the question. Trying to force the eastern end of the pass was equally a suicide mission. The only possible escape route was to go up the side of the cliffs and, using the cover of the rocks, head to the north or south.

They were tucked up against the north side of the pass, and the sheer cliffs above them looked formidable. Were they to try them, they would be under fire from the hostile positions across the pass. The rocks on the south side, however, looked considerably easier and safer to climb. Even though the hostiles held that side, it might be easier, and safer, to risk crossing over and climb there.

The sinking sun shone through a gap in the peaks. For the first time, Rosemont saw the ruins of an ancient fortress on the mountainside across from him. The weathered, jagged walls blended in so well with the natural rocks that he hadn't noticed it earlier. Now he knew that he wasn't the first guy who had gotten himself hung up in this pass. From the looks of it, the old fort was several thousand years old and had been built to guard the pass.

Suddenly Rosemont realized that the fort, which seemed unoccupied by the hostiles, might be a way out for them. From his readings of military history, he knew that mountaintop forts almost always had a trail leading out the back for easy resupply and escape if the walls were stormed. If he could get his

people up there unseen, they might be able to exfil-
trate by the old trail. Since it was on the hostile-
controlled side, it was risky, but it was better than
sitting where they were.

"How's your team at mountain climbing?" he
asked Kat.

"Our free-form's only so-so but we're real good
with ropes."

"Unless you brought some rope, 'biners and pi-
tons in your pack, I'm afraid that it's going to be
free-form this time."

"What do you have in mind?"

Rosemont pointed to the ruins of the fortress
above them. "As soon as it's dark, I want to go up
there."

Kat surveyed the cliff face in front of her with a
professional's eye. "As long as it's not too well
guarded, I think we can do it."

"I don't see any signs of troops up there. You
want to try it?"

Kat grinned. "Why not? All we're doing down
here is getting the shit shot out of us."

BACK AT THE USEF operations center, Major Jim
Collins of Bravo Company gritted his teeth in frustration. Now that it looked as if a major battle was
finally shaping up, there was no way for him to drop
his Hulks in to assist the beleaguered grunts. If Echo
Company had ever needed help, it was now, and if
anyone could help them, it was the Bravo Bulls in

their heavy infantry fighting suits. But with the battle area under fire from the missiles, it was no use sending his people up to be shot down while they were still in their assault transports.

Even if they could survive in the air, with the broken terrain in the mountainous region, the nearest suitable DZ for the Hulks was some twenty klicks away and that was a long hump, even in a powered fighting suit. But it looked as if they were either going to make the long walk or miss out on the battle.

He quickly put a plan together that called for the Valkyrie drop ships to launch his company from their maximum flight altitude and let them steer their drop capsules into that one drop zone. With the powered suits, his people should be able to cover the twenty klicks in two hours if they didn't run into resistance.

MICK SULLIVAN had a similar problem. His First Platoon had broken up into recon teams for the sweep and while he had been able to assemble three of his teams in the same place, since they were on foot, they were kilometers from being able to go to Rosemont's rescue and night was rapidly falling.

Ashley and her team were closer to the contact and she was already on the move. If Mick was going to get there before Ashley, he needed air transport desperately. But force HQ had grounded all flights in a fifty-kilometer radius of the contact area until they could get some Wild Weasel missile-suppression fighters in to take out the missiles. No one remembered why the odd name had been given to the specialized attack planes; it probably dated back to the time of the Vietnam War.

As SOON AS THE SUN went down over the high mountain pass, Rosemont wanted to try to get to get Ironstone and the other two recon grunts over to his location under the cover of darkness. Since Ironstone was farthest away, he made the attempt first and made it to safety without being spotted.

Brown, the second man, was still several meters away when a single shot rang out. Folding at the middle, he went down and his beacon blinked out.

"Shit," Rosemont hissed. "They've got night-vision gear up there."

"Maybe not all of them."

"We can't risk it," he said. "We've got two dead now and still have that last man out there on his own. I've got to get a little close air support to create a diversion to cover us."

"But what about those missiles?" Ironstone asked.

Rosemont smiled behind his visor as he keyed his comlink. "I'm going to see if they can send a couple of Bats with a bad attitude."

ORBITING A SAFE DISTANCE from the missile threat, a UAV mother ship launched her clutch of four Bat recon flyers. This time, however, they weren't equipped with harmless recon sensors in their bellies. The space was filled instead with an enhanced high-explosive package. Two more EHE bombs were slung beneath the wings, turning the small unmanned craft into remote-controlled dive-bombers.

With their skins set to dull night black and their ECM modules turned on full blast, the small flyers were invisible to both radar and bare eyeballs as they sped through the moonless sky to the contact area.

The single Bat already circling over the battle area didn't have its skin dialed to dull black. Instead, it was gloss white and as visible as a beacon as it flew low over the hostile positions. Every time it dipped down and flashed over the commandos, someone opened up on it. When their assault rifles couldn't hit the speeding craft, some of the commandos turned their machine guns on it, but were still unable to score a hit. On its second pass, a Broad Arrow gunner had tried to lock on, but even with the LIR seeker head, the missile had not been able to acquire the small craft.

On each pass, the Bat's sensors picked out the hostile positions and relayed the data to the mother ship. At his monitor, the UAV controller filtered out the readings from the light weapons that had been fired, but logged the positions of machine guns and other heavy weaponry.

When he had a list of targets, he transmitted the data to the Bat bombers circling high overhead. One by one the silent UAVs dropped down out of the sky.

This time the hostiles didn't see or hear the small craft as they unloaded their external bombs one at a time. They only knew they were under attack when a brilliant flash of EHE appeared over one of their positions.

When both their underwing bombs had been expended, each Bat became a guided bomb with even more accuracy. One at a time, the controller switched over to the miniature cameras in the noses of the flyers and, superimposing the target grids over the camera pictures, guided the Bats to their targets. Each time he attacked a target, he had the sensation that he was in the small craft as it made its suicide run. As many times as he had controlled bombed-up flyers, he had never gotten used to the feeling that he was flying into oblivion along with them. By the time he was on the second of his four suicide runs, sweat was rolling down his forehead.

28

In the Mountains—21 June

Under the diversion of the Bat bombing attack, Lindberg, the last of Kat's recon grunts, joined up with Rosemont and the reduced team quickly set out to make their escape. Moving from rock to rock, they quickly reached a point across from the ruined fortress. Checking the far cliff through his night imager, Rosemont found what looked like a relatively easy route leading up to the western corner of the fort.

"I think I've found a route," he told Kat and the two grunts. "Next time one of those bombs go off, run for the base of the cliff."

No sooner had he spoken than another explosion shattered the night. Breaking into the open, the team dashed across the narrow pass and took cover in the rocks on the opposite side. While Rosemont and the others secured their gear for the climb, Ironstone checked the route with his sniper scope. "It looks clear from here, sir."

"Okay," Rosemont said. "I want Kat to follow me, then Ironstone and Lindberg. All you have to do is stay close enough to the person in front of you that you can see where he puts his feet and hands. It doesn't look too bad from here, and I'll go slowly.

"Now, if anyone pops their head up, flatten yourself against the rocks. Don't shoot unless absolutely necessary. If we get in a pissing contest halfway up, we're dead meat."

As soon as everyone had secured their weapons, Rosemont started up the face of the cliff. As he had seen, there were more than enough secure hand- and footholds even for inexperienced climbers. In fact, the biggest problem was that he had to keep from climbing too fast for the others to keep up with him. The only other problem was the sudden explosions from the Bat attacks. One of the bombs detonated less than a hundred meters from the climbers, showering them with rocks and dust.

"Everyone okay?" he whispered.

When he got affirms from the others, he continued on his way. After a few more meters, the glare from another explosion illuminated the top of the cliff, and he whispered a warning for the others to wait while he went up alone. Peering over the top of the rock, he spotted a shadowy shape standing with his back to the wall of the ruined fortress.

Rosemont ducked back down. "I've got a guard twenty meters to my right," he whispered over the comlink. "Hold tight while I to try to take him out."

"Be careful," Kat sent back.

Pulling the 10 mm pistol from his holster, he quickly attached the silencer and switched on the laser sight. Pulling himself up to the top of the rocks again, he took a two-handed firing stance, sighted in on the guard and took up the slack on the trigger, activating the laser sight. When the red dot was centered on the man's temple, he squeezed the trigger.

The pistol bucked in his hand, but not even a pop was heard as the big round drilled the guard in the head, killing him instantly. The commando dropped to the ground with only a faint clatter when his assault rifle fell from his nerveless fingers.

Rosemont climbed over the top of the cliff and reached the base of the wall. "Okay," he whispered over the comlink. "It's clear."

Kat scrambled up the last few meters and joined him in the deep shadows of the broken walls. Ironstone and Lindberg quickly followed.

"Now what do we do?" she asked as Ironstone unlimbered his sniper rifle and checked for more guards.

"Let's see if we can sneak around back and find the trail out of here."

"Take the point," Kat said, snapping her IR imager down, "and I'll take your slack. The Indian and Lindberg can cover our ass."

With their chameleon suits dialed to dull night black, Rosemont and the recon grunts moved from shadow to shadow as they worked around the western wall to the rear of the fort. At one point a rockfall had left a small gap in the narrow ledge at the base of the wall, but they were able to cross it by climbing partway up the wall itself.

At the southwest corner, Rosemont stopped and checked for guards. The south wall of the fort was built on a small plateau a hundred meters wide, which ended against the peak that loomed over the fortress. Leaving the others under cover, he dashed across the open space to scout the trail. Just as he had expected, there was a faint path cut into the rocks leading away from the fort. It wasn't much of a trail and, over the centuries, rockfalls had blocked parts of it, but it could be followed and it led away from the hostiles. He signaled the others to join him.

Now that they weren't climbing rocks, Kat took the point again with Rosemont covering her. Leading a small team through hostile territory at night was her specialty, and he didn't mind following her. He kept her in sight as they worked along the narrow path. As soon as the fort was out of sight around a bend in the trail, he started to relax until Kat flashed an alert. They froze against the rocks while she checked out the problem.

Crouching in the shadows, Kat saw on her imager five shapes huddled around a machine-gun emplacement in the rocks overlooking the trail. As she watched, four more commandos joined their comrades.

"We're screwed," she radioed to Rosemont. "I've got nine hostiles at a crew-served weapons position less than a hundred meters in front of us."

"Wait one. I'm coming up."

Dropping down beside Kat, Rosemont made a quick assessment of the situation. She was right; they were screwed. The hostile position was well sited and commanded the trail perfectly. Even if he used Ironstone's marksmanship to pick off a couple of them, there were still too damned many for only four people to deal with.

He shook his head. "There's too many of the bastards. We've got to try to get around them."

Kat looked up at the mountain looming over the trail. Even in daylight it would be next to impossible to climb. At night it was simply suicidal. "You sure you want to do that?"

"What other choice do we have?"

THE BAT BOMBS had all been expended by the time Ashley and her team reached the crest of the mountains to the south. By coming in from that direction, she hoped to bypass most of the hostile positions overlooking the pass. Checking her position on her nav display, she decided to contact Rosemont before picking her final route into the pass. She had linked up with another of her teams and now had ten people, counting herself, but that still wasn't enough to try to bull her way through this kind of enemy-controlled territory.

"Bold Lancer, Bold Lancer," she transmitted. "This is Bold Strider."

"Lancer, go."

"Lancer, we're approaching from the south and we're about a klick from the pass. Send your location."

"Glad you could make it, Strider. We're in the mountains on the south side of the pass." He flashed his location to her. "There's a trail leading away from the fort, and we're on it. Right now, though, we're held up by a machine-gun nest."

When she saw the enemy's position, Ashley realized that she wasn't far from Rosemont and the hostiles who were preventing his escape. "If you can, hold there for a few more minutes," she said. "We can come in on them from the other side."

"Lancer, affirm. We'll be waiting for you."

ROSEMONT'S COMLINK transmission to Ashley was shielded, but Francillion's EMT detectors still picked it up and an alarm went off on his battle console. The mercenary had been so busy concentrating on the effects of the Bat attacks that he had neglected the readouts from the battery of sensors protecting the fortress. He cursed when he saw that the monitors indicated the Americans had scaled the cliff in front of the fort and were making an escape south over the mountains.

Merde! This is what came of his not having a properly trained battle staff to assist him. He had asked one of the technicians to watch the monitors, but the fool had completely missed seeing the alarms when they had gone off.

Punching up the display showing the disposition of his forces, he saw that a small security team held the southern trail five hundred meters from the fort. Another two dozen men were in position slightly to the west, as well. Snatching up his microphone, he ordered the commandos to be on the alert for the Americans.

ROSEMONT BROUGHT Ironstone and Lindberg up as they waited for Ashley's people to hit the machine-gun position from the far side. If all went according to plan, Ashley's troops would take out the hostiles, then link up with them to make good their escape. If they got into another fight, they would be badly outnumbered, but Rosemont wasn't looking for a fight. The line companies were moving in and it was time for the recon troops to get the hell out of the area and let them go to work.

Within a few minutes, Ashley was back on the comlink. "Lancer," she said. "This is Strider. We're moving into our assault positions now. Wait for my signal."

"Lancer, affirm."

As the team got ready to support Ashley's attack, Ironstone focused his sniper scope on the gun crew. Dropping the guy manning the machine gun at the right time would make a lot of difference in how this turned out. With the target indicator pip centered on the gunner's chest, the Indian went into slow, controlled breathing, the rifle's muzzle not wavering from his aiming point. At Ashley's signal, he squeezed the trigger.

The muffled pop of the silenced rifle was lost in the roar of small-arms fire as both teams opened up. When one of the commandos tried to drag the body of his comrade away from the gun, Ironstone fired again. There was no need for him to fire a third time. Caught between Ashley's and Rosemont's teams, the hostile outpost was quickly eliminated.

Rosemont stepped into the open as Ashley led her troops down to the trail. "Good to see you, Wells," he said. "You saved our asses."

"It ain't over yet, Major. We still have to get out of here, so let's get our asses moving." Apparently the long walk in had done nothing to improve Ashley's temperament.

"Lead off, we'll follow."

The group had gone only a few meters when a sudden storm of fire broke from the rocks above them. One of Ashley's men was caught out in the open and went down. The others quickly took cover and returned fire.

This time they couldn't break through. The hostiles had the advantage of the high ground, blocking their escape to the south, and they were well dug in. If they tried to stay and fight where they were, they would be massacred.

"Head back for the fort!" Rosemont ordered. "We can hold them off there!"

MICK SULLIVAN CURSED when he heard that Ashley had reached Rosemont and was already in contact with the hostiles. Even pushing his people overland as fast as he could go, he was still too far away to reach them before daybreak. Damn it, anyway! Now he would have to listen to her bragging again when they got back to Benning.

"This is Mick," he sent to his troops. "Ash and Trash has reached Rosemont, and they're fighting on the south side of the pass. If we don't want to get left out of the party, people, we'd better get moving."

A chorus of affirms answered him as the pointman broke out in a double time. It was dangerous for a troop unit to run at night, particularly in broken terrain. But as Mick had said, the party was starting without them.

COVERING EACH OTHER with fire and movement, the grunts leapfrogged back to the protection of the ancient rock walls. One of Ashley's men took a minor wound, but the others were able to break contact in the darkness and weren't pursued. The fort's south wall was several meters high in most places and gave the grunts good cover as they took up their positions.

Leaving Ashley to organize the defense, Rosemont reported his situation to force HQ. Not knowing if the Bat bombs had taken out all of the hostile's antiaircraft missiles, force was still reluctant to lose any more gunships unless Rosemont's situation was completely untenable. He told the ops officer that he thought he could hold out till daybreak, when Bravo Company was due to arrive. The colonel put two Tilt Wings on station fifteen minutes away in case the situation became serious and they had to risk the missiles to evacuate the teams.

"We've got to try to hold till dawn," Rosemont told everyone over the comlink. "The Bulls are on their way already and should be here by then. If we get into serious shit, however, the Old man's got two Tilt Wings on call and they'll try to get us out. So while we still have time, get yourselves dug in. I think we'll have visitors before too long."

He turned to Kat. "I want you to check this place out thoroughly and see if there's some place we can make a last stand if we get pushed off the walls."

Kat nodded.

"Ironstone?"

"Yo."

"Find a good place for your rifle. I want you to zero anyone who comes into sight as soon as you see them. Don't let them get in close."

"Affirm, Major."

"Wells," he said. "Concentrate on covering the southern and eastern approaches, but don't overlook the west wall. We came in that way and they can, too."

While everyone prepared to make their stand, Rosemont thought it was too bad that Mick Sullivan wasn't with them. He had talked nostalgically about the old Foreign Legion movies, and this was the classical plot for that genre. The small force cut off from reinforcement and all the hostiles in the world swarming over them. Sullivan might appreciate their situation, but Rosemont wasn't looking forward to it. He knew how most of those movies turned out.

ROSEMONT SCANNED the open ground in front of the south wall, wishing that he had brought a basic load of Whacker antipersonnel mines with him. As soon as the commandos got organized, they were going to storm the fort and he could use something extra to help even the odds. But he didn't have it, so they were going to have to do it with their LARs on full auto.

He was heading over to have a last word with Ashley when Kat's urgent voice came over his earphones. "Major! Quick! Over here!"

Rosemont hurried over and found her crouching low against the southwest corner of the wall. "What is it?"

"Here," she whispered, taking his hand and placing it under an overhanging rock. "It's warm air, and I hear a blower somewhere underground."

"Son of a bitch," Rosemont whispered. "We found them. They've got to be hidden under the fort."

Just then, Ironstone called. "Major, I'm at the base of the tower to your left. I've found a bunch of antennae over here. What do you want me to do with them?"

That clinched it. He had stumbled onto the jackpot by pure accident. The question was, what could he do about it with only the fourteen people he had? Probably damned little right now, but the Bulls were coming and they could crack the place like an egg.

"Major," Ironstone called again, "you want me to destroy these antennae?"

"No, leave them for now and get into position. We don't have much time."

"Affirm."

29

In the Mountain Fortress—21 June

The intruder alarms on Francillion's console
screamed that the Americans were right above his
head. The mercenary jumped up and, snatching the
Beretta 9 mm submachine gun clipped to the back
of his chair, ran to make sure that the outer door
was locked tight. He closed the inner door as he
came back through the tunnel.

When the mercenary returned to his operations
room, he studied the sensor readings from the
monitors installed inside the fort and detected at
least a dozen Peacekeepers. Hugging the protection
of the walls, they seemed to have a good defensive
position, but he could bring over a hundred men to
bear against them. The attacker's losses would be
incredibly high, that was true. But the best thing
about working with the Brotherhood was that they
liked to die in combat.

He quickly raised the commando leaders on the
comlink and ordered them to attack.

As ROSEMONT REPORTED their amazing find to headquarters, Kat looked for a way to get underground. It only made sense that the entrance would be concealed somewhere within the ruins so that whoever was down there could move in and out without being seen. As she was moving away from the wall, her threat-warning went off and she flattened against the rocks.

Studying the readouts on her display, she saw that she was under observation from some kind of motion detector. "Major," she reported. "They've got sensors inside the fort and they're watching us."

"Find 'em and knock 'em out!"

Just then Ironstone spotted a target across the open ground. Drawing a careful bead, he squeezed off a single round. His shot was the signal for the rocks behind the fort to light up with the flames of a hundred muzzle-flashes.

The sudden storm of fire drove the Peacekeepers lower behind their cover. Seeing no resistance from their enemies, the commandos jumped from their hiding places in the rocks and raced across the open ground for the south wall. Ashley sprang into action at that moment, her LAR blazing as she burned off a 100-round magazine on full auto.

Following her example, the Peacekeepers opened up on the attackers, turning the small plateau into a deadly killing zone. The commandos caught in the open went down like grain in a hailstorm. But true to their belief that dying in battle was a quick trip to paradise, they continued to attack.

FRANCILLION PACED back and forth in front of his battle console, his submachine gun slung under his right shoulder, the grip within easy reach. With the Peacekeepers behind the old stone walls, his commandos were having to fight their way across the open ground to the south of the fort. As he had predicted, they were taking casualties, but they had the Americans pinned down.

Hassain and the civilian technicians gathered outside Francillion's operations center. Even as deeply underground as they were, the sounds of the fighting still reached them. When the mercenary continued to ignore them, Caproni volunteered to be their spokesman and walked into the control center. "Can you tell us what is going on up there, Colonel?" he asked.

"It's a battle, you idiot!" Francillion snapped, not taking his eyes from the screens. "What do you think?"

"This wasn't supposed to happen. We were promised that we would be safe here."

"Tell that to the Americans up there," Francillion sneered.

"I insist that you get this stopped immediately, Colonel!" Caproni's face was pale and his fear was palatable. "We are not combatants."

Francillion turned to fully face him, reaching for the pistol grip of the submachine gun. "You do not insist on anything, mister. You and your friends are in this up to your necks right along with me. If you don't want to end up dead, you had better think about fighting for your miserable lives like men."

Caproni looked like a man who had been hit in the back of the head. The possibility of being killed by the Peacekeepers wasn't in his contract. "But—"

"Out of here!" Francillion roared.

Caproni fled.

With Francillion busy at his console, the technicians withdrew to the other end of the control room and whispered among themselves. With a glance over his shoulder to make sure the colonel wasn't watching, one of the holotechs dashed for the passageway leading up to the fort. He was halfway to the outer door before the sensor in the tunnel announced his intentions to Francillion. The mercenary spun around and raced for the entrance.

All the way at the end of the tunnel, the technician had started climbing the rungs to the outer hatch when Francillion got within range. Sighting in carefully, he sent a short burst of 9 mm bullets into the man's back. Sure of his aim, he turned and ran back to his operations center.

The technician fell from the rungs, landing on the locking handle to the outer hatch and releasing it.

FROM HER POSITION at the base of the tower, Kat's audio input picked up the muffled sound of a submachine gun firing close by. The short burst was followed by a death scream. It sounded as though the shots had come from under a large boulder a few feet away from her.

"Major," she called over the comlink, "I think I found the entrance to whatever's under us and I just heard firing from down there."

This was all Rosemont needed right now—hostiles inside his perimeter ready to attack from the rear. "Take your team and secure that entrance ASAP."

"That's affirm."

By the time Ironstone and Lindberg joined her, Kat had figured out how the hidden entrance worked. With the two grunts holding their weapons on it, she pivoted the boulder to the right and swung it out of the way to uncover a hatch. She slowly opened the hatch and, seeing it was safe, peered inside. A man in a white labcoat was crumpled at the bottom of the hatchway, but beyond that she could see nothing more.

"I'm going inside," she whispered. "Cover me."

"The Major said to secure it, not invade it," Ironstone whispered.

"Screw it," she snapped. "I'm going down there. You with me?"

The Indian nodded. Kat's blood was up, and this was no time to argue with her.

"Let's do it."

With her knife in her right hand and her silenced pistol in her left, Kat dropped down through the hatch. The passageway leading away from it was dark; obviously the lights were rigged to switch off when the outer door was opened. Her night imager showed that, except for the corpse at her feet, the tunnel was clear all the way to a door at the other end. She silently signaled for Ironstone and Lindberg to join her.

Reaching the door, Kat flattened herself against one side of the tunnel. Sheathing her knife, she placed her hand on the door latch. "Ready?"

The two grunts nodded.

As Kat pushed the door open, an alarm went off on Francillion's console. He burst from his cubicle and fired a quick burst toward the opening door. A return burst of automatic fire as the door swung open sent him scrambling for cover. Grabbing one of the technicians around the neck, he used the man as a shield as he backed away.

Rolling to one side as she entered, Kat caught a flash of a figure in white holding a weapon. Bringing her pistol up, she fired three times before taking cover behind a desk. Two of her three shots took Francillion's shield in the chest, and only then did she see the mercenary behind him.

Still holding the corpse, Francillion ripped off a long burst at Kat, but was driven back by Ironstone's and Lindberg's combined fire. Dropping the corpse, he spun around and sprinted for a passage leading down into the lower chamber of the cistern.

Ignoring the others in the room, Kat concentrated on the man in the uniform. He was obviously the man in charge here, the one who was responsible for the commandos who had captured her. She had already racked up several commando kills since she had been released, but that had, more or less, simply been business. This kill would be pure pleasure.

"No, Ironstone!" she shouted when she saw the Indian snatch an EHE grenade from his ammo pouch and swing to throw it down the passageway. "No grenades! That fucker's mine!"

"Guard these assholes!" Ironstone shouted to Lindberg as he dashed after his team leader. This wasn't the best time or place for her to go mental on him again.

THE SLOPING PASSAGEWAY took Kat down into a huge underground chamber. It was only dimly lit by glow strips set into the ceiling, but she could see that, unlike the finished room above, the walls were bare rock and only the floor was finished. Messy stacks of supplies and machinery filled most of the space. Other than the passageway she had taken, Kat didn't see any exits, so he had to be hiding in there somewhere.

As Ironstone joined her, she signaled him to cover the left side of the chamber. Scanning with her IR sensors, the way looked clear and she darted out of cover. A burst back of 9 mm fire echoed in the underground chamber, but she was undercover when the bullets sang overhead. Swinging her weapon into play, she triggered off a return burst to let Ironstone get into position.

"I'm in place," he sent over the comlink.

"Keep him busy, Ironman," Kat said. "I'm going to try to get around on his flank."

"Watch yourself."

Before she could move, a long burst came from a cluster of machinery at the dark end of the chamber. Francillion's burst was answered when Ironstone threw a flash-bang grenade into the open space in front of his hiding place. Knowing that her visor would blank out when the grenade went off, Kat waited a second for the detonation before dashing out from cover.

Catching Kat's movement from the corner of his eye, Francillion ripped off a burst, bouncing the bullets off the rock wall in front of her. The ricocheting 9 mm rounds hit her chest armor and smashed into the receiver of her LAR, knocking the weapon from her hands. She snatched it back and found the action had jammed. Dropping the useless rifle, she smiled as she slid up her visor and drew the fighting knife from her boot sheath.

It was fitting that she should have a chance to take this guy with her blade. He had hurt the Kat, and now she had her chance to use her claws on him. The problem was that there was no way she could get within arm's reach. That meant she would have to throw the knife.

Throwing a knife with enough force to kill was a tricky proposition even under the best of circumstances. Not only was it difficult, but it wasn't a militarily sound way to use a knife. If she missed her target, she'd be completely screwed. But since it was the only way she had to make the kill, she was willing to take the risk. She didn't want to have to owe Ironstone for this one.

Trying for a chest or back shot was out of the question—her teflon blade wasn't heavy enough to cut through his ribs and would be deflected. The neck was also out, since it was too small a target. But if she could get a face-on shot, she could go for the abdomen, right under the breastbone, into the diaphragm and the aorta. First, though, she had to get close enough to him to make the throw.

"Ironman," she sent, "keep him busy."

He answered her by ripping off a short burst, followed by two more. When Francillion answered his fire, she slipped out of her hiding place and dashed across the open area, diving behind a stack of supplies. "Keep on him, Ironman. I'm almost there."

There was another long exchange of gunfire, and she used the noise to mask any sounds she might make as she crawled the last few meters to her chosen spot, a broad pillar about five meters from Francillion's hiding place. Once she was sure he hadn't seen her, she measured off the distance in the dim light and, slowly risking, moved back half a step into the shadows.

Unlike in the holoflicks, success at throwing a knife depended upon being exactly the right distance from the intended target, and that distance depended solely on the length of the knife. She had practiced throwing her knife so many times that she knew the correct distance as well as she knew the length of her own arm. Holding the blade in the palm of her right hand, she drew her arm back.

"Yo, dickhead!" she yelled.

Francillion spun around, his submachine gun leveled, and Kat threw the knife. He triggered off a quick burst, but Kat had dropped back behind the pillar and he missed. She didn't, however. She had judged the distance accurately and the blade made a precise turn and a half as it flashed through the air. When the knife reached him, the point drove deep into the pit of his stomach.

The submachine gun fell from the mercenary's suddenly limp fingers as he slowly slid to the floor. A look of shocked amazement was on his face as his hand clutched at the hilt of the knife buried right under his rib cage.

Kat dashed out, snatched the fallen submachine gun and turned to face him. Francillion raised himself up on one elbow. "Please, your name," he gasped. "You have to tell me your name."

Kat hesitated just a moment before answering. It was an unusual, but completely understandable request, so why not tell him? Raising the muzzle of the Beretta a fraction of an inch, she triggered off a long burst into his chest. When the bolt locked back on an empty magazine, she lowered the smoking weapon.

"Staff Sergeant Katrina T. Wallenska," she proudly told his corpse. "United States Expeditionary Force."

30

In the Mountain Pass—22 June

The first tendrils of dawn were streaking the sky over the Zagros Mountains when the battle for the pass ended. A half hour earlier, while it was still dark, the Bravo Bulls had arrived at the western entrance of the pass. Though they were tired from their long forced march overland, Major Collins didn't waste another minute and immediately threw the Hulks into the attack.

Even though the commandos held the high ground, most of their heavy weaponry had been taken out by the Bat bombs, and infantry small arms against powered heavy infantry fighting suits was no contest. True to their nickname, the Bulls bulled their way through the pass and fanned out to dig the enemy out of the rocks.

Much to the shock and dismay of the commandos, the Hulks in their bulky fighting suits scampered up the rock cliffs like mountain goats with night eyes and a bad attitude, their M-18 8mm heavy infantry rifles taking a fearful toll. Their HIRs fired at a slower rate than the light infantry LARs, but the heavier-caliber ammunition included armor-piercing and enhanced high-explosive rounds that blasted the rocks to jagged splinters.

When the 8mm AP and HE rounds couldn't reach the targets, the 30 mm grenade launchers built into the rifles went into action. Firing the full-strength rounds, they dropped into crevices and behind boulders, blasting the commandos from their hiding places.

The hostiles fought back, but the Hulk suits soaked up their small-arms fire as though they were BBs. Faced by men they couldn't kill, the commandos panicked and tried to run, but all that did was raise the Bulls' body count.

Mick Sullivan's grunts even got in on the tail end of the fight as the commandos fled from the onslaught of Bravo Company. Deploying in the eastern end of the pass, they blocked their escape and turned the narrow defile into a bloody killing zone.

The oath of the Brotherhood commandos demanded that they fight to the death, but they had never fought the Peacekeepers in the open before. They had never come up against the full-strength firepower of the USEF. They were fanatics, but even the most fanatical of them saw only death, and their will to live was stronger than the oath. Slowly, by ones and twos, they dropped their weapons and raised their arms over their heads.

INSIDE the underground facility, Rosemont monitored the end of the battle on his comlink as he looked over the holo transmission equipment. "What time are the morning prayers around here?" he asked Ironstone.

The Indian grunt had to stop and think. "Right after dawn, about 0700 hours, I believe."

"Good, we still have time."

"What do you mean?"

"This isn't over yet. We still have to get this Mahdi fraud stopped before we can go home. Get that phony Imam in here ASAP and tell him to get into his costume. He has one last appearance to make."

Rosemont turned to the man in the white labcoat. "You're in charge here, right?"

Now that Francillion was dead, Caproni no longer feared for his life and was quickly recovering his composure. "Yes, I am. Dr. Alfredo Caproni at your service, sir."

Rosemont had no time for social bullshit right now. "Is your broadcast system still working?"

"Yes, it is."

"How many holo receivers do you have set up?"

"There are fourteen altogether."

"Can you transmit to all of them at once?"

"It is difficult—" Caproni started to say.

"Can it be done?" Rosemont snapped. The strain of the past twenty-four hours was finally getting to him, and he was in no mood to take any shit from these people. Even though they were civilians and hadn't pulled any triggers themselves, they were equally responsible for the death and destruction that had been visited on the Middle East in the name of the Twelfth Imam.

"Yes, sir."

"Then set it up fast! I want to be on the air in five minutes."

While Caproni scurried off to set up the broadcast, Ironstone came back with Hassain. The young Lebanese was in the same ancient Arabic costume he had been wearing in the photographs Rosemont had seen. "What do you want me to say, sir?" he asked in heavily accented English.

"I want you to tell your audience that you're a fake and this whole thing was a setup."

"Please, sir," Hassain said, not understanding. "A setup?"

"Damn it," Rosemont said. "Just tell them that you're not a messenger from God and tell them to stop destroying everything in sight."

That the Lebanese understood. "Yes, sir."

Caproni approached Rosemont. "Everything is ready to transmit, Major."

"Okay." Rosemont pointed to Hassain. "You're on, mister, and you'd better make it good."

Hassain mounted the platform and turned to face the holocams. *"Allah Akbar!"* he shouted when Caproni gave him the cue. "God is great."

He paused for effect before continuing. "Hear my words! I am not the returned Mahdi," he said in modern Arabic as he unwound the green turban from his head. "I am an imposter, a mortal man playing the role of the great Imam. Evil men paid me to act the part of the Mahdi for their own evil purposes. And, may Allah the Merciful forgive me, I willingly agreed to do this evil for them.

"My image was sent to you not from God, but by a hologram. This has not been a holy miracle—it has been a fraud to make you hate your neighbors and rise up in rebellion against your rightful rulers. This jihad was not called for by God to right a wrong in his eyes. It was ordered by mortal men and not even men of Islam. The jihad is dead. Put away your weapons and go back to your homes in peace.

"Know that Allah is a merciful God and He will forgive what you have done in His name. In His infinite mercy, may He also forgive me. Peace be upon you and all your houses."

He stood silent for a moment, and Caproni cut the transmission. "How did I do?" he asked Ironstone.

The Indian nodded. "Not bad, they should get the message. At least you had better hope the hell they do."

"What will happen to me now?" Hassain asked Rosemont fearfully.

"We will keep you safe from the mobs," Rosemont told him, "until we can get you out of the Middle East. After that, it's up to the World Court. But I have a feeling that it's going to be a long long time before you walk the streets of Paris again."

Rosemont turned to Ironstone. "Take charge of this prisoner."

"Yes, sir."

THROUGHOUT THE DAY, Echo Company guarded the ruined fortress while a team from force headquarters sorted through the underground facility and interviewed Hassain and Francillion's technicians before taking them away. Now that it was late afternoon, their work was almost done and the Tilt Wings were on their way to take Rosemont and the rest of his people back to Saudi Arabia.

Rosemont found Ashley moving her teams out to the open ground behind the fort to await their transport. "Have you seen Kat?" he asked, his voice pleasant but neutral.

Ashley's eyes were guarded. "I think she's over on the north side of the wall, sir."

"Thanks."

Her eyes followed him. Since the battle the night before, he had said nothing to her except in the direct line of duty. That was not too surprising considering everything that had been going on, but she had noticed that he was being quite talkative with everyone else in the fort except her. This was what she had thought she wanted, but now that she had it, it seemed wrong.

He had praised her for having rescued him and Kat's team and for her defense of the fort, so she obviously didn't have to worry about being transferred out of the company now. But that didn't make her feel any better. Something had changed, and she didn't know what it was. She was certain that whatever it was, it had to do with Kat Wallenska.

Rosemont found Kat standing alone looking down over the broken stone wall into the pass below. The POW teams were still processing the last of the Brotherhood prisoners and tending to their wounded. The hostile bodies were still lying where they had fallen and would be left for the locals to dispose of. That was another standard Peacekeeper practice. They recovered all of their downed equipment, but they always left the hostile dead behind so there would be no questions about who had won the battle.

The Peacekeepers had imposed peace once again,

and no one would ever question how it had been done.

Kat smiled when she saw Rosemont approach. "Good afternoon, Major."

"Good afternoon, Kat."

For a moment he stood silently and looked down into the pass.

"Can I do something for you, sir?"

Rosemont shook his head and smiled. "No," he said. "I just wanted to tell you that I put you in for an award."

The surprise showed in her eyes. "I thought you were going to bring me up on charges for killing Francillion."

"No," he said, "I figured out that you owed him one."

She took a deep breath. "You know what happened, then?"

He shook his head. "Not the details, of course, but I think I know."

Neither one said anything for a long moment.

"Are you okay now?" he finally asked.

A secret smile came across her face. "I'm doing pretty good," she admitted with a nod. "But there's one more thing I need to do before I'm back to one hundred percent."

"What's that?"

Her green eyes traveled up and down his tall, trim

body. "I need to take me a little R and R." She grinned broadly. "What're you doing for the next couple of weeks?"

Before Rosemont could answer, his comlink beeped with a message from force HQ. "It looks like we're moving out immediately," he said after taking the message. "The Tilt Wings are inbound.

"But—" he smiled slowly "—when we get back to Benning, I think I could use a little R and R myself."

EPILOGUE

With the final holocast of the Twelfth Imam, the jihad collapsed and the Middle East fell quiet once again. Civil governments quickly regained control of their nations, and the process of rebuilding the destruction slowly began. But what had come to be known as the "Time of Madness" had forever changed the face of the region.

With more-pressing damage that needed to be undone, the ambitious desalinization and irrigation projects in the Middle East were abandoned forever. Without freshwater, the reforested areas that hadn't been burned to stumps quickly died out and returned to desert. And without the trees to trap the moisture from the Persian Gulf, rain clouds formed over southern Europe once more.

In the south of France, a soft, welcome rain fell on a small vineyard, reviving the withered vines. But the owner of the vineyard wasn't there to see the new shoots sprout or to celebrate the end of the drought.

The year is 2030 and the world is in a state of political and territorial unrest. The Peacekeepers, an elite military force, will not negotiate for peace—they're ready to impose it with the ultimate in 21st-century weaponry.

2030
by MICHAEL KASNER

Introducing the follow-up miniseries to the WARKEEP 2030 title published in November 1992.

In Book 1: **KILLING FIELDS,** the Peacekeepers join forces with spear-throwing Zulus as violence erupts in black-ruled South Africa—violence backed by money, fanaticism and four neutron bombs.

TAKE 'EM FREE
4 action-packed novels plus a mystery bonus

NO RISK
NO OBLIGATION TO BUY